TORTURE

TERRAWAY
BOOK THREE

MARY E. TWOMEY

MARY E. TWOMEY, LLC

TORTURE

BOOK THREE IN THE TERRAWAY SERIES

By

Mary E. Twomey

COPYRIGHT

DEDICATION

For Brittney and Michelle,

The sisters who love me,
even when I make no sense,
and am basically a big dork.

And as a side note to the precious little smackhole who inspired
the character of Deli Frank,
you know who you are, and you make me crazy.
Chapter 32 is dedicated to you.

1

THE PERFECT GUY

The worst thing about being alone with your thoughts is ignoring the ones you have no control over. The fears about my possible death if King Geon of Sakuna continued starving me were one thing. I could deal with those with some amount of quiet dignity. No, it was the childhood bag of crapfest that unleashed itself on me in the unending dark. Visions of the flies trying to burrow under our bedroom door plagued me, especially when Andy's body began to rot after it became painfully obvious that I'd killed him.

Lang had been sneaking in to feed me bits of the *baga* root, a handful of berries or two and a canteen of water I didn't have it in me to resist anymore. I'd begged him to take away Andy's body, but he told me his father wanted me as uncomfortable as possible, so sleeping with a corpse became my norm.

I tried to reconcile my screaming guilt over my homicidal rage with the logic that I'd killed Andy in self-defense. I tried to assuage my horror at the lowlife I'd always known was lurking inside me by telling myself that it was either him or me. I knew I would skirt to safety in a court of law, but my own personal jury had me guilty as charged. I didn't even know Andy all that well, and now he was dead.

And rotting.

The maggots started in after who knows how long. Those gave birth to flies. These were fat, hairy flies that had a whole body to feast on, and they did so with gusto. I'd promised myself when Ollie and Allie finally busted me out of Bev's place that I would never let myself live like that again. I didn't so much mind anymore when adults broke their word to me, but breaking my own promise to myself felt like a new blow I wasn't sure I would recover from in a day.

Or two.

My days were broken up by sporadic visits from Geon, demanding to know where I'd hidden the sagrado stone. He'd come in with a platter of meat, my stomach lurching until he informed me it was roasted sigbin. After he left when I remained unwilling to divulge my secrets, I cried with the hope that Geon hadn't cooked up Edward, the sigbin monster puppy I loved.

I fell asleep, restless and freezing, choking out a cry of relief when Philip appeared in front of the fire pit I conjured to warm my dream self. I ran to Philip, stumbling with my stiff joints, desperate to find some comfort, some connection in the stifling darkness. "Philip? Help me!" I crashed into him, pretending the dream warmth was just as good as actual heat.

"What happened? Are you still in King Geon's prison?"

I blinked up at him as I buried my fingers under his shirt to warm them up. "Yes. And I don't think anyone's coming for me."

Philip held me, warming my body and rubbing my back and arms to soothe my panic. "Are you hurt?"

"I'm okay. The dark's getting to me, though. I'm trying with everything in me not to lose it. Geon's keeping me here to hold me for Sama's army. This Sama jackhole wants to keep me locked up so everyone goes to him for help, instead of being able to feed themselves. It's so stupid! The whole thing, I hate it!"

Philip was stiff. "I'm sure this Sama character doesn't know you're being held in such terrible conditions. Are you well fed?"

"No! Geon's starving me, and I'm sitting in a cell with a rotting body that's got bugs in it. Help me," I begged, wishing I was strong enough to break down the irons and save myself. "Come find me, Philip. Don't leave me here by myself. I'm so scared." My arms banded around my stomach as the confession rolled out of me. "I killed some-one! I killed a guy I don't even really know! He was

Duwende. Andy was going to take my will so I'd tell him where the sagrado stone is. I didn't have a choice!"

Philip gripped my arms. "You know where the sagrado stone is?"

"Of course I do. Or, I did anyways. Hopefully Edward hid it somewhere safe."

"Who's Edward?"

"My puppy."

"You're not making any sense. Where's the stone?"

There was too much edge to his voice. It was like he cared about the stone more than he cared about me. "I don't want to talk about a stupid rock that's done nothing but ruin my life! You're supposed to be the perfect guy!" I started beating on his chest. "You're supposed to love me so much better than real people. I can't even imagine up a fake guy who cares that I'm starving and lying in a cold jail with a dead body? You suck, Philip! You suck!" I pounded on him over and over, taking out my frustration on the hard body he hadn't even had to work at to earn.

Philip softened, letting me beat on him with angry fists. "I *am* the perfect guy. I'm the one you can tell all your secrets to." He held me and slowly sunk to the grass, keeping me close as I broke down into shameful tears that fell into his shirt. "Talk to me. Geon's got you in a dark cell. He's starving you. What else?"

"I want to go home. He's got Von and Mason somewhere, and I know he's hurting them! I can feel it. I can feel something's very, very wrong."

"Mason can handle it. I'm sure Von can, too. Matruculans can endure a great deal. And if your half-vampire's resisted the transition this long, I'm sure he has strength enough for a little torture."

"I don't care about strength! I hate Terraway! It's ugly and mean here. All they do is use me. I was doing just fine until they came along." I gripped Philip's shirt, desperate for a connection, however fabricated. "I need my medication. I'm going crazy, and I worked so hard not to be crazy! I'm losing my mind! I need it, or I'll get lost again. I don't remember what happened when I went off it a couple years ago. It was a week before Ollie found me. A week! He was gone and I was alone. When he found me, I was a basket case. Like, I could barely talk without counting. I was bashing my head against the wall and hadn't eaten or showered in days. I can't go back to that! I can't go under again! You have to help me. I work so hard not to be crazy. I'm not crazy! I'm not crazy!"

Philip's hands scrambled to hold me together as I openly sobbed in his arms. "Quiet now, little one. We can't have you losing your mind. I'll come find you. My people are on their way. They'll get you out of there and take you to my place. We'll get you some food. My own special recipe. I don't want you crazy or dead. I want you with me, by my side." He clutched me, and I make-believed that he cared deeply about who I was, not what I could do for the kingdom. "I'll see to it Geon's punished."

I snorted my disbelief. "You're not real, though. I need

actual help. I need my brother. I need Ollie." I let out a loud wail. "Allie! Allie left us, and she's not coming back!"

He kissed my cheek tenderly. "Tell me about Allison."

"My sister never would've let me live like this. She did everything to make sure I never had to live with bugs and rotting things. Now she's gone. She stopped loving me, but I never stopped needing her! If she was back, she would make me that chicken soup with the noodles Ollie loves and hold me so I didn't hurt myself. She would sing to me and wrap me in heavy blankets until I felt warm and calmed down."

"She loved you."

"She was perfect, and she left us. She knows I'm too much. She knows I can't be fixed. I can't be fixed! I can't be fixed," I moaned in Philip's arms.

He held my head to his shoulder, clutching me to him and providing the deep pressure that always calmed me down when I floated away from myself. "I can put you back together," he promised, and with everything in me, I wished my perfect guy was real.

But he wasn't.

2

THE ONE WHO HOLDS YOU TIGHT

I awoke with a jolt when a fly crawled into my nose, seeking to make me his new home. The black bugs buzzed around me as I cried silently and rocked myself back and forth, certain that if I made a noise, someone would come in and finish me off. My stomach growled like the insatiable monster it was, trapped inside an impenetrable cage. The more desperate my hunger became, the more distressed I was. I had no ability to tell time to mark the passing days, but I knew the agony of hunger, and this had surpassed even Bev's negligence. I clawed at my arms, opening up scabs that had crusted over in my too-short slumber.

I lost count of how many days were spent like that, surviving on berries and dirty water that Lang snuck me as he kept me alive with *baga* root. I couldn't tell how many nights I cried incoherently in fake Philip's arms, confessing details of my childhood even Ollie didn't know.

I missed Ollie, and hated that I still needed my brother for anything. If I was a true adult, I would be able to handle imprisonment just fine.

That logic gave me pause. I'd seen many a grown man weep himself to sleep on his cot in prison. Perhaps it was okay to miss my brother in these dire circumstances. Ollie came with a superhero cape in my imagination, sweeping me away from the horrors of the current doom. If Ollie was here, he'd know what to do.

I touched the bars of my cage, but only made it to twenty. It was a nice, round number divisible by ten. Any closer and I risked touching Andy.

Eighteen, nineteen, twenty. Twenty. I breathed a little easier each time I reached twenty. Then I started touching each bar twenty times for the grand finale, crawling on the floor like a beast.

My mania only stopped when the door opened, still letting in no light. "October?" called Lang through the empty space.

"Lang?" I whispered, scrambling to my feet.

"I'm here to get you out. You're released to go back to Ezra." He stepped toward the cell. "Ezra's waiting outside in the courtyard for you."

"Are you serious? I can go? Just like that? What about Von and Mason?"

"They were released hours ago. Father's been holding

onto you until the last possible second, hoping Sama's army would make it in time to intervene. Then Sama sent word to have you released. He's actually holding back the rations he's sending until you're freed."

"What? Sama wants me set free? I thought he wanted me locked up so I couldn't reap, and everyone would have to go to him to use his rations."

"Apparently Father's so off his rocker that even a megalomaniac like Sama thought he was over the edge." Lang fumbled with the key in the lock. "I guess it's good to know Sama doesn't want you dead. That's news to the council, who are all in the courtyard demanding Father give you up, by the way. Kabayo brought his army, which was the only thing Ezra was lacking."

I attacked Lang when he stepped into the cell, though not in the same way I had Andy. Though I barely knew the guy, I grabbed onto his arms and yanked him to me, gravitating to the warmth of his body until I was engulfed in a hug my body shuddered through.

I'd never been much of a hugger, but I was past the point of reason. Warmth. I needed to feel my fingers again. My limbs were too stiff, making me feel like a barely living corpse. Lang hissed and sucked in his stomach as I pressed my fingers into him. "Oh, you're freezing!"

"It's over!" I howled into his chest, feeling the firm leather of his breastplate brushing my cheek.

"There, there. I told you I'd take care of it. It just took me longer than I would've liked." His arms wrapped me tight, holding me together while I fell apart. A shudder ripped through me as Lang's warm body reminded mine just how cold it was. "You're too thin now. I tried to feed you as often as I could sneak in here, but it wasn't often enough. I had my hands full with Mason and Von."

Lang shook his head and rubbed my arms and my back as if he cared about me. I let myself fall for the comfort and fall into him, closing my eyes as I gripped his skin under his shirt and leather armor.

"Okay, alright. Easy, now. I'm here. I told you I wouldn't let you die. Captain Finn got here this morning. Father knows not to cross a Kataw. Finn's ruthless." Lang led me out of the cell, both his arms still surrounding me in the beefy muscles that heated my frozen insides. "Kabayo brought a small army with him, and they aren't leaving until I come out with you. Captain Finn convinced them to start tearing down the gate separating the main city from the rest of the country, which was when Father started to cave. Father wouldn't want to get any poor on him, and the gate's the one thing that separates his home from the civilians. If I don't bring you out soon, we'll be on the business end of them storming the castle."

"Get me out of here!" I whispered, terrified of the dead body I was leaving behind, and what it said about me that I could leave a man to rot. Andy had been the only witness to my crazy in the cell. His cracked skull had watched me count the bars over and over, touching the irons habitually and rocking in the dark. My foot brushed over Andy's arm as we stepped out of the cell, and I felt something icy zap me like an electric shock. The jolt stayed inside of me, making me yelp through my shiver.

Lang stopped as we reached the door. "I'm supposed to have you cleaned up before taking you out to Ezra, but I don't want to hide my father's sins."

I nodded. "I don't care how I look. Just don't let go of me; I'm so cold!"

"The stones are uneven, and I know you can't see in the dark like we can. I can't have you tripping and bleeding. Von's out of his mind with hunger. I'm carrying you out." He spoke it like a command that was laced with a threat.

"Take me home, Lang. Please! Take me home." I don't know why he expected I had the energy to protest, but the urge did rise up in me when Lang swept me up in his arms, carrying me like the baby I was through the many hallways I didn't care to see. As we moved through the castle, the air grew progressively warmer, though I could tell my body wouldn't be coerced into relaxing. I shivered violently in Lang's arms, and he held me tighter in response.

Not a bad guy, the one who holds you tight.

3

VINDICATED

I didn't open my eyes until I heard shouts and felt the open air touching my bare skin. "Give her to me!" and "October Grace! I'm here!" reached my ears, letting me know that, among the others who were shouting for my release, Ezra was there.

I'd had my appendix out as a teenager, and Bev hadn't come to the hospital. She was "just about to" a million times before I was released to go home with Allie and Ollie, who hadn't left my side the entire time I was laid up. That Ezra came for me when I was down and out? It meant something. Something big.

The moon was out, and I desperately wished for that sauna-like sun to warm me, but I took what I could get. Lang leaned his head down and said to me, "The men will rally more if you can't walk. Let them rally. Let them pay my father back for what he's done to you."

I went one further and lolled my head back as if I didn't have the strength to hold my own neck up (which actually wasn't too far off the mark).

I didn't mean to scare Ezra, but the man nearly lost his mind, his feet pounding the earth as he ran to me. "Give her to me! Give me my daughter!"

My eyes watered at his bold declaration. I'd been distant to him when last I'd seen his face. He'd been trying to be kind to me, but I was too jaded to see his sincerity. I saw it now. I looked through my blurry vision and saw the dad I'd always secretly wanted, coming to rescue me from a dungeon in a castle. It was like I was the daughter of a real king.

"She's ice cold! What have they done to her? October Grace, can you hear me?"

"She'll be okay," Lang said quietly to Ezra. I was lowered to the ground so Ezra could smooth feeling back into my cheeks.

I looked up and saw Finn and Kabayo running toward us, their faces filled with anger and fear when they took in the state of my deterioration.

"What's King Geon done to her?" Finn demanded, looking every bit like the captain he was in his black clothes and brown leather armor. The gills around his neck always threw me. He knelt next to Ezra and cupped his hand, pressing the side to my cracked lips. "Drink from me. My water's clean. You look about an hour from death." His hand that was empty filled with water, reminding me that he was from Dagat, which was the Mermaid country. Apparently they controlled water. I gulped at the gift, my throat painfully constricting as the Sahara finally found its oasis.

"More," I begged when he tried to pull away after a minute.

Ezra moved to the side to give Finn a better angle. Finn's other arm tucked under me so he and Lang held me together, sandwiching me between them so I had body heat on both sides. "He'll pay for this," Finn promised me.

"Cold," I worked out through a painful shudder. I cuddled into the new source of warmth, my body limp against Finn's arm as he fed me more water that kept replenishing in the well of his palm.

When my head migrated to his shoulder, Finn stiffened, as if he'd never held a woman on the brink of death before. Slowly his rigid posture began to relax, even going so far as to slide me away from Lang and onto his lap. He tucked my forehead under his chin, his body curving around mine as I clung to the near stranger. "I'm here, and I'll take care of it. You get to rest now. No one crosses the council and lives to brag about it. It's all over. I'll take it from here."

"Cold," I whispered, to which he held me tighter. He thumbed my cheek affectionately to warm my face.

"Rest with your father. I'll bring you back King Geon's head to mount on your bedroom wall." He stood with flawless agility and handed me to Ezra.

Kabayo leaned in to observe me and then straightened to address the soldiers. Kabayo's black horse head was huge, and when his muzzle turned in the direction of the army, he shouted with authority. "King Geon compromised your food supplier! Storm the castle! Free the prisoners and bring me the rest!" He turned back to me, his giant glassy black horse eyes meeting mine with the determination of a promise. "They'll pay for this." Then Kabayo reached out his human hand and held my fingers, flinching at the cold. "Help me inspire the men. Let them see what's happened to you."

Ezra surrendered me to Kabayo, who slid my arm over his horse neck and human shoulders, and held me like a bride. Or a baby. I couldn't decide which anymore. Kabayo was easily seven feet tall, and when he stood with me in his arms, my breath caught in my throat at being so high off the ground. I let my limbs go limp to further inspire the horse-men soldiers. Shoot, I'd pee myself if it meant they'd go after King Geon with everything in their arsenals. Luckily it didn't come to that.

Kabayo lifted me up to be level with his shoulders, shouting at his men in a voice with passion to rival Braveheart's. "Your Omen wants to end the famine in Terraway, and this is the thanks she gets? Your Omen would see all the nations fed, and every child grow without the hard marks of the field tearing them down, and this is the thanks she gets? Your Omen freed you from the Goblins, and this is the thanks she gets?" He straightened his arms out from his body, holding me up to the men like a limp and filthy sacrifice ready for the slaughter. "King Geon thanked her by torturing her Pullers and leaving her for dead! If not for your swift answer to her cry of distress, she would no doubt be gone from us, and with her, all of Terraway! King Geon would see your lands shrivel up and burn under the sun! King Geon cares nothing for the children your Omen has been sacrificing herself to save." The angry outcry reached me in waves of fury and pent-up aggression, ready to be unleashed. Kabayo raised me higher so I was on the level of his dark eyes. "Do you want to live?"

They all shouted, breaking out into thunderous snorts and the clanging of hundreds of swords on shields.

I was shaking, terrified of the impending war I'd somehow become a talisman of.

"Then thank your Omen and bring me back King Geon, bound and ready for my prison!" Then he dropped me down two feet, making me gasp when I thought he might throw me to the mud in some dramatic gesture. "Attack!" he cried, and my heart swelled with the overwhelming vindication of it all. A whole army showed up to save us. There weren't tears enough for that.

Kabayo handed me off to Ezra so he could join his men in leading the fight he'd been raring for. Finn put his hand on Lang's shoulder. "You and your allies stay by my side, or you'll be slaughtered for sure."

"They're already out. Do what you must." Lang held

my thinned wrist, rubbing feeling back into my arm. "Let Kabayo's men do what they do. I can't watch my father's house fall. I was sent to stay with the Omen, so let's move her. Let's take her to her home."

"*My* home," Ezra corrected. "Mason's already there, and so is Von." Then quietly to me, he whispered, "Your little sigbin monster, Edward, brought me the rest of the stone. It's safe in my home. You did well, and now it's time for you to rest."

Lang's furrowed eyebrows were directed at Ezra. "Can Von handle being under the same roof as her? He was rabid when I saw him last."

"He's locked up until he comes back to himself. I'm taking her now before Sama comes to steal her." Ezra was distraught, and hugged me to him as he stood in the mud. He clutched my frail body to his chest, taking a deep breath before the sucking sensation drew me upwards, where I prayed no magical creatures would ever find me again.

4

MARIANG, MY NEW SISTER

I breathed easier in Ezra's house. I'm not sure if that was due to the half hour-long shower, the constant pulling Danny did upon my arrival to mute my OCD, the breathable air or the warm fuzzy pink pajama pants and lavender thermal shirt that awaited me when I emerged. My skin was scrubbed raw, though it somehow still felt filthy.

Mariang had bags under her eyes from too many days spent crying for us and working at a job that had long since been too much for her to shoulder alone. She sat on the toilet lid while I showered and helped me get dressed when my limbs were too clumsy to figure out balancing on one foot to get the fuzzy pants on. She sat me on the toilet lid and got down on her knees to rub lotion into my legs and feet, helping me above and beyond without being asked. Then she rolled on socks that looked like a skinned muppet's fur and felt like they'd just come out of a microwave.

"You're being nice to me," I said, my chin quivering. I wanted to lean on her, but she was so frail looking. I didn't want to think of the damage I could do if I fell on her, and I was on the brink.

"Of course I am. You're my sister." Her sweet declaration tugged at my heart, and I tried not to miss Allie with everything inside of me.

She didn't ask what they did to me. The only things that came out of her were tears and words that were so kind, I could barely understand how a person who had only met me a few months ago could say them. "You're doing splendid. I'm so proud of you for making it out alive. Prince Langgam told us you didn't tell them where you hid the stone. Is that true?"

I nodded. "I'm sorry I let us get captured. You've been reaping on your own this whole time. I know that's stressful."

Mariang waved off my concern and ran a brush through my hair, being super gentle not to rip through my tangles. Then she pulled up my auburn curls into a bun atop my head to match hers. We were sister ballerinas, and in that moment, I was grateful she was mine.

Mariang offered her arm to lean on as I brushed my teeth with a new red toothbrush. "You're doing great. Move slowly." Then she pulled her head away from me and shouted down the mansion's upstairs hallway. "Danny! Help me with October!"

Danny was a good soldier, and came running up the stairs. He bounded toward us, his eyes wide at my bedraggled but clean state. He stood on my other side and wrapped his beefy arm around my waist, walking with the care he usually used when he ushered Mariang around.

I was shocked he was being so nice to me. I mean, most of the time I was the bane of his existence. My bones ached, and I was so weak, my knees buckled a few times on the way to the room he and Mariang led me to. I remember being able to defend myself against even the giant inmates. Not well, but enough to not get myself stabbed all too often. Now I was worried about the damage I would do to myself if I tripped.

"You'll sleep in here with us," he said, opening the door to the peach room that had clearly been decorated by Mariang. The peach walls had gold accents and hardware throughout the expansive space, bespeaking of opulence I'd not been exposed to growing up.

The bed was so soft, I didn't protest even when I thought of the germs I knew were inside the sheets. Probably dandruff. Probably Danny's semen. I shuddered, but was too tired to do anything else. The sliver of light coming in through the peach curtain told me it was not the middle of the night, as it had been in Terraway. "What time is it?"

"It's around ten in the morning. But that doesn't matter. You should rest as long as you like." Mariang sat on the side of the bed and brushed a few stray strands of auburn hair from my face that had come loose from the bun. "Can I get you anything?"

I wanted to tear up at her kindness. She looked down on my face with love that couldn't be faked. She had no agenda other than being my sister. "I... You're so nice to me," I repeated, sounding like a moron. It was meant as a thank you, but I was so confused by the sweetness, I didn't know how else to say it.

"Who wouldn't be nice to you? You've been through a dreadful ordeal." She took my hand and pressed it between her thin ones. "You're still cold. Not as bad as you were when Dad brought you home, but still too chilly for you to be comfortable." She blew on my fingers and rubbed while Danny watched our exchange.

"You have to tell us what happened," Danny said quietly. "Von's still not a person yet, and Mason's too devastated to talk. What did they do?"

I didn't know where to start, so I picked a topic at random. "Geon poisoned all the pregnant women to lose their babies, so when the soldiers came to take me to the castle, the civilians revolted. I mean, shrapnel and gun powder kind of uprising. Lots of bodies on both sides." I paused for Mariang's gasp. "Then soldiers found Mason, Von and me and brought us in. I don't know how many days I was in there."

"You've been in Terraway for two weeks," Danny informed me.

"Oh, jeez. Well, I was locked in a cell for a long time, then. Mason and Von were taken somewhere else, so I was alone in the cell until I murdered Andy." I ignored Danny's outcry and continued. "He tried to pull me to mindlessness so he could get out of me where the sagrado stone was hidden."

"No! He was a spy?" Mariang was horrified while Danny merely hung his head. I knew he'd had a hand in hiring Andy, and the shame was palpable.

I waited for Danny's humiliation to be discreetly swallowed down a few seconds later. When I spoke, I was quiet, afraid my presence and my voice weren't welcome here. "Lang snuck me berries and water, and made sure I had enough *baga* root to breathe, but I need to eat something more substantial, if it's not too much trouble. Does anyone know where my keys are? I can go get takeout." I was pretty sure I could drive. I might need someone to help me to the car, but I was decently confident I could take it from there.

Danny's face turned to frustration. "You must be joking if you think you're going anywhere. You can barely walk. I'll go downstairs and grab you something."

A thought flickered in my brain, giving me new life. "Do you have my backpack?"

"Yeah. It's in your room down the hall."

Oh, right. I have a bedroom here. "Would you mind grabbing it for me? I need to get something out of it."

Danny got up without being asked and came back a few minutes later with the bag that made my heart leap in my chest. I ripped open the front pouch and pulled out my medication, nearly letting out a cry of relief when I shook a tiny pill into my hand and downed it without water. I didn't care that Danny and Mariang were watching me. I knew that by the time it took to work its way through my system, I would be a little more myself, and that was a powerful promise.

So focused on my mental sanity was I that I didn't notice the bowl of beef until Danny placed the blissful deliciousness in my hands. It was beef bourguignon, and I was in heaven. I mean, really it could have been a greasy fast food slider and it would've had the same effect. I wasn't picky at this point, but I appreciated the fanciness of the dish all the same.

"Keep talking," Danny instructed me, his arms crossed over his chest as he leaned on Mariang's white lacquer desk.

"That's all I know. Lang has two friends who helped us and tried to get Von and Mason out. I haven't seen either of them since I got locked up. King Geon wanted me to give him the whole stone, so he kept me in the cell, thinking he'd starve me until I caved. Plus he wanted to punish the countries who didn't come to his aid when the famine hit his people hardest."

"Ezra has the stone now," Danny told me. "So you don't have to worry about that. He confirmed the broken-off part was dropped in the well. And Geon's going to be locked up in Kabayo's prison, so Prince Aranya's in charge of Sakuna for now. King Aranya now, I guess. I can't decide if that makes things worse or the same, but at least the people won't be starving anymore."

I pulled the spoon from my mouth. "They didn't kill Geon?"

"No. He'll have to be tried for each crime he committed. That could take months, if not a year."

"Awesome," I deadpanned.

"You did it!" Mariang squeezed my knee. "You got the piece of the sagrado to one of the nations and made it out alive! You have no idea how amazing that is."

I chewed the beef, not feeling anything like amazing, but girlfriend was in full-on cheer-me-up mode, so I didn't argue. "Tell me about Mason and Von."

Danny swallowed. "Von's useless for information right now. They bled him dry."

I gasped. "I thought he was still alive! Bled dry? No!" Panic hit me hard as tears I didn't even know I still had stored up began to well in my eyes. "Why didn't you tell me sooner? No!"

"No, no. Vampires can't die from blood loss. They just go rabid until they start to deteriorate. Von's still in the rabid stage. Ruiz and Klark brought him back bound from head to toe and put him in the cage Ezra had made for him in the basement." Danny motioned with a wave of a hand to his face. "Black bag over his head so he couldn't bite anyone." I could tell by the hollow look in his eyes that he didn't like the use of the black bag one bit.

"Are you kidding me?" Though the beef screamed at me with its siren song, I was out of the bed in the next breath. "Von doesn't belong in a cage. Get him out!"

I stalked toward the door, but didn't make it more than a few steps before Danny intercepted me. "Von requested Ezra have it made when he started working for the household, in case anything like this ever happened. Von isn't a person right now. All he can see is blood. We're feeding it to him in doses so he can come back to himself, but until then, he's not safe to be around."

"I'm going to see him. I won't let him be alone while he's losing his mind. Where is he?"

Danny sighed. "I guess showing you won't hurt anything. You might not like what you see."

"I haven't liked one bit of my life in weeks, so I don't care about that. I need to be with Von."

Danny and Mariang exchanged dark looks as they led me down the hallway and through the mansion to see my vampire.

5

GET OVER IT

I heard the howling before I saw the man. In the basement, there was a cell in the corner occupied by one Mr. Brady. When we came into view, Von lunged at the bars, his jaw snapping as he fought with the iron to get at me. The bag over his head was gone and his bindings had been cut, but the sight still broke my heart all the same. Von didn't have words, only growls and wails of agony that tore at my tender insides. I wanted to go to him, but Danny was firm I wouldn't be allowed within four feet of the cell. "He needs more blood!" I cried. "Can I give him some of mine?"

"No! Are you mad?" Danny shouted, as if I was inches from slitting my wrists to let Von drink fresh from the source.

Mariang was more gracious in her response, taking the time to re-explain things to me. "Human blood's the worst thing for him right now. He can't be allowed a drop of human blood. It'll only make him insane to get more, and it'll bring him one step closer to this being his permanent state if he transitions."

I rubbed my forehead, remembering the vital details I shouldn't have forgotten. "Oh, yeah."

"He has to gain control of himself." Danny placed his hand on my shoulder to keep me from inching closer to the cell, but I shrugged off his touch.

My mouth fell open when Von reached through the bars to claw at me, stretching as far as he could reach to grab any part of my body. His eyes were the usual: one gold and one blue, but the gold one seemed impossibly more vibrant than usual, the wanton desire driving him always forward toward the blood. He was beyond language, and I was beyond... just beyond.

I cast around for a chair, my eyes landing with unhappiness on the one I'd been tied to way back when this whole mess started. I walked over to it in the vast concrete basement and made to drag it over with what was left of my energy.

"What are you doing?" Danny asked, intercepting my effort. He was starting to treat me like he did Mariang when she was ready to pass out. This acted as a rapid fuel for me to get better fast.

"I'm staying with Von until he comes back to himself. Can you get me a book from his bedroom? Maybe if I read to him it would calm him down."

Danny blanched. "You're not serious. October, he doesn't even see you as you. All you are to him is a giant blood sack. Whatever gesture you're trying to make, he won't see it."

"The gesture isn't for him, it's for me. Von stayed with me while I was sorting through stuff. He stuck by my side and gave up his life to spend it with me. I know it's for the greater good and not for just me, but it can't be one way. I'm not a taker. This is finally a way I can be there for him."

Danny shook his head, setting the chair down six feet from the cage, but he stood next to it wearing his angry face, so I didn't dare go near Von. "That's not your job. Your job is to reap souls, not be his therapist."

"I'm allowed to be friends with my Pullers, Danny. If Mason's well enough, could you send him down here? The three of us are in this together. When one of us is broken, we should all feel it."

"No. You're getting this backwards. When you're broken, *they* should feel it. They're not allowed to burden you with being broken."

"Oh, you're hopeless. This is what family is," I informed him, feeling like I was a first grade teacher, and Danny was the mouthy kid at the back of the class.

"Whatever. I'll send Mason down to make sure you don't get eaten by your family pet."

My tone turned sharp. "You'll not run Von down in front of me anymore. He just went through something in Sakuna, and this is all you've got for him? The same old bag of flipped-up garbage? Your brother was being tortured in prison! What's the matter with you? Whatever sibling stuff you two've been married to for this long, get over it."

Danny reared back, and I saw out of the corner of my eyes Mariang retreating up the stairs to escape our fight. "Get over it? Get over it? You've known him only a few months. Von's got a trail of wreckage behind him, but he's a tortured artist half-vamp, so it's all okay."

I remained firm. "Get over it."

"He let my car get dinged when he was teaching Bishop to drive!"

"Get over it."

"He slept with the girl I liked in high school!"

"Oh, boo-hoo! Get over it."

"He's... He's irresponsible, but the worst part is that he didn't used to be. He knows how to do right by us, but he gave up."

"Get over it."

"He was a prostitute! That's the lowest kind of profession for Duwendes. He's a disgrace!"

I heard Von whining to snatch at me. Though I knew he couldn't understand that I was standing up for him, I felt finally right in my own skin at putting a stop to the aggression Danny always had ready. I lowered my voice and tried to iron out the frustration from my tone. "Danny, I know it's hard, but trust me, I'm telling you to get over it for you, not for Von. I know the boat you're in."

Danny scoffed, his Frankenstein eyebrows pushing together. "You couldn't possibly."

"No?" My temper started swinging like a pendulum. "Bev forgets us on Christmas every year. Allie and Ollie used to buy a present, wrap it and say it was from her. Bev let men into the house who were... They were the worst kind of men who shouldn't be allowed around young girls." I shivered. Perhaps it was because of the cold I still couldn't shake, or maybe it was from the memory of Bev's old boyfriend Gideon always trying to "accidentally" brush up against me and touch me where he shouldn't.

Danny's eyes went wide as his mouth closed, ceding the fight for the moment.

"Bev didn't feed me, drive me to school, take me to the doctor, come to graduations – none of it. And you know what I had to do? I had to get over it. Sure, it still stings, but being mad at this point? It only hurts me. You being mad at Von for something he did in high school? You're hurting yourself, not just Von. Did he even know you liked that girl before he slept with her?"

"No, but he should've. I only sat at the same lunch table with her every day for a month."

I let out a raspberry of disbelief. "Wow. And I thought I had problems. Can you really be the best at your job if you're carrying around all that anger? You have to find a way to let it go. Anger clouds your judgment, and you can't afford to be compromised on the job like this. Find a way to look at Von and not see all the ways he's failed you. It's a sucky way to look at people, how you're doing it. It's toxic, and you're addicted to the poison."

Danny chewed on his bottom lip, his arms crossed over his chest like armor to shield his heart so my words couldn't touch the tender, shriveled organ. "I can't see him any other way. Von knows how to be great. He was the best big brother when we were younger. Now he chooses not to be worthwhile. He chooses the gutter. Bev was always hopeless, but seeing your own personal Superman choosing the gutter? I can't stand for it."

I shrugged. "Then you'll just keep being unhappy. You'll keep hurting yourself." I looked up into his blue eyes, searching for something human lurking beneath all the steel he wore just to make it through the day. I saw the overburdened brother clearly, and felt truly sad for the Ollie of it all. "Danny, you're so tired. You work so hard. Can you really afford to carry around all this extra weight? Man, that must've been a high pedestal you had him on before he fell off of it. It's a wonder Von can stand at all."

With his mouth in a tight line, Danny watched my face, searching out signs that I was wrong or trying to get him to let his guard down for some shady purpose. "You... Don't... I don't care how dreamy you think Von is, you're not staying down here without Mason or me to watch you."

I nodded, expecting as much. "That's fine. And for the record, Von's my friend, nothing more. It's Mason I was aiming at."

"Was?"

"It's complicated. You'll be happy to know it's more complicated than I have the energy for. Your buddy's safe from my womanly wiles, as is your brother." My legs were tired from the mere effort of standing. I hadn't finished my stew, and was still starving and worn out.

Danny seemed to see all of this. He was well-trained at anticipating needs that might interfere with a Death Omen's ability to do her job. He moved the chair toward me and lowered me down into it by holding onto my elbows. "Steady," he warned me when my arms started shaking. After I was safely seated, he leaned my temple into his hip to make sure I didn't fall over. "You're still cold."

I took a few breaths, trying to iron out my weakness that threatened to make me pass right out in the middle of the basement. My eyes widened when I felt Danny's fingers brush back the errant curls that had come loose from my bun. He... He was being nice to me. I wasn't sure if I liked him better like this, or if I preferred him shouting like a fool. At least I could predict the fool.

"You know," he began, his voice quiet, "I'm going to have to tell Ezra everything. I haven't told him about Bev's trailer yet because I thought you should know before I did, but it's coming. He deserves to know the pile he's stepping into."

My lashes swept shut, fending off the arguing I wanted to do. "I don't want to take things away from Ezra. If Bev makes him happy, he should have that."

"Bev won't make him happy if she's this person you're telling me she is."

I didn't want to lean on him, but staying upright was problematic after enduring such malnourishment. "If they don't get married, then there goes my chance at having a dad." Moisture pricked at my eyes. "Could you go? I'm about to lose it, and you're like, the last person on the planet I want to cry in front of." I heard Von's grating howl to get at me, and I welcomed the distraction from my pain.

Danny palmed the side of my face and squeezed me to his hip. It was his version of a hug, and it served us both fine – jaded as we were. He exited up the stairs, leaving me alone with the monster who used to be Von. I soaked in my vampire's growls and snarls; they were far more eloquent than the taunting of the voices in my head.

6

JUST ONE KISS

One look at Mason took my breath away. Von had changed in the couple of weeks we'd been locked up, but Mason had been altered on too many levels. His seven long dreads had been cut off. Actually, he'd been shaved. I didn't know everything about the Matruculan race my biological father and Mason stemmed from, but I remembered one key element: their inhuman strength was tied to not cutting their hair. It was why Ezra wasn't a Hulk of a man, and I wasn't body slamming people more than the average girl with nine chips on her shoulder.

Mason's spirit was utterly crushed. Though I could now see his handsome face more fully without his beard (and truthfully, he looked a lot more like a hot guy from my world than a ruthless Viking), he was not himself. I'd fallen hard for Mason, and what Sakuna returned to me was a pretty shell. Mason came to me because Danny made him watch to make sure Von didn't eat me, but I could tell he'd rather be anywhere else.

"A lot of good I could do if Von actually broke loose," Mason countered.

Danny's thin lips were set in a tight line as he took in the tenor of his best friend's sunken mood. "You're every bit as strong as I am now. I'm not Matruculan, and I can guard my charge well enough. You still have strength; you'll just have to work a little harder for it from here on out. And your body compensates for what October needs to stay safe, so it's actually easy for you, me and Von to build muscle."

Mason pfft'd and sat down on the concrete floor, not bothering to spread out the blankets Danny had brought down for us. He didn't want comfort. I couldn't say I didn't understand. There were soft beds aplenty upstairs, but I was adamant about not leaving Von when he was so distraught.

Danny sighed, a hard look in his eyes as he watched his best friend sulk in what felt like a new permanence rather than a passing rough patch. When I got up off the chair to fan out the thick blankets Danny brought down for us, Danny helped me spread them on the floor, reaching out and brushing my fingers when we were finished making a nest for Mason and me. "You're still freezing. You shouldn't sleep down here. You know it's warmer upstairs."

"I won't leave one of my team when they're down and out. I don't want Von to come back to himself all alone. He doesn't deserve that. They were tortured because they were with me. I can be a little uncomfortable for them."

Danny shook his head at me, on the edge of exasperation. "You don't understand how this thing works. We follow you. You don't follow us."

"I don't much care how it's supposed to work. This is who I am. Deal with it."

So focused on smoothing out the wrinkles was I that I didn't see the luscious bowl of beef Danny set down beside me. I barely chewed as I wolfed down the remainder of the meal, so grateful to be full and on the way to feeling normal again.

Danny still didn't get why I needed my little team to stick together through Von's torment, but he didn't say anything more about it. He simply sat on the blankets near my head after I laid down, watching Mason stare off vacantly from his seat on the concrete.

"Danny?" I said just loud enough to be heard over Von's growls and snorts.

"Yeah?"

"Do you ever resent Mariang for all the work you have to do?"

Danny was thoughtful for a moment. "Some days are more intense than others, but in the end I know I chose this life. Why?"

I pulled the hunter green comforter up to my chin and stared up at the concrete ceiling. It had wood beams running width-wise across it, and not a single cobweb. "I have a hard time living with the fact that I've pretty much ruined their lives." I spoke of Mason as if he wasn't there, which was basically the case. "Sakuna put us in prison, but now that we're out, they're not actually free. They're still sentenced to lifetime duty. I'm wondering at what point they'll start taking their resentment out on me."

When Danny spoke, he sounded confused. "You really care about them."

"Of course I do."

Danny cleared his throat. "I wouldn't worry so much about the resentment thing. It's not a huge issue, no more than it is with any relationship."

I nodded, wishing I could do anything for Von, who was whining to get at us, reaching through the bars of his cage to snatch at me. I wished I could help Mason, who was utterly not himself. I sat up and crawled over to my Viking, kneeling in front of him to show him my hands before placing them on his shoulders. I massaged the meat that was tense from too many zombie-ridden battles, knowing it wouldn't fix him, but it was at least a start. He couldn't look at me, even as I pulled him up to stand. I laid him down in the makeshift bed and scooted in next to him.

"If you don't need anything else, I'm going to go upstairs to be with Mariang. She's had a long day."

"That's fine. Thanks for everything."

"No problem, kid." Danny turned off the overhead lights and left on the stairway bulb so we had just enough illumination to see.

When we were alone, I turned on my side to face Mason, reaching out to touch his shaved cheek. He was even more handsome now, like a cowboy model on a smutty porn-for-women book cover, but utterly destroyed. When his eyes finally met mine, a small amount of life flickered when he whispered, "Kara. I need to see Kara. Please."

My heart sank. Of course he would want his wife in this situation. We barely knew each other. What use could I really be to him? I was the conduit for giving him access to the woman he truly loved. Though it tore me up, I felt like I owed him that for all he'd suffered through on my account.

"Sure, buddy. Anything you need. Just one kiss, though, okay?"

"Okay. Thank you for this."

I sighed, gearing myself up to rip my heart in two all over again. I closed the gap between us and stroked his lips with mine. They were soft and supple, tasting like the beef he'd no doubt been fed earlier. He was delicious. My intention was to take it slow as I indulged us, but by the second kiss, our passion took my senses by storm. The red and yellow colors blasted into my vision, swirling around Mason and tying us together in our nest.

My stomach jumped up, did a backflip into my esophagus and landed with a splash in my midsection. Soon I was the desperate one, clinging to his hard body with hands that read his chest like it was covered in Braille.

He was warm, like sun-baked earth, and I had been so cold.

And then he was crying. I didn't have a ton of experience making out with older men, but something told me that tasting tears wasn't as sexy as, well, not. I pulled back to gauge his expression, but when we parted those few inches, he grew immediately frustrated. "Where is she? Kara? Kara!" He grabbed my face like he wanted to punish it, and crashed his lips down on mine, rolling atop me. Then he pulled back with a mournful wail. "No! Kara! Come back to me!"

The pleasant sensory overload melted away, and I lay beneath him, horrified. I apologized for not being able to produce his deceased wife on command, unable to stop myself. "I'm sorry, Mason. I don't know what happened. You can't see her anymore?"

"I know she's in there! Let's try again."

"I don't think we should. Mason, let's..." But Mason swallowed the rest of my protest in another kiss. The flutes were screaming at me now as the colors flung themselves on my body like the splash of a rotten tomato, as if warning me to get away.

Believe me, I was trying. "Mason, it's enough. I can't..." His body was heavy, and weighted my weakened one so I couldn't get out from under him. My pulse spiked when I realized that this wasn't a kiss; it was an attack. "Mason, calm down a little. That's too rough!"

"You're being stubborn! Give my wife back to me!" His

cry broke my heart for too many reasons.

Mason pinned my arms out to the sides when I tried to gently extract myself, his demanding lips seeking out mine that were now protesting his bruising force to no avail. "Mason! Stop it! Let me go!" When his hips pressed down atop mine, fear lit me up like a Christmas tree on fire. I screamed to the upstairs for help, but Mason ignored me, frantically searching my lips for someone that just plain wasn't there. Maybe I could've thrown him off on my own, but the whole thing was so confusing and scary. I didn't think I had the wherewithal to hold my head up under the crushing weight of the worst love life in the world. Also, I was pretty undernourished, and didn't have my usual throw-a-Viking-off-me oomph.

"Give her to me!" Mason shouted as he mashed his lips to mine again through my scream, rough and angry, like he wanted to punish me for not producing his wife on command. "Kara!"

Von's first human words erupted from his pained expression as he gripped the bars like he wanted to bend them. "Danny! Help!" Then he went back to growling and snapping his teeth to get at me.

I heard heavy footsteps pounding down toward us. "Ah, guys! I thought you were in trouble," Danny groused, embarrassed as he turned to stomp back up.

"Help! Get him off me!" I shouted, trying to twist away, but unable to escape from under him. Mason caged me in with his arms, shoving his lips down on me again, searching in vain for something I didn't even know how to give him.

The next thing I knew, Mason was ripped off of me, looking like a wild animal in Danny's grip. Danny had him around the chest and the waist from behind, his eyes wide as he tried to make the scenario mean anything other than what he'd seen. "Get ahold of yourself, mate!" Danny squeezed, and Mason started to view the room with new clarity.

I crawled away from Mason, tears pricking my eyes. I knew he was distraught and not himself, but I couldn't look the other way on this. It was violation on top of pain, and now all I could see when I looked at him was the fear he'd just instilled in me. Von was a monster, and Mason was a selfish prick. I wasn't sure which one was more dangerous.

Danny called for Ezra, who padded down the steps, still in his day clothes. I wondered, at this rate, when any of us would find rest again. Danny released Mason, who turned away to hide the tears that stained his shaven face.

Ezra demanded.

Danny explained.

Mason confessed.

I kept my mouth shut as I cried into my hands in the dark corner. I jumped when Ezra put his hand on my shoulder, breaking me out of my bubble of pain. Very slowly, Ezra pulled me up, and without a word walked me up the stairs so I didn't have to see Danny sort Mason out.

7

ICY INSIDE

I slept with Danny and Mariang that night. Mariang was the best kind of mom-sister and simply held me while I cried into her nightgown. Occasionally Danny would reach over Mariang to pat my back in a "hang in there, kid" kind of way. I cried until I exhausted myself, falling asleep in Mariang's thin arms that somehow felt like the safest place in the world.

I didn't leave her bed that day, or that night. The next morning I stayed in her bed, not willing to get out and face the world. It wasn't until Mariang came back up with a bowl of oatmeal that I even registered it was nearly ten o'clock in the morning, and I was sleeping in like a lazy waste of space.

"I think you should eat something," she said in her caring way. She waited for me to sit up in her bed, and then handed me the warm bowl that smelled like brown sugar and freshly cut apples. When I didn't speak, she started in on the events of the morning I'd missed. "Von's doing better. Dad's going to let him out of his cell soon. He's completely himself now, but he's staying inside on his own will. Von's pretty good about that. He knows when he's too dangerous to be around, and he won't allow Dad to get him out until he's certain he's safe to us."

I nodded, taking a bite of food. It was the right kind of too hot. It warmed me in my cold spots that I wasn't sure I would ever be able to shake at this point.

"Danny and Dad sorted Mason out. I... I've known Mason for years, and I still can't believe something like that happened. But Danny told me Mason confessed to how he's been using you." She shook her head, her black hair swishing from side to side. "You don't deserve that."

"If it's all the same to everyone, I'd rather not talk about it. I got out of prison and walked smack into that. I'm on the edge of bowing out, so you might want to spread it around not to push me today."

"That's understandable. Danny and I are leaving soon to start the workday. I would invite you to join us, but I can't imagine you or Mason are ready to jump back into reaping."

"You imagine right. I'm going back to my house as soon as I finish breakfast."

"I don't think that's wise," came Ezra's steady voice from the doorway. He was freshly showered and wearing khaki pants with a blue button-down that had lavender pinstripes. He was fastening his cufflinks, frowning at me with an air of paternal scolding. "Your house isn't nearly as safe as mine."

"I've given up on being safe. You know as well as I do that it's a pipe dream. It doesn't seem to be an option no matter where I land. I don't live here, Ezra."

Ezra's eyes were earnest, and his voice was firm, but gentle. "But if you did, I could protect you better."

"But I don't." I wasn't trying to be bull-headed; I just wanted my own bed. "I appreciate everything you've done for me. Really, Ezra. You're like, the nicest man I've ever met. And Mariang?" I turned my attention to the girl who sat on the edge of the bed in her khaki skirt and pink sweater. She looked as if I'd just run over her puppy. "Mariang's top notch. But seeing as I'm not up to working today, I think I've earned a day off to blow in bed. My own bed."

Ezra was hesitant, but eventually he nodded. "Okay. I'll send people to your house to reinforce the protective charms."

"So long as they're gone by the time I get home, that's fine."

Ezra stood straighter, gearing himself up to make a speech. "I apologize for Mason's behavior. I had no idea he was still using you to see his wife again. It's unacceptable, and I've sent him to a friend's for the day so he could get some space and clarity. He'll be ready for reaping in a day or two, but you won't have to see him until then, and definitely not without Von there to monitor his behavior."

"Thanks." My voice came out in a croak I wished I could make sound more refined, but after another night of crying and weeks of dehydration, a froggy throat was the best I got.

Mariang and Ezra left me to my breakfast. After I choked down my food and dressed in new clothes that had been laid out for me with the tags still on, I was ready to go home.

Terence the Taurus had missed me just as much as I'd missed him. Danny had brought my car to the mansion for me, which made it on the expanding list of reasons why I was grateful for him. With the windows cracked a little, the fresh air revived me, giving me new life to sit up straighter and snap out of my funk. I had the heat on full blast, but I was still shivering. I hadn't managed to shake the cold that felt settled in my bones.

Mason was a tool, I'd been naïve, and that was the extent of it. Nothing more complicated or magical than that. I tried not to foster the fear of him that was steadily growing, but chalked it up to a bad choice after the worst couple weeks of his life. Losing his Superman strength was pretty traumatic. I decided to walk away from the hurt instead of examine it too closely. I also decided I would never kiss him again.

My house wasn't exactly as I had left it, but I expected as much. The closets and doors had all been thrown open, and the rooms had been rifled through. Don't get me started on the fingerprints on my windows. We'd slipped out under cover of night and subterfuge, and I guessed the guards had done a thorough search for us. My shower felt the same, though, and so did the thick pajamas I covered myself in.

I collapsed onto my bed and burrowed under my covers. I never thought I would miss sleeping with two delicious smelling men hogging my pillows, but I did. Not so much Mason, since the sting of his desperation was still too fresh, but Von for sure.

I closed my eyes and willed myself to feel safe and content in my bed, grateful I wasn't sleeping in the mud in Sakuna or in the cell. The cell had been so cold that I still felt the sting of the chill that seemed deep-set somewhere inside me. I got out of bed to slide on another pair of socks and tug an oversized gray sweater from Ollie's castoff pile over my head. I didn't care what I looked like, only that I was warm.

Only I wasn't warm. I was icy inside, and part of me wondered if that would ever go away.

8

OUTSOURCING BATHING

I didn't expect Team Terraway to leave me alone for the whole day and night, but when I awoke to it being late morning without interruption or threat of death, I was pleasantly shocked. I checked through the house, and there was nothing. No Von eating all my food or Danny drinking juice from the container, or Lang sending his trail of bugs to spy on me. I actually had my house to myself.

And I knew just what to do with it.

After a decent meal, I got out my cleaning supplies and went to town scrubbing, washing, folding, polishing and disinfecting until I exhausted myself. It was a good kind of tired, not the kind you got from being starved and locked up with a dead body.

As I showered the stink of the morning off me, I winced at the thought of Andy, probably still rotting in the cell. I worried about Kabayo's men, and the loss they might've suffered trying to vindicate me. It was a heavy weight I felt, having seen so many thinned Sakuna civilians die in the revolt.

No matter how much hot water I used, I still felt icy. When I got out, I adjusted the thermostat, raising it to seventy-three degrees, which was about four degrees hotter than I could usually stand to keep my house at. I had my fleece pajamas on, fuzzy thick purple socks, a heavy baseball jersey and a black hoodie I prayed would warm me up. But still I shivered, wrapped in a cream wool blanket on the couch as I flipped around for something interesting to distract me from the cold that only seemed to be growing.

There was nothing with Bruce Campbell on, which meant that all the TV stations sucked, and there was nothing good to watch.

I shivered as I tried to summon up the muscular control to go make myself some hot tea. When even that debate grew too tenuous, I realized something was very wrong. I was so cold, and the constant shivering was exhausting me. I laid down on the couch and closed my eyes, huddling under the wool blanket that had always made me sweat. I couldn't figure out why I had no body heat, and was too scared to call Ezra and get to the bottom of whatever weird leprechaun flu I'd contracted.

I drifted off some time in the evening on the couch, and was awakened only by the sound of the doorbell. My feet were too cold and inflexible to be put to use, so when the person on the other side of the door grew impatient and started banging, I called for them to calm down. I was still trying to stand up without falling immediately back onto the couch when I heard keys jangling in the front door. My shallow breath quickened, and I wasn't sure if I should be excited that Ollie was home early, or afraid because Ollie certainly was not home, and someone was trying to break into my house.

I shrieked when Danny came barreling through the door, eyes almost as wide as mine. His muscles were tensed, as if expecting a fight. His chest moved in and out with too much force. "What's the problem? Couldn't be bothered to answer your own door? Didn't you hear us knocking? I've been calling you all day!"

I wanted to spout back at him what a jerk he was being, but the effort was too great. "Keys," I observed, pointing to his hand. "You used a k-key."

"Of course I did, no thanks to you!"

"Where did you g-get a key to my house?"

"I had one made when you were abducted. Have you noticed you haven't been attacked here? It's because I increased a few protection charms around your property while you were gone."

"You have a copy of the k-key to my house?" I was shocked, not even greeting Von, who strolled in with a backpack, a six-pack and four pizzas. My favorite vampire made himself at home, setting his food in my kitchen.

Danny glared at me in lieu of an apology. "Why didn't you answer the door? Or the phone?"

"Give me the k-key," I demanded, extending my hand the few inches it would go before my joints stiffened in protest.

Danny was distracted from our fight by my immobile body that usually would've been raring to go if an intruder came in the door. "What's wrong?"

"Are you k-kidding? You stole my k-keys! You broke into my h-house!"

Danny closed the distance between us and tore the sleeve up my arm, exposing the skin beneath that was paler than my usual glow. "Von!" he shouted. "Von, get in here!" I tried to rip my arm away from him, but I was ashamed at how weak and ineffectual my effort was. When Von trotted into the living room, Danny's voice was tinged with a note of growing fear as he got in my face. "You can't reap without one of them here! You're like ice! Von, hurry, get the corroded soul out of her."

Since Danny was still gripping my arm, Von smoothed his thumbs starting at my forehead, and then slid them down around my cheeks. He pulled a layer of stress and something icy from my bones I hadn't been able to get rid of even with a hot shower and too many layers.

Without willing my body to do so, I slumped forward, nearly passing out at the relief from the warmth that started to trickle into me. I whimpered pathetically as Von and Danny caught me and lowered me down on the couch.

Danny was barking orders at Von, but I couldn't make heads or tails of anything. All I felt was chocolate slowly melting into my veins, taking its gooey time warming up my insides.

Von disappeared, and then came back to take off my hoodie and socks. My baseball jersey slipped up and over my head, leaving me in my white camisole. Another shiver ripped through me, choking a cry out of my shaking body as Von wrapped me in a hug. The hug was the only thing I could feel in my maze of ice that wasn't completely gone, so I clung to it. I clung to him.

I was floating in the air somehow, and then a minute later I was being submerged in my large oval bathtub, the heat finally giving me its full attention. The tub was big enough for my legs to stretch out, which was the main reason Allie had voted for this house.

The relief that flooded through me was incredible. I'd never been high, but I imagined this was what it must feel like. I was boneless and couldn't think clearly enough to form sentences. All I wanted was more of the warmth, so I sunk down into the water, content as the heat closed over my head.

Von ripped me out of the tub by my shoulders, shouting in my face with uncharacteristic alarm I didn't like seeing on him. He was too good a kidder to be painted with such distress marring his handsome features. He wasn't nearly as wild as he'd been when I'd seen him last. It looked like he'd shaved, showered and had enough blood to put some color in his cheeks. Or maybe that was from the steam in the bathroom from my bath. His arms wrapped around me and squeezed, not caring about keeping his green garage rock band t-shirt dry.

Danny came in behind him, a pile of my clean clothes in his arm that he laid down on the toilet lid. I could hear them murmuring to each other, but I was too out of it with the bliss of heat to care to decode the words. I wish I'd been paying a little more attention, though, because Von surrendered me to Danny, who crushed me to his chest so my limp body didn't go back under. Von tore off his shirt and unbuckled his pants, letting his jeans drop to the tiled floor. I wanted to protest, but the sight was so strange, I didn't care to make a fuss about it. My mouth popped open when I saw dozens of slices all over Von's torso and legs. The torture he'd endured was too much to quantify into a single emotion.

Danny leaned me forward, and Von climbed into the water behind me, pulling me onto his lap. I'd never taken a bath with a guy – least of all with my clothes still on. I knew I should want to squirm away and tell him to get his own flippin' tub, but he was so warm. The water was soothing, and I'd been so cold for so long. I cuddled up in Von's lap, my cheek on his bare shoulder and my hand resting in the smattering of hair on his chest that reminded me he was very much a man – despite his boyish ways. He waved Danny away, and I closed my eyes as he stroked my cheek and rubbed my back under my camisole. Von pulled away layers of ice and stress I'd not been able to slaughter on my own.

"Hey, Peach. Did you hear me?" He lightly pinched my arm, and I only just realized he'd been talking to me. I'd heard a murmuring, but nothing more audible than that.

"Huh?"

"I asked if you were sweating yet. Hot bath, hot guy?"

I snuggled further into his chest, not wanting to soak in his silly jokes just yet. "I'm too cozy to smile through what passes for your humor. Now hush up and be pretty and warm."

"Yes on the pretty and warm, no on the shutting up. You haven't told me about your time at Hotel Prison Sakuna. Did they have the tiny bottles of shampoo and soaps? Did they fluff your pillow?"

"Something like that. I ate slightly more than a pillow mint, if that counts."

"Lang mentioned you were being starved. He said he did what he could to sneak you food. Geon isn't exactly an expert at looking after humans, the git. I hope Kabayo kills him after a good long stretch of sport."

"I'm not a fan of torture, but Geon needs to be put down for what he did to you and Mason." I noticed Von had a little smudge of something on his collarbone. I reached up, noting the flexibility that was coming back into my joints, and swiped my wet hand over top of the bar of soap on the ledge of the blue tiled wall. I rubbed my sudsy hand on Von's collar, a smile touching my lips when he tilted his chin back so I could give his neck a thorough scrub.

"Mm. That feels nice. Will you do my arms?" When I hesitated, considering our already too casual friendship, Von batted his lashes at me. "Please? I've been tortured."

I smiled at him, reaching up to bring down the bar of soap to get a good lather. "You're going to milk that one for a while, huh."

"You know it. I might need a foot rub and a pint later. You know, because of all the torture." He said it in jest, but I saw the haunting truth he tried to cover up. He wasn't over any of it; Von was scared.

"Worst weeks of your life takes a toll on a person. It's okay to call a spade a spade."

Von swallowed. "Those weren't my worst weeks, but definitely top five."

"What was your worst? Bad hair day?" Maybe I shouldn't have asked.

Von was quiet a few moments before answering. "A long stretch of weeks spent in Dagat – that's the country with the Merpeople. The one Captain Finn oversees. Those were the worst of my life. Getting kicked out of the Academy was probably up there, too."

"What happened in Dagat?"

He kissed my cheek. "That's a conversation for an empty house. I think Danny might still be out there."

"Okay." I was gentle as I soaped up his left arm, getting in between his fingers and even going up under his arm, smirking when he squirmed at the unintentional tickle. "Hold still," I chided, turning in his lap to wash his right arm. I gave his forearm a light massage he groaned at.

"You know, this would be the part where we started making out if we were in a movie," he observed, burying his nose in my hair. "This probably isn't the sexy talk the viewers dreamed of, but man, your blood smells amazing. You're heating up and I can smell you so clearly. Like peaches, nice and ripe." There was too much longing in his tone, and I shivered in his lap. He shifted beneath me and cleared his throat, shaking his head to rid himself of the trance he was falling into. "Change the subject. Tell me all the ways Geon's a rat bastard."

"Only the usual ways. I don't really want to talk about it. I'm alive. Lang deserves a raise. That's the end of it. How about you? Danny said they bled you dry?"

Von turned his chin from side to side. "I don't want to talk about it either. Suffice it to say, Geon wanted the stone quite badly. He wasn't sure which one of us would crack, so he tried all three of us."

"I can't believe he did that to Mason. Took away his strength? I mean, I'll be okay eventually. You're looking much better. But to permanently clip Mason's wings like that? It's the worst kind of cruel."

"Speaking of Mason," Von began with too much hinting in his voice. "I missed out on being rescued, but I was starting to see again when that went down. He shouldn't have kept kissing you like that. He knows it now, but hindsight's not worth a whole lot in that kind of situation."

"I don't really have anything to say about it. Mason will come back because he has to. I'll be civil. I've worked with all kinds of people who didn't listen to me. But yeah, that's long over."

Von took the soap from me and surprised me by starting in on my arms, massaging with real pressure that did me lots of good and made my already limp body lean back into him, my spine on his chest. I sighed, enjoying the breadth of the snuggle that lapped at us. "I'm sorry he did that. I wanted to pull him off you, but I couldn't get out. Even if I could've, I'm fairly certain I'd only have added to the problem."

"It's fine." I hmm'd when Von leaned me forward and massaged my back with soapy hands, sliding my straps down my arms so he could grind his thumbs into the meat on my shoulders.

"It's really not fine, but I appreciate you being the team player in it all. Word of advice? When Mason comes groveling back, don't play the whole 'it's fine' card. Tell him you forgive him or that you don't, but nothing about what he did was fine. Kissing you to see another woman? Then not stopping when you screamed for him to get off you?" Von closed his eyes and then coiled his arms around my torso, pulling me to his chest and leaning back. His thumb found my navel through my thin white camisole and traced a circle around it. He rolled up the hem a few inches so he could palm my stomach, sending a naughty thrill through us both. "Of all the things I wish I could scrub from my brain, your screaming haunts me most."

I reached my hand up behind me and stroked his shaved cheek. "I'm okay now."

"What's this scar on your arm from?" Von asked, thumbing the puckered jagged pink line on the upper crest of my bicep. I always hid it from Ollie by not wearing tank tops when he was around.

I squirmed uncomfortably. "It's old. It's nothing."

Von sent infinite chills through me when his lips dragged up the slope of the side of my neck. My head leaned back on his shoulder involuntarily. "What's it from?"

My brain was turning to mush while Von played my body as easily as strumming a guitar. Pain and starvation didn't work on getting information out of me, but kissing my neck? I sang for Von without hesitation after that. "An old work injury."

"What'd you cut yourself with?"

"I didn't cut myself. It's from one of the inmates. Pistola stuck me with a shiv I didn't see on him. I was treating him for bang-ups during a yard fight. He doesn't like women."

Von's lips removed themselves from my neck. "Are you serious?"

"Yeah, but Ollie doesn't know, so keep that to yourself. He'd freak."

"He'd freak over his sister getting shivved by a terri-fying inmate? What an overprotective wanker."

I chuckled, still relaxed against him. "It's all fine. I lived. Pistola got solitary."

Von tangled his fingers through mine under the water, studying how our hands looked when they were so very intertwined. "You're more than just the job to me. You're like my best girlfriend. Like a sister or something."

I chuckled, my stomach moving his hand up and down with the motion. "I've got news for you, champ. Ollie and I never did this. I'll take the best girlfriend label, if it's all the same to you."

"Works for me. But that means I'll be expecting more of this. If I can outsource bathing myself to you, that'd really free up a lot of time and effort on my part."

"Von?" My finger traced one of the deeper cuts on his arm that looked on its way to healing.

"November?"

I reached up behind me and clumsily pressed my hand to his cheek, closing my eyes when he leaned into my palm to press a kiss there for me to hold. "I don't like that they hurt you. Just the thought of how you got all these cuts is grating at my conscience. If not for me, they wouldn't have taken you. I'm so sorry."

"*Hani*," he whispered, his breath tickling the shell of my ear. "I'm alright. I'm just glad I didn't scare you too bad with the aftereffects."

"Von?"

"November?"

I waited until the water stopped moving, needing absolute quiet to eke out the words I'd known for a while to be true. "You're my best friend, too."

Von smirked before placing a kiss on my naked shoulder. He tightened his grip around me, bringing my hand back up to his cheek just to savor the feel of it. It was intimate in a way I hadn't let myself be with a man before Von came into my world. My whole body hummed at the luxury. Von's gentle caresses made my body feel beautiful instead of just useful. In his arms, I was a woman.

For all the sanity the doctor prescribed me, that night Von was my good medicine, and he held me in the bath until the water went cold. Then finally, I was warm.

LEPRECHAUN FLU

*V*on and I got out of the tub, drying each other off with careful fingers. I feathered the towel through his hair, messing it to perfection. I could feel him watching me as I styled which parts of his hair I preferred spiked and which should stay tamed. We turned around to give the other one a little privacy as we stepped into our clean and dry clothes. We went out into the living room a thousand times more relaxed than when we'd entered the bathroom. Danny had picked me out some fleece leggings I only wore around the house, a fresh tank top and my black hoodie with a pair of my lacy black panties I wish dude hadn't seen.

I probably shouldn't have been surprised to find Danny pacing in the living room, but his surly mug found us with something to say about our contented expressions. "Well, it's about time. Are you warm yet?"

I nodded. "Good to see you, too, chief. I guess it was some weird leprechaun flu or something."

"You can't go reaping without one of us there. I mean it. What you did was dangerous, and could've had lasting consequences. Mariang's skin? That's what happened before I was hired in. You don't want that."

"Yes, sir." I flopped onto the couch, gearing up for whatever lecture was coming next. "But I didn't reap anyone. I mean, I would know if I had, right? I was locked in a cell, Danny. No humans down there at all but for little old me. I was taken straight from the dungeon to Ezra's. No time for extracurricular reaping."

Danny grimaced, looking a little like the Frankenstein monster sucking on a sour Jolly Rancher. "That's not possible. You had a rotting soul in you. Von pulled it out." He looked to Von, who confirmed it all with a nod as he slid onto the couch next to me.

Von motioned for me to hand him my foot, but I couldn't imagine for what. I lifted my leg a few inches in his direction, and he caught it up and pulled it onto his lap, rubbing my toes with his warm fingers. My eyelids shut without needing me to command them to rest. Von slid the wool blanket over me, sealing in the heat I feared would escape in the open air.

"Von!" Danny barked. "Knock it off. I'm trying to get to the bottom of this, and you're distracting her."

Von tickled the arch of my foot, earning himself a light kick to the elbow. I sat up so I could focus more clearly, but left my feet in Von's lap so he could play with my toes. "I don't know what you expect me to say, Danny. I mean, the only dead person I was near was Andy in the cell after I…" I swallowed. "You know, after I killed him. But Andy's not human. Doesn't reaping only work on humans?"

"Yeah. It can't be Andy. But who else?" His eyebrows pushed together as he studied me, as if my face might tell him answers my mouth couldn't. "I don't like this. Von, not out of your sight. I mean it, if she's reaping people we can't keep track of, that's dangerous."

Von saluted Danny. "Yes, sir. Not out of my sight."

Danny ran his hands over his face. "I picked up some takeout while you were in the bathroom. I figure you'll be pulling from her for a while, and there's not much pizza left. There's a blood bag in the fridge in case you need it. I'll be back tomorrow with Mason, so you know, be ready to start working in the morning." His eyes narrowed on Von's. "Morning means be ready by seven, not noon."

"Yes, supreme leader." Von bowed his head in Danny's direction, earning him a glower. "Isn't he adorable when he orders me around?"

"Simply precious," I agreed.

Danny gathered up his coat and keys and then turned to me, jabbing his finger in my face. "You," he said in an accusing tone. "You know, I'm, well, I'm glad you're okay. Call me next time something's wrong like this."

I touched my knuckle to the tip of his finger. "Thanks

for stealing my keys and barging in." I looked up and blinked at him. "Truly."

"Yes, well. Whatever." He cracked his neck twice. "Call me if Von's being a problem. Otherwise, I've got to go home and pull from Mariang so she can work tomorrow."

"I hope you have a good night, Danny."

I don't know why he seemed confused at my normal parting greeting, but he paused as if considering my words for hidden meaning before nodding. "Alright, kid. You, too."

Von squeezed my toes when Danny finally left. "Do you get the feeling that he's warming up to you? I mean, that was almost civil just then."

"Yes, Danny's learning manners. It's an uphill battle." I squirmed when Von pulled up my foot to kiss my big toe before setting it down on the couch when he stood. He went to the kitchen and brought back two takeout boxes with Chinese food inside that made both of us groan when he opened them.

"Tuck on in here, Peach. Dibs on the steak. Or the chicken. I can't decide."

I snatched the Kung-Pow chicken from him and slid my chopsticks out of the red paper sleeve. I clicked on the TV and let Von scoop me to his side. We settled on a B-Horror movie, which were my absolute favorite. Especially the chainsaw-wielding variety. You could do so much with a simple chainsaw.

So content was I under the blanket on the couch eating

Chinese food next to Von that I didn't even care when he picked a piece of chicken from my box. "Lean your head back," he said as the opening credits concluded. The movie started in on a busty girl tiptoeing through the woods in the dead of night in her skimpy prom dress. *What could possibly go wrong?* I cozied into Von's nook, leaning my head back on his shoulder. I tore my eyes from the screen when he chuckled. "Well, that's just adorable. But I meant *tilt* your head back. Open your mouth. You've got to try this." I did as he instructed, and he reached high above me, dangling a too-long noodle overhead and draping it into my mouth. "Now lean back on me like that again. I've got to say, I like this whole platonic girlfriend thing."

"Whatever. You just like double the Chinese food."

We ate while laughing at the cheesy script and took turns trading little cheek kisses until the movie ended. It was barely eight o'clock, but when Von suggested I carry him to bed, I decided the day had been filled with enough adventure. The constant shivering had taken a lot out of me, and my body was tapped out.

Von and I got ready for bed and climbed into the queen-sized cloud haven of feather comforters and soft sheets. Our toes tangled with each other's as we tried to give the other person space, but realized we preferred the closeness after the week of torture and isolation. Von slept clad only in his blue cotton boxer briefs, tucking me into his nook. Our legs wound around each other, somehow unable to get close enough. He moved to turn off the lamp, but my childish fear stopped him. "Wait! I was kind of hoping we could sleep with the lamp on." I caught myself too late, and shook my head. "Never mind. That's stupid. Go ahead and turn it off."

He quirked an eyebrow at me. "Afraid of the dark, are we?"

I didn't want to admit that he'd hit the nail on the head. I gulped, strangling the chicken inside of me. "Geon kept me alone in the cell in pitch black for days."

Von's expression turned tender. "Darling. Do you want to talk about it yet?"

I shook my head. "You can turn off the lamp. I was being a dork about it. I'll be fine."

Von got out of bed, turned on the light in the living room, and shut our door, letting a little illumination filter in through the bottom. Then he turned off the lamp that shone too brightly for either of us to get any sleep if it was kept on. "Is that better?"

"Much," I said with a sigh of relief. "Thank you. And thanks for not... I know I'm being high maintenance."

Von climbed back under the blankets, rolling atop me to cover my body with his. "You were starved and locked in a dungeon. It's quite alright to feel a bit turned around. You should always tell me what you want." He nipped at my lips, my cheeks, and finally planted a kiss on my nose. Our eyes met with heat that felt laced with too many layers of things neither of us were ready to put words to just yet.

When he rolled off me to lay on his side, our separation lasted a handful of agonized seconds before we were holding hands and twining our legs together under the sheets again. "Von?"

"November?"

"What happened in Dagat?"

Von cleared his throat, and I could tell he was fishing for a PG version of the truth. "That's where I started up as a male escort. Not exactly my high point. Tried to raise funds to pay off some gambling debt. Didn't go as planned. Turns out, a stripper with a heart of gold is slightly less glamorous in real life."

My mouth dropped open. Danny had called him out on being a male prostitute before, and though Von hadn't argued with the accusation, part of me sort of assumed Danny was just being a jag.

I was cutesy cuddling a male prostitute, my legs looped through his while we held hands. I didn't have the words, which ranged from "Ack! STDs!" to "What a poor puppy." After a moment of confusion, I realized that this was Von, and there was precious little he could say that would make me turn away from him.

I kept my words censored as I opened my arms and waved him to come even closer. I wrapped my arms around him, crushing my front to his as we lay on our sides to let him know that no matter what, we were in this whole thing together. "I'm so sorry being tortured in a prison wasn't the worst part of your life. Is all that behind you now? You don't still sleep with women for money, do you?" Von was gorgeous; I couldn't imagine him not making a killing selling his body and his sexy smirk to the highest bidder.

"I haven't done that since I left Dagat." He relaxed in my embrace, snaking his arm around my waist under the sheets. "You didn't send me to go sleep on the couch."

"Of course not. You belong right here with me."

Von rubbed my back, and when he spoke, his voice came out choked. "I haven't belonged anywhere in a long time." He delivered a closed-mouth kiss to my lips.

My lashes fluttered shut on instinct, and I scolded myself for indulging in the sweetness that made my cheeks turn pink. "You kiss my mouth, even though it's against your rules."

He shrank sheepishly. "Yeah, I know. I can't help myself. Scares the pants off me with anyone else. I don't know why, but it feels safe with you." He watched my face for signs of flight. "Was that okay?"

I nodded slowly. "I like how we are. I'm just never expecting it." My toes brushed up the back of his bare leg. "And you don't have any pants on to scare off tonight, so I think we're safe."

His lazy smile returned, relaxing us both. "Darling, don't you know never to get used to me? I'm full of surprises." He pecked my lips again, his long, dark lashes sweeping shut mere seconds before mine. The kisses were light, and not deep enough to invoke the psychedelic sensory overload, which made them absolutely perfect.

We talked and played for another half an hour before I drifted off, contemplating my sea of unfortunate events, and wondering how I got to be so lucky.

10

MAGIC PILL

I awoke to the sounds of voices in my house and groaned. I snuggled into Von's side and scratched a light line across his toned belly, rousing him just enough. "I think Danny's here."

"Tell him to go away. My alarm's set for six forty-five. I was having a really filthy dream."

I kissed his cheek and sat up, stretching before I placed my feet on the lush white carpet I loved. "I'll go see why they're here so early. It's barely six."

Von threw his hands into the air, frustrated. "See? Now the dream's gone because you left my side. Danny ruins everything."

I stood and stretched, taking the opportunity while Von was yawning and facing the other way to slide off my leggings and put on jeans. "What was the dream about?"

"All sorts of ungentlemanly things." He pulled on his

jeans and shoved his arms through a navy blue t-shirt that hugged his muscles and showed off the fact that he was a physically fit vampire well suited for seduction.

We went out into the living room and found Mariang and Danny sitting at the kitchen table eating a breakfast that looked homemade. "Lynna?" Von inquired, forking several pancakes and starting in on one without needing a plate to slow him down.

"Yeah." Danny jerked his thumb to the front door. "Mason's on the porch. Said he doesn't deserve to come inside or something like that. Ezra's ordered he only be a wolf Topside from now until, I don't know, a long time. It'll limit... you know, what happened last time."

I nodded at the suggestion that seemed reasonable. Mariang handed me a plate and I filled it with probably too many pancakes. I poured maple syrup over the top and stabbed into the fluffy goodness with excitement when I realized it was real maple syrup, and not the artificial kind. Allie would've loved it.

"You pulled a lot from her last night?" Mariang asked of Von's full plate. "I thought taking a day or two off from reaping would help things go smoother while you lot healed from your abduction."

"Nah. I'm just refueling from all the raucous sex we had. Takes a lot out of a bloke. November's absolutely bananas in bed. Took my virginity all over again, she did." Von tossed Mariang a smile when Danny choked on his orange juice.

I kept eating, not at all put off at Von's crass jokes. "Yes. We had lots of sex. Tell me, sweet cheeks, next time can it last a whole three minutes? I'd really like that." Von scoffed and offered some rebuttal, but I couldn't hear a word of it since his mouth was full of pancakes. I turned and kissed his cheek. "You can work up to the three minutes, if you like." Then I tucked my finger into the waist of his jeans and gave a slight tug, smirking when his eyes widened. "I believe in you, little buddy."

"Little?" Von choked out, astonished that my jokes were better than his.

"If we're done with this, then we can drum up a plan for the day." Danny was surly, which was to say, business as usual. We decided on going to the hospital nearby, and started an uneventful day of sucking the souls out of people.

Von stayed by my side morning, noon and night for the next week while we muddled through reaping duties. We had to store up souls so I could take the sagrado stone down to the next country in Terraway and do my thing. While I'd been able to do dozens before in a single work-day, Von insisted we take it slow, meeting the minimum quota, plus one or two extra. While I'd wanted to argue, I was starting to feel winded when we hit eight reapings. I knew being starved for weeks couldn't be fixed in a day, so I tried to be patient with our sluggish progress.

"You nervous?" Von asked me as he shut the bedroom door so we could wind down for the night. Mason roamed around near my dresser, giving the bed a wide berth while Von and I turned the covers down. "Hopefully this next journey won't be as harrowing as the last. I mean, this one will be properly planned out."

I shrugged, unwilling to admit that my stomach was in knots. "I'm fine." Then I groaned when Von handed me the clear jar he'd put on the shelf of my nightstand that he'd labeled "Denial Jar". I yanked a dollar from my messenger bag and shoved it inside.

"Shall we try that again?"

"I hope it's not as rough as the last time. I mean, we're taking healing to their country. You'd think that would be a good thing, but it feels like we're doomed the second we step into Terraway." I straightened my pillow on the bed before I climbed in under the covers, exhausted. Mason hopped up next to me, and I reminded myself to be cool. We'd fallen into a good rhythm, especially since Mason couldn't speak, which meant we couldn't have the dreaded talk about how it all went so wrong. I fished for an engaging topic that would distract me from my discomfort. "So, this Sama character. Super bad guy?"

"Super immortal bad guy, which is like, the worst kind."

"Tell me about him. Long mustache to twirl? Tying damsels to train tracks?"

"Honestly, I only know the headlines. He's like, over a hundred years old or something. He was an apprentice with some other bloke under the last Kapre."

"What's a Kapre? I forget."

"It's an extinct species now. They used to be these incredible giants who smoked fat cigars and told you riddles. They fancied gems and important stones. They were fascinated with the sagrado stones. The last Kapre was in possession of the spare sagrado stone, and when Sama and the other bloke killed him, the last stone went missing." He flopped down in the bed next to me on my other side. "That is, until it showed up in your mum's home."

"That's crazy."

"Yeah." Von scratched his toned stomach. "You sure I can't smoke in here? I'm itching for a cigar right now."

"You can smoke all you want outside. I already caved and said you can sleep in your underwear." That was with the firm understanding that he would wear pajama pants again once Mason was allowed to be human.

"Yes, but you put your foot down on you not sleeping in just your knickers, as well. That cuts off half the fun. And now no cigars in bed on top of that? You're one cruel mistress."

"Oh, brother. My bedroom's my perfectly clean place. I need one clean space in my life. You know that."

"Yes, yes. I know. I just figured if I keep whining about it, maybe you'll realize your long lost love for smoking cigars, as well. Then we can spend our nights smoking together before we turn in. Doesn't that just sound sexy?"

"Oh, Von. You're my favorite bad habit, and I only allow

myself one of those at a time." My foot found his under the covers. "Tell me more about Sama. The villain in the movie tonight died too easily. Bruce Campbell's just too incredible for his own good."

Von chuckled at my Bruce Campbell obsession. "Let's see. Where were we? Ah, yes. Bedtime stories about evil geniuses who can't be killed. When they were apprentices for the last Kapre, Sama and the other bloke found a way to make themselves immortal using a self-inflicted curse, powered by one of the magical gemstones the Kapre collected. Sama was then doubly cursed by his Kapre master, imprisoned on an island."

"So he'd live forever, but alone? That sucks."

"Indeed. Sama's a powerful one, though. He's always trying to get off the island, sending his soul to inhabit the weak. He's got a whole army he controls without ever having to leave his island. It's how he killed the last Kapre from his remote location, without ever laying a finger on him."

"Yikes."

"Sama uses the undead who haven't been properly buried. That's why what Mason did was so important. There were fewer zombies for Sama to call to himself." He reached over me to pat Mason's furry head. "Now Sama's army is growing every day, I'd imagine."

"That's terrible! What are we going to do to stop him? There must be some kind of magical pill or something that can kill an immortal."

Von tugged me close, pecking my lips. "Solving all the world's problems in a conversation, are we? Sorry, love. There's no such pill. Hence the whole 'immortal' aspect of it all."

"Stop saying 'hence'. I know you're trying to turn me on with your fancy words."

He chuckled at my humor. "Well, I had to give it a shot." He drew my hand to rest on his stomach, sighing contentedly at the intimate contact he only enjoyed from me. He loved sleeping in his underwear, and I loved the warmth he exuded, so it was a win-win. "Must sleep, darling. We'll figure out that whole magic pill thing in the morning, yeah?"

"Yeah, okay. Night, Von. Night, Mason."

Mason had kept to his wolf form that entire week. He and I slept with our spines pressed together while I dozed in Von's arms, dreaming about Philip.

11

THREE DAYS

I drove Terence the Taurus with Von in the passenger seat and Mason sprawled out in the back as we made our way to Ezra Manor to discuss the next leg of our journey through Terraway. It was the first time Mason had not been a wolf since the incident, and things were a little tense. Von kept his hand on my knee, maintaining a constant stream of gentle pulling until I cut the engine in Ezra's driveway. I'd been weak for a while, but this morning, I was starting to feel more myself. I was getting stronger again, with my brain firing on all cylinders after a week of eating properly and reaping only a modest amount while I recouped.

For half a minute, I just sat in my seat, unwilling to get out of the car and face the next assignment. While I'd gotten back a bit of my strength and clarity, I didn't feel ready to tackle Narnia just yet. Von tugged on my ponytail. "I think it's time, Peach."

"I know. I'm working my way up to opening the door." I looked over at him. "You sure we can't FedEx the sagrado stone to the next territory? I mean, does it have to be me?"

Mason answered when Von wavered. "It has to be you, and it has to be now. Terraway's waited long enough." It was the first thing he'd said to me since he'd pinned me down and forced me to keep kissing him. Not quite an apology, but whatever.

Ezra trotted out to greet us, opening my door and ushering me out like a gentleman – a gentleman who couldn't wait another minute for me to get on the ball. Ezra displayed his hands before wrapping them around me in a hug I tried to get used to. Ezra's chest was solid, and he smelled of aftershave and fresh coffee. "You're looking much better than when last I saw you. I don't like this distance, you living an hour away. I worry."

For seven solid seconds, I let myself pretend that he was worried about just me, and not Terraway's food supply. I leaned my head on Ezra's shoulder, indulging in the paternal glow of it all. It was one of the few times I let Ezra hold me without squirming to get away. He felt the difference, squeezing tighter when he sensed I needed the boost. "I'm worried this trip's going to end up like the last one. I didn't like being locked up like that."

Ezra rubbed my back to soothe me, and I let him. "We're far better prepared this time around. You'll be going to Kabayo's land, and since Kabayo's the king, he's granting you free passage through his country. It won't be the same war trying to sneak through. And I'll be with you the whole time, yeah?"

"I guess that's a little better."

"Mariang's coming, too. It'll be like a family camping trip," Ezra said with a smile.

"Isn't that kind of hard for her? I mean, are you sure that's best?" I tried to picture her frail body sleeping on the ground and winced.

"Not best, but necessary. Kabayo's wife requested to see her."

"Wife? I didn't know Kabayo was married." I couldn't picture him romantic or soft. Or as anything but an equine warrior king.

"Yes, if you can believe it." Ezra turned and led me into the mansion with one arm still wrapped around my shoulders. He dipped his head in my direction to speak quietly to me after Von and Mason went into the conference room ahead of us. "Things are okay with Mason?"

I shrugged. "I guess they have to be. We haven't talked about what happened. Von's a good buffer, though."

Ezra turned to face me to make sure I was paying attention. "Should you feel uncomfortable around Mason, I want you to tell me first thing. The Omen and Puller bond is sacred; he shouldn't have treated it so unkindly."

"How are things going with Bev?" I wasn't sure what Danny had told him.

Ezra forced a polite smile. "They're alright. She wasn't thrilled that I found out about Allie, and I wasn't thrilled that she kept a whole child from me. We're working through it. My forthcoming absence didn't go over well, but that's to be expected." He shook his head. "You don't need to worry about your mother. I'll be sure to conduct myself like a gentleman."

I wanted to tell him it wasn't her I was worried about, but the words stayed stuck in my throat. "I have no doubt."

Ezra led me into the room where the first thing I heard was bickering. The first thing I saw was a massive dead horse head on the round table. I gasped, taking in the foam on the horse's maw and the lifeless glassy eyes that stared in no particular direction. The nurse in me wanted to investigate the green tinge to his maw, but Ezra stopped me when I tried to reach out to examine it. "King Kabayo, why don't you fill our newcomers in about your recent predicament," he said as he lowered me to a chair.

I saw Finn, Lang and Sylvia, who all dipped their heads at me in formal greeting. Kabayo stood, placing his hands on the table, towering over everyone there. He was easily seven feet tall, and his black horse head looked menacing as he addressed the group. "Ever since Sakuna received their piece of the sagrado stone, our people have been hit hard with some sort of plague. The Omens have been keeping up with their reapings, so our *buhay* crops are starting to grow stronger, but we're no match for this. I'm certain it's a curse." He pointed to the horse's mouth to indicate the crusted and dried foam. "We don't know what's causing it, but it seems to be something they're ingesting. And it's only affecting those of us not taking Sama's rations, so I know he's not poisoning us that way. If we can get the sagrado to the main water source, like you did in Sakuna, I think that could help. The stone has healing powers, and we've never needed them more than we do now. I've lost forty Tikbalangs to this plague, and it's barely been a week."

Lang lifted my backpack off the floor and set it on the table in front of me, so I had something to focus on other than the giant dead horse man. "Here's what's left of your stone, Lady October. Ruiz, Klark and I are ready to assist you on your journey."

Sylvia shook her crescent moon-shaped head. "I wish I could help, but my land's on the brink of a civil war. Factions have been splitting off, and the country's divided – those who want me to continue my rule and those who would see others in my place. Me being here for this meeting is the most time I can spend away from my people."

Ezra nodded. "Understandable. Just make sure when it comes time for our journey through your land, that it's safer than what we found in Sakuna."

"That's exactly what I'm working on."

Finn was sitting back in his chair, his long fingers folded over his abdomen. His blondish-brownish hair had just enough wave to it, and his deep green eyes and full lips drew my gaze. He always appeared outside of whatever drama was happening, and today proved no exception. His expression was hard to read, since it looked like he could have been concentrating on his favorite TV show instead of studying a dead horse. He didn't speak, but Ezra's eyes kept sweeping toward him as if to gauge how to proceed. While everyone deferred to Ezra, I could now see how Ezra relied on them every bit as much.

Kabayo didn't believe in deferring, so he pushed on. "How long until enough souls are stored up? How soon can the stone come to us?"

Ezra looked to me for an answer, and I stiffened. Apparently I was the weakest link, so the journey depended on how soon I could get my act together. "Depending on how many souls we can find in a day, I can be ready no problem. How many do we need stored up?"

"At least fifty if we're to be gone five days," Ezra replied, his tone dubious that I could get the job done in a time-frame that would suit Kabayo. "Remember, we're still behind on what was lacking before you were awakened."

I'd been working at the bare minimum for the past week, but it seemed now was the time to crank it up a notch. I ran my hand over my face, adding up that cost versus the effort I had in me. "Give me three days. Can y'all be ready by then?"

This number seemed to please them. They nodded and some stood to ready for departure back to their home-land, but Finn remained seated, his gaze shifting to me with that same indifferent calculation. "You and Mariang can reap that many in three days? You look on the edge of collapse."

Whatever weariness I felt at the mere act of sitting while I was still on the mend, I shook off in that instant, bristling as I met his gaze with probably a little too much defiance. "You're not so beautiful yourself," I lied. Finn was gorgeous in that "how should I care what I look like, I hit the genetic lottery" kind of way. "I was held in a prison for weeks and starved while my Duwendes were tortured. What's your excuse?"

Finn's answering smile was heard. The 'oh, snap' looks that fizzled and spun around us from the others were ignored. "Apologies, milady. I only meant to ask if you were sure three days was enough time for you and Lady Mariang. You look terrible."

I leaned back in my chair, mirroring his body language. I knew his type. I'd seen enough mafia henchmen and upper management in prison to know they only respected the ones who disrespected them to their face. They revered unwavering strength, which I had in spades when my abilities to get a job done were questioned. "I don't plan on Mariang working these next few days. She'll be resting and packing for the journey. I can do fifty souls on my own in three days just fine. Or would you rather I drag it out so I can go get my nails done? I haven't scheduled a manicure in ages." I tried to appear bored as I studied my nails that had never actually seen the inside of a salon.

Finn examined my small movements. "You always give me something pretty to look at."

I ignored what I'm sure was supposed to be a compliment. "This is the part where you say 'thank you' and move along to your little underwater friends." He opened his mouth to reply, but my raised eyebrow told him not to push it. "Have a good one, guys. See you in three days."

12

A FOURTH WHEEL

Finn remained in his seat while the others shook hands or vanished on sight. When it was just Ezra, me and Finn, Ezra spoke more openly. "Darling, I'm not sure it was wise to promise such a high number in so short a time. You're barely upright."

"I can handle it. No point in letting more of Kabayo's people die while everyone waits for me to feel better. I've powered through and gone to work half-cocked before. This is no different. Same rodeo, different horse is all."

"While I appreciate the bravado, the others will be ready to go in three days' time. Will you?"

"We'll see, won't we?" When this response worried Ezra, I waved off his concern. "I'll get it done, and I'll do it without Mariang. She kept going while I was in prison, least I can do is give her a few days off. She needs it."

"That's kind of you, but she can't even keep up with the

minimum quota of souls. What you're promising…" Ezra shook his head.

I stood, leaning on the table and probably tipping my hand at how under the weather I still was. "Could I make myself a sandwich? And a few for the guys? I don't want to have to stop for lunch once we get going. We're burning daylight, here."

Ezra pulled out his phone and called Lynna, requesting she pack us each several large lunches. "It's done."

"You didn't have to do that. I could've made the sandwich myself."

Ezra tilted his chin to the side, looking at me as if seeing me more clearly than most. "It's okay to lean on me. One day, I hope you understand that."

I didn't know what to say to that, so I shoved my hands in my pockets. "I… um… Well, thanks. I'll try to keep that in mind."

"What else can I get you?"

"Oh, jeez. Nothing. You've got enough on your plate helping Sylvia with her Tombstone-style uprising. Just make sure if Mariang's set on going, that she's ready when it's time."

Finn spoke up, having watched our boring exchange with a skeptical eye. "You ask for too little. You're an Omen; you can demand whatever you like from any of us. What are you hiding? No one's that selfless."

"You're confusing selfless with capable. I'll ask when I

need." I narrowed my eyes at him. "And I don't need your commentary on my life. You don't know the first thing about me."

Finn maintained his laidback position in his chair, scratching one of the gills on his neck. "I know enough."

I looked around at the empty chairs. "Aren't you dismissed? Like, don't you have a kingdom to run for your king or something? I know listening to me talk about making a sandwich can't be the most important thing you've got going today."

"As a matter of fact, it is. *You* are. Banak's kingdom is properly delegated, just like any good organization. I won't allow what happened to you to go down again. I won't let Sama or Sakuna send more spies to abduct you."

"Aw, shucks. Thanks, but I'll pass. I've already got two shadows."

Finn waited in his lazy way, giving me a calculating smile that didn't touch his light green eyes. Ezra answered for him. "Finn would feel better if he could accompany you today."

"You don't say. Thanks, but I don't think those gills you're rocking are going to blend in up here."

"I'll manage. Your wolf king blends in easy enough."

"No," I ruled, staring at him with my best "back off" face.

Ezra's voice remained even to temper the growing argument. "Captain Finn operates under a curse, October. If King Banak orders him to do something, he must obey. It's why Captain Finn makes for such a strong leader while King Banak... distracts himself. King Banak has requested Finn watch out for you to secure his nation's food supply."

There was a hardness to Finn's eyes that tried to appear nonplussed at the mention of his curse. If someone had forced me to obey their will, I'm not sure I'd handle it quite so gracefully.

"Wait, Ezra, talk to this Banak guy. My life's weird enough as it is. I don't need Finn lurking."

I expected my attitude to earn a little in return, but Finn's chest began to shake with silent laughter. "It's no wonder Geon didn't let you go once he knew he wouldn't get the stone from you. You've got some fight in you."

"I'll see you in three days, Ezra." I gave him a two-fingered salute, ignoring Finn as best I could. I didn't expect Finn to follow me, though maybe I should've. His footsteps echoed behind me down the hall, making me cringe. "Dude, I think you know I'm going to tell you to get lost."

"And I think you don't know who you're talking to. I almost prefer it that way. Everyone's got such a healthy fear of me; it gets tiresome after a while."

I rolled my eyes at him. "Blah, blah, blah. Yeah, I get it. You're a badass. Go home to your fishbowl."

Finn ignored me, which was frustrating. Instead of engaging in what I assumed would be yet another fruitless argument, I spun on my heel and made my way down to the kitchen, where Von was sitting on a stool with Mason in wolf form at his feet. Von had been joking with Lynna while she packed us lunches, but swallowed his laughter quickly when Finn entered the room. He stood to attention with a closed expression of disdain, with Mason doing the wolf version of that at his side. I was grateful that Mason had deserted his human form; it made me less anxious. Lynna bowed her head, looking scared that Finn was in her haven.

I waved off their formal greeting before things got out of hand. "No, no. Finn thinks he's coming with us today, but he's not." I pointed to the fearful respect or blatant dislike on each of their faces, my chin jutting out at Finn as I sassed him. "See? This is exactly what I didn't want. We've got enough problems without having to be perfect all the time in front of you. We'll never get anything done this way."

"They seem to be doing just fine. In fact, with me here, I bet they move even faster."

"And they'll be nervous wrecks. Don't you think we've been through enough? Don't you think we've got enough on our plates without you making them all scared?"

Von's wide eyes told me I was treading on dangerous ground, and his words came out with a grudge. I could tell he hated Finn, but had acquired a grave respect of him somewhere along the road. "It's no trouble, Captain Finn. We'd be honored."

"He's lying," I told Finn, who smirked at me. "There isn't room in our car."

"You'll have to make room, dear," Lynna countered, giving me the "now, hush up" look that forced me to obey.

"If we're going to do fifty reapings in the next three days, we can't be slowed down with dead weight. He's not going to blend in. Hello, he's got gills!"

Von broke his formal demeanor to gawk at me. "Since when do you think you can do that many? You were barely upright two nights ago at the end of the workday. Scratch that, you weren't upright! I had to carry you to bed."

I grumbled that he'd mentioned that in mixed company. "You don't need to be bringing that up in front of old Gill, here." I jerked my thumb at Finn.

Von ignored my humor. "Be reasonable. You're not as strong as you were before you were abducted. You're still getting back on your feet. You know this is too much. You're being stubborn."

"Mariang's taking three days off, so let's get cracking." I stretched my arms over my head. "I'm fine. Got a full night's sleep, and I'm good as new. Where do you want to hit up today? A hospital? I think hospice might be easiest." I eyed Finn's gills. "Like shooting fish in a barrel."

Von groaned and Mason whined. "And you already promised them this, didn't you."

"Yup. It's all good, guys. I told you, I feel fine. We can probably knock off half the list today alone. The second half tomorrow, and the third day we can crash and finish the movie marathon we started two nights ago. Easy-peasy."

"If only you were joking." Von handed me my phone. "I turned it on and charged it for you. You missed a call from Ollie, who wasn't thrilled I answered."

I squinted one eye at him. "That makes two of us."

"And you missed a call from Bev, who seemed pretty upset about something. She asked that you call her straightaway."

I took my phone from him and rubbed his fingerprints off on my lavender t-shirt. "Okay, rule one: Don't answer my phone. Rule two: That goes double if it's Bev. She probably found out I took the doorstop." To Von's raised eyebrow, I added, "That's what she was using the sagrado stone as."

Von did a face-palm. "I wouldn't spread that around. When do you want to go, Captain?"

Finn opened his mouth to answer, but I beat him to it. "Oh, Finn's not going. We don't have time for this. Can you be ready to go in five?"

"We're ready now, love." Von grabbed his light black jacket off the back of the chair. "Mason, if we're going to hospice, you need to be human. The one this way doesn't allow dogs."

Mason whined dejectedly and scampered up the stairs. Von's hand on the small of my back was nice, and I didn't even mind that he did it to pull the stress from me at being around Mason again. I didn't want to see him and deal with the mess. I just wanted it to go away. I couldn't wait until this sagrado business was over with so I could get some space. "I'll wait in the car." I was hoping for a few minutes of privacy to call my brother back, but knew that wouldn't happen.

Von's hand slid into mine, and I could tell he was nervous at Finn's watchful eye. "By the book today, Peach. Seriously."

"Okay. You alright?" Von gave a stiff nod as we walked out to the car. "Give me a minute. I've got to call Ollie before he starts to worry."

I shut myself in the car, leaving Von and Finn standing awkwardly in the garage, not looking at each other. I called my brother, who answered on the first ring. "October? Where have you been?!" he shouted into the phone.

"Jeez! What's with the attitude? I called you back."

I could tell I'd said the wrong thing by the fuming I could hear him doing. "Are you joking? You missed your Thursday check-in! Again! I thought you understood that those aren't just 'hey, how's it going' chats. Those are important! I'm not near you, so I need to know that you're safe! How could you do that to me? And that's coming off three weeks where you didn't check in at all until you got back and deigned to pick up the phone. I think I've earned the right to worry. What's going on with you?"

I bit my lip, softening at the worrying I'd unintentionally put him through. I guessed that telling him I hadn't called that first two weeks because I was in a dungeon wouldn't help matters, or that I hadn't been conscious most evenings this past week because I was busy ripping the souls out of dying people. "I'm sorry, Ollie. I went out of town. Took a little vacation. I completely lost track of time. Unacceptable, I know."

"Where were you really?" Ollie shouted. "I know you! You don't take vacations! I know when you're lying to me!"

Flashbacks of Ollie, Allie and Bev screaming at each other flooded my mind, and I no longer felt like a woman who was part of a world-changing team. I was a little girl again, hiding in the trash and hoping the chaos would stop. I'd hoped someone would rescue me and sweep me off to the Brady Bunch. I'd needed it then, and it took too long to come. My voice was small under Ollie's tirade. "Ollie?"

"We're all we have! You get that, don't you? You can't check out on me! You can't forget about me!"

"I didn't..." My protest was laced with hurt, but it didn't matter. He didn't hear a word I said. Ollie rarely yelled at me, so I never really knew how to handle it. I'm guessing hanging up on him wasn't the best way to deal, but it was all I could think of. It was the only way I could run and hide.

The second I ended the call, I was horrified at my actions. I'd never hung up on Ollie before. Panic welled up in me at the awful thing I'd done, but for the life of me, I couldn't bring myself to call back and face him. Ollie and Allie raised me, gave up everything they wanted so I could have a future. What'd I do with that future? I quit my job, shacked up with two dudes, didn't return phone calls and hung up when he finally got in touch. I was awful.

Von opened my door and placed a hand on my arm, correctly sensing that I was nine kinds of crazy right now. "Oh, man. That must've been some phone call. The stress is coming off you in waves."

"I don't know what I just did," I admitted, shocked at my own behavior.

Von pried my phone out of my rigid fingers, shut my door and walked around to sit in the passenger's seat next to me. Finn let himself into the backseat, and I knew he had to be uncomfortable with his longer legs. Mason was a few seconds behind, sliding in behind Von in the back, his posture rigid at sitting with Finn. He handed Finn a blue silk scarf, which Finn artfully tied around his neck to hide his fishier qualities.

Von reached across the console, his hand on my knee as I pulled out of the driveway. "You've got to calm down if we're going to do a ton of reaping today." His warning fell on deaf ears, because as soon as my phone rang, I swerved. "Okay! Hey, that's not calming down. I've got it. How about you just drive, yeah?" He answered the call, and I could feel the anxiety creeping up inside of me like too much vomit on standby. "October's phone. No, this is Von. She's driving, so I'll put you on the Bluetooth."

Ollie's rage was barely contained through succinctly spat words. "What was that?" Before I could answer, Ollie's anger built like one brick on top of the other, every sentence bringing about a worse level of fury until his voice towered over me, turning me into a mouse. "Did you just hang up on me? Did you really just do that? You go radio silent on me for three weeks, and you give me some BS excuse about why you were gone with no notice. I call to make sure you're still alive after you miss yet another check-in, and you hang up on me?"

"Ollie, I'm sorry! You were yelling, and I..."

"Of course I'm yelling! I was scared you were dead! Never! Never in the whole time I've been in New York have we ever missed a Thursday night phone call. And who's answering your phone? Is that why you've completely flaked out on me? You met some guy? That British friend of Ezra's who stayed over that one time on the couch with you? I knew he was trouble!"

Von raised an eyebrow at me, taking pleasure in being the bad boy parents warned their children away from.

I scraped at the skin on my arms, wishing we were not on speakerphone, that I was far, far away, and that Ollie would understand. "No! It's got nothing to do with Von or Mason. I said I was sorry! I was out of town, and I lost track of the days. I was being irresponsible. I didn't think. I didn't mean to worry you, Ollie."

"I know you're lying to me! What I don't know is why? I've never lied to you. Never! What's really going on? And who's Mason? I get nothing from you, and Bev's been calling me every day to apologize for who knows what."

"Huh?"

"She's been crying, actually crying and trying to get me to come home so she can make sure I'm okay. Me! Said she wants us to be a family. Is she high? I've never heard her talk like that. I don't know what she's on, but that Ezra's really done a number on her. I thought you were checking in on her once a week still, or did you forget about that, too?"

"Hey, you told me to stay away from Bev! You told me to get her out of my life. Now you want me to check in on her after I finally take your advice?" I gripped the steering wheel. "You need to call your sponsor. I'm serious, Ollie. You're off the rails, yelling at me like this."

Ollie paused, clearly embarrassed I'd brought up his Anger Management sessions. "I guess I'm not being fair. I just have no idea why Bev's calling trying to make amends. I thought you were handling her."

"None of this is fair!"

Ollie's tone changed when he heard the frustrated emotion tugging at my tone. "Are you... Are you crying?"

"No!" I retorted, feeling foolish. "I know you're mad, but you can't yell at me like that! I've been through the craphole here, and I don't need you shouting at me!"

"I knew you were lying. Talk to me. What's going on, Gracie? Is it that guy? That Von guy?"

I groaned, scratching my neck to relief the anxiety and center myself. "No, Von's fine. He's just a friend. He's been a good friend, actually. My best friend these days. It's nothing. Everything's fine. I told you, I just lost track of the time."

"I never thought I'd have to tell you to stop lying to me twice in one conversation. You didn't lose track of the time. Something's up."

"Look, I've got to go. I don't want to do this right now. We can talk more when you move back home."

Ollie's voice was low and deadly. "Don't you dare hang up on me."

"I'm not hanging up on you, but I'm ending the call. I love you, and I'll see you in a couple weeks."

"I don't like this."

I pulled onto the freeway, holding back my anxiety as much as I could. "Believe me, Ollie, there's nothing about this that I like, either."

13

HEAD IN THE GARBAGE CAN

I tried not to feel the eyes staring at me. "Not a word," I warned them quietly as I drove. The radio was a welcome distraction, so I cranked the music to make sure no one could comment on my personal life.

After two crappy pop songs that really should never be blasted, Von turned the volume down. "Love, you've got to stop. You're going to tear your skin. I'm doing pretty well with controlling myself, but you're going to make things difficult for me if you keep scratching yourself." His hand was still on my knee, but the pulling was too gentle for the tumbleweeds rocketing around inside of me. When my phone rang again, Von checked the caller ID. "It's Bev."

"Please don't answer that. I don't have it in me to handle her today. She'll just yell because I took her doorstop, and I can't handle another person shouting at me this morning."

"Fair enough."

Mason spoke up from the backseat. It was the second time I'd heard him talk since our kiss had turned sour. "How would she even know it's missing?"

"Oh, she knows where all her special things are, and if anyone moves even a piece of paper, she goes ballistic. I don't want to talk about it. Can y'all be cool and let it go? It's barely ten o'clock, and it's already been a long day for me."

"This was a bad idea, you promising all these souls." Von laced his fingers through mine as I drove with one hand and my knee.

"It's done. I want this sagrado nonsense snapped off already. I want my life back. I want to go back to work, and I'm sure Mason wants to go back to Sombi so he can do all the zombie killing to his heart's content. And I'm sure you want to get on with your life, too, Von. Anyone got a problem with me speeding things along so we can get back to our regularly scheduled programs?" When my question was met with crickets, I nodded. "Didn't think so."

We drove the rest of the way in silence, arriving at the hospice facility twenty minutes later. I parked the car and reached for the door, but Mason stopped me. "Wait for us to get the door for you. You and Finn are stations above us, so you don't open your own doors. Captain Finn's here, so we play by the rules."

"Well, when you put it like that, how can a girl not swoon?" I was miffed that the first time he offered to open the door for me was because a big bad baddy was watching. I sighed and turned around to address the peanut gallery, kneeling on my seat. "Look, it's going to be a long day, and I don't want to start it feeling like we're not in this together. Finn, I told you to go home because we do things different than you're probably comfortable with. If you're with us, you're one of us, not above us. You can get your own door."

Finn's chin moved to the left as he held my gaze, sizing up the odd creature he found me to be. I could hear Von swearing under his breath in a stream of nervous curse words as the balance shifted. It was all unnecessarily dramatic. Finally Finn answered, "I can play along, but only this weekend. When the others are around, I expect the respect I've earned. It's the way the system works, and without the system, fools think they can sit where I do, and it's safer for the kingdom that they don't. Understood?"

"Sure." I knew it was as good as I was going to get, so I ended the conversation by opening the door and starting to walk toward the building.

Mason and Von trotted after me, each of them taking one of my hands and making us look, well, kind of weird together. My gut was easy to follow, and the death was ripe for the picking. Finn walked behind us, observing our tag team approach to pulling and the in-and-out way Mariang had taught me to do my job. She was a pro at it, but I'd been a quick study. I barely registered the names of the people I was reaping anymore, coming into the rooms with some lame excuse or no excuse at all. The facility produced thirteen souls that were reaped and then pulled with no incident, only the occasional question or comment from Finn. He actually wasn't such a pain once he realized there would be no bowing and cowering.

I tried not to lean on Von or Mason on our way out, but the exhaustion was starting to creep up on me. I felt cold settling in my chest, but the more they pulled from me on our way to the car, the more that weighted chill dulled. I slumped in the driver's seat, leaning my head back and closing my eyes to give myself half a moment of collecting myself before we ramped up for another round.

"Break for lunch before we go?" Mason suggested, his stomach rumbling.

"Sure. I'll grab the food from the trunk." Von waved us off to the few picnic tables on the other side of the parking lot from the main hospice building. It was picturesque with the tall oaks framing the wooden picnic tables that were clear of graffiti. There was even a swing set further back, no doubt to keep the families with young children occupied while they waited out their great grandparents' last moments.

Mason held his arm out to me, and though I wanted to be far away from him, my feet felt like lead and my breath was too shallow to walk long distances. Like, you know, from one end of the parking lot to the other. What a wuss. Mason was gentle with my unsteady feet, moving slowly and pulling the cold from me as we walked like a true couple to the tables. He lowered me onto the bench with care.

I could tell he'd almost thought he'd gotten away with everything, until he leaned down to kiss my cheek and I flinched. He watched me avoid his gaze and finally sat next to me. He draped his arm around my shoulders as Von and Finn sat across from us. "I'm truly sorry," Mason whispered low in my ear. "There's no excuse for my behavior. I won't indulge in you again."

Indulge in me? Like I was a sinful dessert that was only bad for him. Of course he wouldn't be kissing me again. He couldn't use our connection to see his wife anymore, now that he wasn't in love with me. Thus, kissing me had lost all appeal because being with only me wasn't enough. I don't know why that rock sunk hard in my gut; it wasn't like I was itching for another go at our non-relationship.

I nodded at Mason in lieu of speaking my mind, keeping my eyes away from his face. I didn't feel the need to tell him it was fine. Von was right. It wasn't fine, but there was nothing I could do about it now.

Mason lifted an item out of the midsized cooler, taking a bite that was almost half the meaty sandwich. It was a good thing Lynna packed for a troop. "So what do you think about the Topside?" he asked Finn conversationally. Ever since I laid down the law about the whole us being on equal footing thing, the atmosphere had relaxed a little. Von was still edgy and unhappy that Finn was around, but the fishy guy actually managed a conversation here and there. Von lit his cigar and puffed it between taking bites of his sandwich.

Finn looked around as he chewed. "It's nice. Colder up here, but maybe that'll change once we're free of our burning suns when the climates even out. Maybe things will cool down to this temperature. I think I might like that."

I swallowed a bite of my sandwich before speaking. "What are you going to do without all the famine and heatstroke and whatnot? I mean, so much manpower goes into just surviving, I wonder what Terraway will look like once things aren't so hard."

"I imagine I'll have a lot more work on my hands, keeping everyone busy enough so they don't cause problems for themselves, but that's the lesser of the evils." Finn looked to the swings with a small smile. "It's not always the hardships that reveal who you are; it's often when those hardships are removed and hands grow idle that your true self surfaces."

"Makes sense." Mason and Finn had been equals at one point, and in the quiet shade of the tree, they started speaking like that again. It was nice to see Mason rise to his status of sitting at the cool kids' table he'd cast himself off of so long ago. It was even more gratifying to watch Finn let his guard of distance down to be one of the guys. He even laughed a few times at a couple of my dumber jokes.

Von was not so enthused. He was visibly seething the

more Finn spoke. "And what do you know about hardships? You're the one controlling the harem. You eat the king's stores of *buhay* without having to sell yourself into slavery."

"That you think I enjoy any part of my job, or that working for Banak's childish whims isn't a hardship shows how little you know about the world, *kendi*."

I didn't know what *kendi* meant, but it set Von off. He stood, throwing his arms out and rolling up his sleeves to ready for a fight. "That's it! I shouldn't be expected to have to work with him after everything he... Ezra should know better than this!"

Finn turned to face Von, but didn't get up, demonstrating how little of a threat Von was to him. "Ezra knows about your time in Dagat? And he still hired you?"

"Paying off a debt isn't anything to be ashamed of, and that's all I was doing in your country. Now stand up so I can knock that smarmy smirk off your mug!"

"You want to fight me? I got your sentence reduced, but you want to fight me?"

"What sentence?" I asked, confused by the conversation. Mason put his hand on mine to stop me from getting involved, though he looked just as lost as I did.

"It's because of you I was sentenced at all!"

Finn finally stood, leveling his authoritative glare at Von. "Actually, it's because of you. It didn't have to be you, you know. That was your choice."

Mason stood and walked around the picnic table,

placing a hand on both men's chests and pushing outward. "Settle this on your own time. Von, you can't attack the Captain of Dagat." When Finn shot him a superior look, Mason chided Finn. "And you have to know you can't start stuff with a Reaper. We're just as valuable and irreplaceable as the Omen, so lay off. You're here as a guest, not a captain. The Omen was clear on that. Her ranking's above all of us, so work together, or go home."

The men slowly sank back down into their seats, Mason switching with Von so he didn't have to sit next to Finn. Mason engaged Finn in conversation about Dagat so Von didn't have to be social. My arm slipped around Von's back as he shoved half a sandwich in his mouth. Though I didn't understand what just happened, I knew that Von needed a Puller more than I did at the moment. "Hey, it's alright," I whispered.

Von gave an obligatory snort as he puffed on his cigar. "No, it's not. And you wouldn't look at me like that if you knew all Finn put me through."

"Look at you like what?"

"Like I'm a man worth the light in your eyes."

I gave him a confused smile. "Do you always get poetic when you're pissed off?"

I handed him a water bottle and leaned in when he closed his eyes to rest his temple to mine. "Don't leave me," he whispered in a quiet plea he kept between us.

Mr. Never Get Attached needed me, and I didn't take that privilege lightly. I linked my fingers through his under the table. "Never. Not even if you grew three heads and told me you hated Bruce Campbell."

Von's pained expression lightened with a hint of the smile I adored. "What if I scratched the paint on your car?"

"I wouldn't leave you even then. I'd kick your butt, but I wouldn't leave you."

"What if I forgot to wash my hands after using the restroom?"

I dropped his hand immediately and wiped it off on my jeans. "I wouldn't leave you even if you were gross, but I wouldn't hold your hand so much."

"Understandable. What if I –"

"Von? I don't care what life you had before I met you, unless you want me to care about it. I know who you are, and it's exactly the kind of best friend I need."

He wrapped his arm around me, pulling me into his nook so he could kiss the top of my head and blow his cigar smoke away from my face. "I don't deserve you, you know."

"Buy me a unicorn. That's a good start."

Von laughed, sounding more like himself. He started in on another sandwich while I tuned in to the conversation across the picnic table. Finn and Mason were elbow-deep in their own conversation that I was just beginning to tune in to. Finn leaned his forearm on the table as he spoke. "One thing I don't look forward to is Banak's harem shrinking. If the crops start growing again, the Mermaids won't need the king's food anymore. He's right surly when he doesn't have access to all the tail he can get his hands on. Makes my life a pain." A small tease played on his lips while Von paled, looking like he might be suddenly sick. "I'm sure the king and his son will be the only ones sad to see the famine end." He raised an eyebrow at me when I had nothing to say. "No witty reply? No angry comeback? I'm disappointed. Half the reason I didn't fight Banak on shadowing you is because you were such promising sport."

I laid my head down on the table, exhausted. "Pretend I said something hilarious about you having a small penis. I'm too tired to bother with you right now. Quit trying to wind Von up. I see what you're doing."

Mason had the nerve to apologize for my mouth. "She doesn't know anything about Dagat or who you are."

"No need to apologize for your charge, Mason. She amuses me. Though, the moment her charm grows tiresome, I suggest you educate her on the ways of Dagat before I have to."

"I told you that you didn't want to come out for a day of reaping."

"On the contrary, Lady October. I like to know all I can about my assets. That way if something breaks, I can fix it." His tone darkened. "And if that asset proves problematic, I'll know exactly how I can break it so it never stands in my way again."

I picked up my head to glare at him. "I don't jump for you. I'm only playing along because Lang showed me how bad off his people were. Fear doesn't motivate me. Ask Geon."

"I see you haven't been properly groomed with fear, then. If you don't deliver on your promise of fifty souls in three days, I'll see to remedying that the fun way."

"Yeah, yeah. You're a badass," I droned, rolling my eyes. "You're so big and scary, and I'm just this little woman, fanning myself in the corner thinking, 'Whatever shall I do? How can I please the great Captain Finn?'"

Mason leaned forward, his elbow on the table as he glowered at Finn, his voice low. "Look, threaten her again, and I'll put in a complaint to the council. You ever seen an Omen reap thirteen bodies before lunch?"

"I'll admit, I didn't think that could be done."

"Then trust that she knows her limits. She can handle the work well enough without the threats. If you get her worked up, it only goes against productivity."

Finn sat back, eyeing Mason with a cold calculation. "You gave up your throne, but clearly the ruler's still in you. Shame you never went back to take up your rightful place. Your brother Carter's a drunken joke these days."

Mason held Finn's gaze, their casual back and forth going sour. "I don't regret taking care of my people after they die. I have honor enough to hold my head high when I look in a mirror. I don't need a harem of desperate women to give me my pride. Look down on me all you want; I don't regret my choice. And you'll not talk about my brother like that."

"I never said you made the wrong choice. The shame lies only in leaving the throne without a ruler who has the passion you do for your post. Your brother's just as weak as your father was."

"You're done commenting on my life and my family," Mason ruled.

"You want a different sandwich, November? There's a couple more kinds in here." Von changed the subject and fished around in the cooler, pulling out an egg salad sandwich.

"Nah. I'm alright. Not hungry."

"I know you think that, but you still should eat. You're ripping through a lot of bodies today. You need your strength," Mason urged.

Von gripped the back of my neck and gave it a massage with just the right pressure. I moaned and became even less motivated to pick my head up off the table to join the world.

"My stomach hurts. I honestly don't think I could choke it down."

"You sound like a petulant child," Mason commented good-naturedly with a small smile, the toe of his shoe tapping mine under the table.

"And you sound like someone who needs a faceful of egg salad for busting on me. Too much reaping makes me queasy, and I'm out of practice doing this much in a morning."

Von picked up the teasing just to taunt me. "You want I should feed you, baby bird?"

I lifted my head, scowling at the guys. "Not unless you want to lose a finger. Honestly, I've already got a big brother I'm fighting with. I don't need two more. If I eat a few bites, will that get me a little space from the lectures?"

"I'd feel better," Mason said.

"Well, anything I can do to make *you* feel better. By all means, hand me the sandwich."

"Excuse me," Von said, sliding his phone out of his pocket and motioning for Mason to take his seat so I wasn't without pulling for a whole minute. "Penny's expecting my call. She's all excited about going to a carnival this weekend."

"Where at?"

"Pemberton Elementary. That's her school. Not too far from Ezra's. I might take a lunch break while she's there to go see her, if that's cool."

"Of course."

Von gave me a thumb's up and walked away from our group to talk more privately to his almost-daughter.

The filling in the sandwich was creamy and smelled like just the right amount of mayonnaise with fresh dill mixed in. On any other day, I would've devoured the thing. Today, four bites was all I could muster, and those mouthfuls churned in my gut, making me regret each one. When Mason removed his hand from my back so he could take a drink from his water bottle, the washing machine feeling in my stomach picked up at full speed. I grew dizzy as Mason and Finn chatted pleasantly about the state of Dagat and Sombi, and how they anticipated the sagrado stone helping their territories.

The trash can looked so far away, though I knew it was only a few feet from the picnic table. I barely made it there on trembling legs before the vomit spewed out of me, forcing me over and over to regret taking a chance on the sandwich. Egg salad in reverse is no picnic, even at a picnic. The desire to break down rose up in me when I felt Mason on my left, but I kept my head bent over the can and locked my tears firmly inside. "I'm fine," I choked out when I caught a breath. "Go sit down. You don't want to be here for this."

Mason rubbed his palm down my back. "I'm exactly where I want to be."

It was too sweet, too kind, too loving. I could tell he'd been married and knew how to be good to someone in sickness and in health. Even though he was being compassionate out of practice rather than out of love, the gesture was still significant to me.

My stomach was sick, and now so was my heart. Mason didn't know what he wanted, but he was stuck with me, just as I was stuck. I knew what I didn't want, and that would be enough to give us both solid direction. "I don't want you to see me like this. Please, Mason." Another wave of sick hit me, and I prayed he was gone so I could pretend I had the space to be disgusting without an audience. In the trash can were too many things I didn't want to have my head near. There was a dirty diaper, several old food containers, newspapers, an old sock, flies and who knows what else. I'd tried so hard to distance myself from the trash, but it always found me, like it knew I belonged with it.

"Here." Mason handed me a bottle of water when I finally lifted my head from the garbage can. The thing was crawling with germs, and I'd gripped it to brace myself. I shuddered, unable to touch the bottle of water until my hands were clean. I reached into my messenger bag and pulled out a container of wipes, sanitizing my face, hands, arms and the front of my shirt. Then I ran the wipe over the nape of my neck just to cool myself down.

Mason looked worried, his hand on my elbow. "Oh, you're so pale. Here, sit down."

He helped me to sit on the picnic table bench, but I couldn't look at him. The kiss and the crash of emotions were too ripe when coupled with heaving my guts out. I wished I could sleep away the rest of the day, which was exactly why I knew we had to keep moving. "Let's go. I'm fine." I held up two fingers to excuse myself to Finn. "Sorry about that. We should get going. It's only going to get worse from here. The sooner I can reap a whole mess of people, the better."

Mason shook his head, sitting next to me at the picnic table. "No. Take a real break. We've barely finished eating, and you haven't had anything."

"Well, I can't get anything down, so I'd rather plow through and get it done." When Mason opened his mouth in protest, my tone grew short. "Look, I don't have the energy to argue with you. I'm going. Come if you want." I stood and motioned for Von to join us, packing up the food that made my stomach roil.

Von trotted over to us, ending the call and looking me over with a wary eye. "You sure about this, November? You're looking piqued."

"I'm fine." I pulled out my keys and started walking to my car.

Von snatched them out of my hand. "Alright, but you owe the jar, like, twenty bucks, and I'm driving, you drunken Omen. You can barely walk in a straight line!"

"Yeah, alright. But be careful, understand? I mean it. Actual speed limit, Von. And if you really scratch my car, it'll be the worst butt-kicking of your lifetime."

"You're so adorable when you lecture me, even sweeter when you get the taste of that vomit out of your lovely little mouth." He pulled out a stick of gum from his pocket and handed it to me.

"Thanks. You're a lifesaver." He proffered his arm to me and I took it with gratitude, leaning on him and moving with all the enthusiasm of a snail when he opened the passenger side door for me. Though I wasn't sure how long I would last if I kept up at this pace, I knew I was lucky to have two Reapers who didn't mind helping a girl out, even when she'd just had her head in the garbage can.

14

REAPING PREEMIES

*A*s it turns out, puking makes your gut fickle. Following the twisty feeling in my stomach led to a few missteps as we wandered through the hospital, but eventually I found my groove. After five more reapings, I began to trip over my feet, growing quiet so the guys wouldn't catch on to how much this job was crushing me from the outside as much as the inside. I knew I didn't have much time, so I opted for the place I knew I'd find a few hearts in one room – the NICU. I hated reaping babies. It felt wrong and in poor taste, but business was business, and I had a job to do. Also, the thought of granting the babies a peaceful death soothed my conscience a little. I had to remind myself that I wasn't actually a bringer of death. I wasn't the one killing them. I was merely giving their death a purpose and taking their pain away.

That's what I told myself, anyway. I wasn't so sure how well I believed the line I'd been sold.

Mason waited outside of the ward, since his Matruculan genetics made him crave the taste of freshly born babies. He made himself useful brushing his hand against any doctors, nurses or parents who came in and out of the ward. The gentle pulling allowed us to get close to babies who weren't ours, since security was way tighter in this ward than the others.

Finn remained on his guard when we entered in with our visitor's passes. I could see that being in the baby ward filled with preemies scared him, too. "Are you certain this is the best place?" he asked, treating each of the incubators as if they contained an alien – which, I guess to his species, they kind of did.

"Yeah. These guys don't have a high survival rate. We don't have much time. You never know how effective the pulling's going to be on civilians. Any of these nurses could call security on us for being in here, and then we're out for good." I looked up into his eyes, bucking up so he wouldn't be so scared. "Terraway needs help *now*. They need the sagrado stone *now*. They can't wait a few more weeks for me to take the souls out of adults." When Finn looked like he wanted to turn around and leave for this part, I caught him by the wrist. "Hey, this is the job. You wanted in on it, so here you are. Don't wuss out on me now."

He swallowed, standing straighter and puffing out his chest as if readying to belt out an opera to the back of the auditorium. "Alright. Let's go quick. I don't like babies, and I like them even less when they might up and die near me."

I blinked up at him, fearing my knee was starting to buckle. "With talk like that, you'll have to keep the ladies away with a stick."

Finn took my hand and wrapped it in the crook of his elbow to make sure I didn't fall down. "Steady, now."

Von was chatting up a nurse so I could reap a few babies without drawing suspicion that I was lurking near children that certainly weren't mine. He darted between pulling for me, and then back to the nurse's station to pull for them so they weren't so fussed I was near the newborns.

Finn ran his hand over his shirt several times, wetting his lips as he mulled over how best to get out of the situation he'd put himself in. "I didn't realize Omens had to do this." He seemed to come to himself a little when I squeezed his arm. "Are we almost done for the day?"

"Almost." I softened when I saw the nerves that were not easily soothed. The ghosts haunting his eyes bespoke of too many adult problems for me to guess at. "Hey, I'm sorry. I'm being an irritable jerk. This part of it is hard. You can wait out in the hallway with Mason. You don't need to be here for this. It's okay if it's too much."

This seemed to shake Finn's fears to the bottom, permitting his courage to rise to the top. "It wouldn't be right to expect you to deal with this if I can't. I'm a captain, and you're a young woman. Very young. If you can do it, so can I."

I'd been without Mason or Von for too long. Each minute one of them was not touching me made me feel cold on the inside, and I feared that chill spreading. I caught Von's eye and waved him over. "I'm sorry. I'm totally raining on your parade with Hot Nurse in Pink over there." I took my hand from Finn and slid it into Von's. "Did you at least get her number?"

"I did. But she's in the middle of a divorce that's not quite finalized. I don't like to get messy."

"You found all that out in the two minutes you were over there?"

"I'm just that charming."

I could feel Hot Nurse in Pink staring at Von's hand in mine. I wished I could tell her we were just friends.

We were just friends who lived together, slept together, had bathed together, worked together and pretty much were never separated. I mean, who wouldn't want to get in on that action? I felt terrible for Von, and vowed to push him on Katrina at the next available opportunity.

Three of the babies were sealed off, but there were a fair few I could brush on the toe as I walked by. There were twenty babies in the ward, and eight of them called out to me to be reaped. Eight. Eight out of twenty. The odds choked me around the throat as I stared down the barrel of mortality that was inescapable.

My hands were shaking from how sick I'd gotten at the

picnic. That, coupled with coming off the coattails of the malnourishment I'd suffered while in Geon's cell made for a rough afternoon. I wasn't sure how I was going to get through my quota and out of the hospital without passing clean out in the middle of the ward.

Von caught my anxiety and gripped my hand, brushing my fingers to the toe of a preemie with too many tubes attached to him. The delicate soul went straight into my fingertips and leapt into Von, barely staying in me a whole two seconds. He decided that's how the rest of the babies should be reaped, and I couldn't object. The tiny booty-covered feet, the toothpick-like fingers that would never learn to play the piano or use chopsticks properly after using them five hundred times incorrectly – all of it was about nine kinds of too much.

There was a mother near one of the preemies who was calling out to my gut from across the room, and I wished she hadn't looked up at my face. She had chocolate brown eyes, unwashed tangled chestnut hair in a messy bun and dark circles under her eyes. Her baggy sweats had stains under the armpits, and I could tell she'd been crying and not showering. I wondered how long she'd been in limbo, waiting for her baby girl to get well enough to take home. Wanting a family, but it being just out of reach.

"I think it's time for a little charm," Von suggested, his voice low.

"Charm?" Finn inquired in a whisper. "What kind of charms do you need?"

Von pointed to his smile that flashed from zero to a million kilowatts on command. "Just me. Mason's the intimidator, and I'm the charm. You're the giant fish out of water. Watch and learn. And don't let November fall. She can barely stand as it is." He gripped my shoulder, pulling the radiating stress from me. "Let me know when you're ready, Peach."

I hated myself when I gave Von a nod toward the woman, and he took over with his distracting grin. He was captivating, and lost as she was, his mild flirts gave her a moment of something beautiful to hold onto as she stumbled through her walking nightmare.

Finn's hand in mine brushed the baby's toe when Von had the mother's full attention. The ice of the reap shot through me, taking my breath away and cutting like a million tiny blades through my veins. The dainty soul shot through my body and stayed too long. My legs started to falter, and I knew that last reap was one too many. I clawed at the air, grasping onto Finn's shirt just before I went down. The mama whose daughter I'd just reaped let out a noise of distress for my sake, and in that moment, I truly hated myself.

15

TRUTH TIME IN THE TUB

I awoke to Von and Mason yelling at each other, which if I had to pick, would not make it on my top ten ways to be roused. Mason was irate, and his voice was loudest since it was nearest my head. He shouted with a mouthful of food tucked in his cheek. "I haven't done a thing but my job all day, Von. You don't need to harp on me about stuff that's in the past."

"The past? The past? Are you joking? I've met a lot of delusional blokes in my day, but you're at the top of it. You wrecked her barely a week ago! I swear, I never thought I'd see the day where you were more of an arse than Danny, but then you went and did that."

The warm, burly body beneath me was Mason's. As much as I wanted to get away from him, the lure of his strength that was this time on my side kept me feigning sleep so I could remain in my guilty pleasure a few minutes longer. Finn spoke up from his spot next to me, and I placed the three of us in the backseat of Terence, with Von at the wheel. "What are the hallucinations like?"

Mason sounded frustrated. "Like no drug in Terraway or Topside. It's the best feeling in the world, and far too addictive. Some days I wish I'd never done it, so I wouldn't know what bliss felt like."

I could hear Von speaking through his teeth from the driver's seat. "That's a helluva thing to say about the woman in your arms. You used her, Mason. You used her to see Kara. Never thought I'd see the day where Danny cared about a person more than you did, but you proved me wrong."

"I do care. I wouldn't have seen Kara at all if I hadn't loved her. That's why the hallucinations started going away, because when I started to see Kara through October, I remembered my love for my wife, and it overshadowed what I felt for October. The last time I kissed her, I felt the euphoria of the high, but the visions left me. I lost Kara and October in the same kiss. You want to tell me how seamlessly you'd handle that?"

"Incredible," Finn breathed, and I could tell he was studying my face. "I had no idea Omens were like that."

Von was livid. "I don't give a shite about your loss, Mason! I held her while she cried herself to sleep after what you'd done to her. She was devastated! Two blokes, Mason. Two men her whole life she's kissed. She's pure, and you're wrecking her. One tosser cheated on her with friend, and the other grown-arse man used her to makeout with his wife!" Von's pitch rose, and with it, my heart climbed to new heights of appreciation for him. While I didn't like my business being spilled out for them to dissect, I heard Von. I really heard him. It was that same protective go for the gut that Ollie used when he stuck up for me. "If I catch you kissing her again, I swear to you. People think my unbalanced days are behind me? It's nothing to how I'll unleash on you if you mess with her ever again."

"Von, I heard you the first time you went off on me. And the second. I get it. She's important to you. She's important to me, too. I won't kiss her again. It messed us both up, so you don't have to worry. I love her enough to know I'm not right for her, or anyone, for that matter." His arms tightened, and I felt his affection for me, the regret at something that could've been beautiful turning dark before it had the chance to bloom. "You have to drive faster, Von. She's still icy."

I heard the accelerator whine as Von coaxed Terence to climb past the speed limit. Mason stroked my cheek, pulling until I was deliriously out of it. I opened my eyes and shook my head. "I'm going to pass out again if you keep pulling so hard. Where are we?" I kept my temple pressed to his shoulder, not wanting to leave the only source of warmth I had.

"Hey, love. You alright? You gave us a fright back there. Passed clean out in the middle of the ward."

"I'm fine."

Von groaned dramatically. "I hate when you say that. I swear, I've never despised two words more. It's almost always a lie, or wishful thinking."

"Well, this time it's true. I'm just tired."

"We're about fifteen minutes from the mansion. Hold on, Peach."

"How many souls did we get?" I asked, not remembering the math of it all.

"Twenty-six," Finn answered. "It was really something to watch an Omen in action. I've never seen that many reapings in a single day. Wait until the council hears about this."

"No," Mason and Von both answered with a definitive gavel. Mason explained, "It was foolish of her to promise that many in the first place. Terraway's in desperate need of the sagrado stone, otherwise she wouldn't have worked herself to the brink like this. It's not safe, what she did today, and the whole council should burn for letting her try it. If they know she's capable of this? They'll push her till her heart gives out, and she's capable of doing that on her own with no additional prodding."

I tried to lift my hand to give Mason a comforting pat, but it flopped lifelessly into my lap, heavy with ice. "It's got to happen this way," I mumbled. "When it's all over, I'll take a break. Mariang can't keep up at the rate she was going. Girlfriend needed to rest up."

"Would it help if I spoke to the council on her behalf?"

Finn suggested, his eyebrows furrowed. "Asked them for a few more days? I didn't realize... I didn't know she'd be like this at the end of day one."

"I can do it. I picked the number. I know my limits."

"You have no limits!" Von shouted from the front seat, livid. "Do you understand how long you've been out, you daft girl? Half an hour, October!"

I didn't like it when Von used my actual name. I didn't like it when he yelled, or was serious beyond repair. I cuddled into Mason's warmth, wishing it was ten degrees hotter.

Mason and Von had a few more spirited back and forths while Finn watched me shiver in Mason's arms. Mason lifted his shirt and stretched it over my head for lack of a blanket. His bare skin was hairy and warm, causing my eyes to roll back gratuitously. I indulged myself in pressing as much of my body to his toned torso as possible.

Mason threw his head back and let out a bitten off noise of distress. "So cold! Ah! Von, something's wrong. She should be fine by now. Should've been warmed up a few seconds after the last soul left her." He gripped me hard. "I can't pull this much for this long! I'm starving, and if I don't get more food, I'll shift back into a wolf and bite her!"

Finn opened the cooler and ripped a sandwich out of a bag, shoving it in Mason's hand. He ate loudly and with gusto, breathing hard like he was fighting off wolfing out with every breath.

"Almost home," Von responded through gritted teeth, taking a turn too sharp. We rocked in the backseat, me clinging to Mason, and the two men gripping the doors as Von gave Terence the workout of his life. Von whipped out his phone. "Danny, start running a hot bath in the big tub upstairs. Hot as you can stand it." He glanced in the rearview mirror. "It's bad, Danny. Not sure how bad yet." He ended the call just as Danny was getting revved up on the other end.

Von and Mason went back and forth, throwing out different conjectures I couldn't focus on enough to follow. Instead my eyes fell on Finn, locking in on his hardened gaze that seemed to be saying something to me, though I couldn't tell what. He didn't break eye contact as he untied his scarf, leaned forward and looped it around my neck. He took his time tying the knot, pausing his world to brush his knuckle to my cheek. "Hold on, *kendi*."

Von hissed under his breath. "Don't you dare call her that."

Finn straightened. "I think you've forgotten your place."

Von tightened his knuckles around the steering wheel. "We're equals on this trip, remember? She's my charge, and I don't want you calling her that. Don't even think about it." He pulled into the long driveway. "And I'll know if you're thinking about it."

"That's enough out of you."

Von cut the ignition and ran around to extract me from Mason, who was starting to shiver from the cold I couldn't help but exude. Ezra ran out to meet us, his perfect hair not daring to fall out of place. "No! What's happened to her?"

Von didn't bother answering. He hefted me up, clinging to my rigid body. He ran me into the house, past Danny, Lynna and Mariang and up the stairs to the bathroom. He laid me on the floor with great care, and it was only then I noticed that I couldn't move my arms or legs more than an inch back and forth. The shivering was uncontrollable, and my muscles had locked from the ice that felt somehow permanent. Von tore his clothes off down to his boxer briefs and took off my shoes and socks. Then he stepped into the steaming tub Danny had filled for us, wincing at the high temperature.

I didn't want Finn to lift me up, but he inched into the bathroom to lend a hand. I didn't trust him to hold me or watch out for me when I couldn't look out for myself. His arms were muscular, and I didn't want to know how he went about obtaining the strength he had. I had a feeling it was more bashing skulls than lifting weights. He had that sinister, no conscience look to him that gave me pause. But Finn was surprisingly gentle in the bathroom. He lowered me fully clothed onto Von's lap once my Puller was settled in the hot water.

The water was an instant relief, turning my skin rosy

and relaxing me. After a minute of partial submersion, I was a limp noodle in Von's arms. I could tell he was keeping up a constant stream of pulling to calm my body. I couldn't help but marvel how he'd gone from lazy playboy who couldn't adhere to a schedule, to a details-oriented coworker I counted on for nearly everything these days. Somehow we'd gotten to that elusive place where I could lean on him when I wasn't able to stand on my own.

It was a few minutes into the best bath of my life before I realized conversation was going on around me. Finn had been replaced by Ezra, who was barking at Von. "Never again!" Ezra thundered as he tossed a blood bag at Von, who wasted no time in guzzling it down. "I don't ever want to see her barely alive like that. You should all know better than to compromise her. It's too much!"

"Funny that you think we let her do anything. This was all her suicide mission. This was her doing, and she promised this feat under your supervision, Ezra. Mason and I weren't in the council meeting when this was decided."

"October Grace, don't you dare test me on this. I know what I'm talking about. Having two Pullers doesn't make you invincible! I watched my daughter diminish because Terraway pushed her too hard. I'll not watch another daughter of mine go out in the same way!"

I could barely lift my head to point my face in Ezra's direction, but I caught his eye to examine his sincerity, taking it in to see if it could be dismantled by a stiff breeze. "You think of me as your daughter?"

Ezra paused his tirade to cast me a look that showed the state of his wounded heart. "Of course I do. You really can't see my affection for you?"

I shook my head uncertainly. "I don't know. Sometimes I think I do, but then I remember that I'm the job. I'm the commodity, and that's why you care."

Ezra rubbed his forehead, exhaling a bit of his disbelief at my cold heart I feared might never thaw. He was softer when he answered, gentler with the doubt I held tight in a fist I wanted to shake at the world. "When I marry your mother, it'll be official, but even without that piece of paper, I look at you and see a daughter. I'm afraid I can't help it. I adored you from the very first day I met you."

"B-But I shoved you when I first met you."

"Yes, and no matter how often you shove me, my love for you won't change."

I blinked up at him, wet, still a little cold and very, very confused. "You're not just using me to save Terraway?"

Ezra dropped to his knees, reached into the tub and held my icy hands. He winced at the chill and dunked my fingers under the water. "Oliver has no use for Terraway, and I love him much the same. I've called him once a week for months just to get to know him better. I see you, and I'm glad you're my daughter."

Ezra had too much good in him to be lying. I'd been lied to over and over, so many times that I developed a sixth sense about it. I searched his face, taking in the slight crinkles at the outside corners of his eyes, his Ken doll hair and the dress pants and pressed shirt he didn't mind wrinkling if it meant I understood my place here better. The words were too good to be true, but somehow they were real.

I took a chance and leaned forward, wrapping my arms around his neck in probably the worst hug of his life. I was freezing and soaking, but he didn't pull away. I kept waiting for the separation that told me I was too messy for his perfect family, but it never came. He held me tight, pressing me to his firm chest with so much love, it threatened to choke the emotion right out of me. I was the girl born in trash, but he didn't care. He saw me through the garbage and clung to me, as if I was the treasure he wanted to keep. As if I was too important to him to be thrown away.

That last note of realization hit me hard. My own mama had thrown me away. Every item she brought into the house to edge us out cut a nick in my heart, whittling away the softness until I feared there was nothing left of me but the hard shell of scars and walls I had to have to keep myself alive and my heart beating. Ezra added to my life with his kindness, spackling in the cracks Bev had cut me with. He showed me I didn't have to be alone. I could lean on him, and even though my childhood was sometimes too heavy for me to carry, Ezra was strong enough.

"I'm scared it's a lie," I whispered, shivering in his arms.

"That you'll get to know me more and see something you don't like. Then you'll split, and it'll hurt."

Ezra held me tighter, not caring that I'd soaked his shirt through. "Then tell me. Tell me the things you're afraid I'll abandon you over. Test me. I promise you, I won't run."

I'm sure he hadn't meant right then, but I couldn't chance my moment slipping away. If this was real, I wouldn't give myself the escape route to run out on the best thing that could happen to a nobody like me. A real dad was something I'd wanted too badly to be able to say out loud. Now that one was right here? I decided to jump at the test he offered up. I nodded into his shoulder. I kind of wished I could send Von away, but I knew I couldn't be without a Puller after such a hard day. "Okay. What do you want to know?"

"Only everything." Ezra lowered me back onto Von's lap, but remained at the side of the tub, holding my hand in the water as a sign that he wouldn't run. My grip was arthritic, and it held him probably too tight, but I was scared if I loosened my grasp, he'd run away when my story grew too awful.

"How is the water getting tepid already? It was steaming just a few minutes ago." Ezra leaned over and let out a little of the barely warm water. Then he turned on the hot spigot to give me back a little feeling in my limbs.

"It's her. She's cooling the water down faster than it can heat her up. Let more of the cold water out first." Von leaned forward and shut off the hot water while Ezra put the towels on the floor next to the heating vent. Once the water drained, Von plugged up the tub and hissed as the scalding water hit his bare toes.

"Oh, Von. I'm sorry. I'm b-burning your skin!"

"It's fine. I don't mind." He banded his arms around me, holding me tight as the heat started to rise in my quaking limbs. "Talk to Ezra. Tell him everything. I promise you, Peach, you can't tell him anything that'll scare him off. Trust me, I've tried."

Ezra held my hand, not caring that his clothes were wet, that I was a mess, and that I was about to hand him more than a qualified shrink could deal with. He was sincere, and I'd been devastated by too many broken promises not to see the difference in Ezra. "Okay," I said, clearing my throat as my shivering lessened. "Has Danny told you about her trailer?"

Ezra's eyes hardened. "Yes. Just this morning, actually. I couldn't believe Danny would ever lie to me to try and break up our engagement, but there you have it."

"It's not a lie. I'll take you there sometime, if you want. I just need you to promise me something."

Ezra was hesitant, no doubt rethinking what he'd assumed was Danny's propaganda. "Yes?"

"I need you to still marry Bev. No matter what I tell you or what I show you, you have to marry her!" My voice cracked from distress and desperation, but I didn't have the strength to feel ashamed of the blatant weakness. "I need someone to help me with her, Ezra. I can't look after her all by myself! Ollie's away, Allie's completely gone. It's just me, and I'm tired! I'm so tired. Promise me you'll still be my dad even after you find out what she's really like."

Ezra took in my odd plea warily. "I have no intention of leaving my fiancée because she doesn't have a housekeeper. I love your mother."

My eyes closed as I leaned on Von, who was there for me at my most vulnerable. "Alright. Good. Then go get my phone from my bag. I don't have to tell you anything. I can just show you."

"Ezra, I need another blood bad," Von requested as Ezra stood.

Ezra left to grab a blood bag and my phone from wherever it had landed, giving me a moment to calm down in the hot water with Von. The heat was staying in my body longer this time, which dialed down my fear a few notches. Von played with the hairs at the base of my neck, as if there was no tension in the room, as if we were just old pals who sat around watching the Brady Bunch on a Sunday morning together. I kinda loved him for it.

"I feel like the bottom's about to drop, Peach. What's the deal with your mum?"

"She's fun and tells great stories and can charm anyone. Bev's also mentally ill. She isn't the person Ezra thinks she is." Von fished around in the water and held my hand to keep me from scratching it and breaking the skin. "Thanks."

"I love how highly you must think of me to try to tear open your skin when I can already smell your blood heating in the water. You smell…" He pressed his nose to my cheek and took in a long drag, closing his eyes in ecstasy. "Don't cut yourself. I'm barely holding on, here. Distract me. Tell me about the drama."

I leaned up and kissed Von's cheek, softening us both. "You don't want to bite me. You care about me, and I care about you. Even when you lost yourself in the cage when you were trying to eat me, you found yourself enough to call for Danny when Mason got out of hand."

He craned his chin to look me in the eye. "You're right. I do care about you. You're my best friend, and I don't say that about women. Total waste of a great rack, if you ask me."

I clung to him in the water, needing something immovable to hold onto through my valley of vulnerability.

16

MACARONI AND CHEESE

When Ezra rejoined us, he gave us a look that was one of a father taking in the tenor of a heated moment he'd interrupted between his daughter and her guy. Only he hadn't, and was just jumping to conclusions. He handed Von a blood bag, and then set down a fresh outfit for me, and one for Von. I couldn't not like Ezra; he was above and beyond kind, serving when he didn't have to and anticipating needs out of sheer thoughtfulness. "I'm ready to listen, October."

I took a deep breath before shattering his world. "You want to know who Bev is? I took the sagrado stone. I snuck into her trailer when she wasn't there and took it. She was using it as a doorstop, and it was buried under a mountain of crap. Bev's a hoarder, Ezra. She edged Allie, Ollie and me out when we were kids. Ollie had to seal our bedroom door shut to keep her from putting trash in our room, and to keep the bugs from crawling all over us while we slept." I watched Ezra's distrust grow and his eyes widen. "Bev lives in a house of garbage that she can't part from. It's a sickness I can't fix. Somehow she knows if one thing in her hoard is missing, and she'll come scream at me first thing if she suspects something's gone. Play the voicemail. She doesn't love us; she loves her stuff." I felt the need to add the defense of, "She's not a bad person; she just has a problem, is all."

Ezra shook his head, so confused at the barrage of new information that he simply obeyed instead of responding.

Von finished off the blood bag just as the voicemail started up. He was able to hold me without wanting to eat me, which was a good thing. I hadn't had someone to hold me while Bev went off on me in years, and cherished the rock Von was for me in that moment. I closed my eyes as Bev's voice sounded through the bathroom on speakerphone. Her sinister tone gave me a sick feeling in my gut. My mouth wanted to apologize to Bev over and over, but I kept my lips pressed firmly shut.

"It was you, and I know it! You snuck in here and stole my doorstop. How would you like it if I stole something from your perfect life, you fat little freak! Give me back the rock! It's mine! You can get your own doorstop with all your rich nursing money you don't deserve. You never buy anything! Don't you know what I could do with your paycheck? I could buy all sorts of treasures to make your place nicer. Just give me a hundred dollars, and I'll show you how great your house could look."

Her tone dipped again to that snake-like place I hated. My stomach turned, and the familiar tightness in my chest resurfaced when Bev's recorded voice laid into me further. "You don't need that money. I put a roof over your head for eleven years before you abandoned me! You owe me rent! All three of you do! I'm your mother, and you should chip in! Give me back my rock!" she yelled, causing Ezra to jump. "I know it was you who stole it. Allie's off whoring herself to who knows what kind of lowlife, Ollie's gone to make money in New York and keep it all for himself! Your brother is the greediest bastard alive! You're the only one left, so I know it was you! When I find you, I'll take the price of that rock outta your hide, girl! Don't think I won't beat that rock outta you! I've had that doorstop longer than I've had you! It's more mine than you are!"

The machine cut off her tirade. "You can erase the message," I told Ezra, who fumbled with my phone to simply turn the whole mess off.

Ezra was pale and horrified as he looked up at me. "What was that?"

"You asked me to get the sagrado stone, so I did. Bev doesn't know what it is; she just uses it as a doorstop. That's what happens when I move something in her trailer, which I never do. Ollie did a couple years ago on one of his visits. Bev thought it was me, and she beat me something awful." I shuddered at the memory. "But she can't knock me around anymore. I know how to defend myself now."

"Stop it," Von said to me, separating my hands I hadn't realized were scratching each other. "Here, scratch me. Will that help?"

I tried his idea, but it didn't have the same effect. It helped a little, but not as much. "It's not the same. It only feels better when it hurts. I can't explain it right."

"Hurt me, then. I can't take it when you scratch yourself."

"But I don't like it when you're hurting," I admitted.

Von draped one of my arms around his shoulders so I couldn't injure myself. "Well, then we're in quite the predicament."

"I don't understand. She must know about the sagrado stone's power to guard it so fiercely," Ezra commented, staring at my phone as if it had lied to him. "Beverly isn't like that. She's funny and kindhearted."

"Trust me, she doesn't know about the stone or Terraway. She's like that with everything. When Allie took a box of macaroni and cheese once when we were hungry, Bev locked us out of the trailer for the night. It was December." I remembered that night well. Sandy, the pit bull next door had nudged us toward his owner's house, but as usual, no one was home. Ollie was firm that we weren't the type of people to break into someone's home and steal their food, no matter how much Sandy seemed to insist we were welcome there.

"No. No, that's not possible. Bev's a good person. She's kind to Mariang," Ezra protested, though I could see the sick feeling rising up in him, too. He'd been had, and he was starting to see the cracks in the perfection, too.

I flipped through the highlights of that awful night in a quiet voice. "Allie cried and said she was never going to eat another bite of food, so Ollie and I had to talk her down from starving herself again. It was snowing, and we knew we couldn't sleep outside. Ollie carried me all the way to the school in my pink footie pajamas. He and Allie broke in, and we slept together in the women's locker room. We took showers, ate apples and bananas from the school's cafeteria, and pretended we were camping to try and cheer Allie up. I remember watching her eat her apple to make sure she finished it, to make sure she didn't starve herself again. She was always so thin. It was scary." I closed my eyes to shut out the horrified looks from the guys. "Bev's a lot of fun, but she doesn't know how to take care of people. She's sick, not mean. There's a difference between someone who can't help themselves and someone who can. Bev can't." I looked up at Von's angry expression. "So that's why Ollie was yelling on the phone this morning. He gets scared when he doesn't know where I'm at, when he thinks Bev's got her hooks in me and he can't do anything to stop it."

"I... If you'll excuse me. I seem to've..." Ezra patted his breast pockets for who knows what and stood, completely at a loss. He made to exit, but then stopped, stalwart in his frustration. "I need more proof. I believe you, but if I'm going to talk to Beverly about any of this, I need more than your word against hers."

I nodded. "Sure. Call Ollie. He's my first speed dial. Ask him about the coat hangers. That's a good story."

Ezra dialed the number, and my heart nearly broke when Ollie answered in a panic on speakerphone. "October? I'm sorry. I'm so sorry I yelled. I've been leaving you messages to tell you how awful I feel about the whole thing, and now your mailbox is full."

"It's fine. I know you were just worried. But I didn't call about that. I called because I told Ezra about Bev."

"Oh, wow. Really? What'd you tell him?"

"The time with the macaroni and cheese and breaking into the school for the night."

"Oh, man. I really hoped he'd go through with the wedding, too. I wanted him to take her off your hands. What happened? Your conscience get the better of you? Or did he see her trailer?"

"Actually, Ezra's right here. He wants you to confirm the macaroni story so he can talk to Bev about it."

"Hello, Oliver."

I almost could hear Ollie sitting up straighter on the other end. "Hello, Ezra, sir."

"No need for the formalities, son. I just want to know what I'm walking into. If I've been fleeced, I deserve to know. Mariang deserves to know."

I heard Ollie's long exhale and knew he was preparing

to dig into the muck we tried not to get too near. "Alright, what do you want to know? I mean, just showing up at her trailer will tell you enough."

"I want to know how it is October's told me a completely different version of the woman I fell in love with."

"Alright." Ollie spoke slowly, thinking through his response and ironing out the hurt he tried never to feel. "Bev's a great performer when she wants something, so she pulls out all the stops. You're rich, so she was on her A-game. Don't feel bad, Ezra. You're not the first guy to be totally fooled by her. You're the first one I've felt bad was fooled, though. You're a decent man. I actually look forward to our weekly phone calls."

"Thank you."

"If you're going to break it off with her, make sure to tell her I ratted her out, not October. She gets physical when she's mad, and I don't want this to come back on my sister. Seriously, Ezra. I'm states away. I won't be there when this blows up."

"Physical how?"

I shook my head. "I can handle myself, Ollie. You know I don't let her get a punch in anymore."

Ezra was horrified, but Ollie kept his cool. "Sure, but I don't want her taking swings at you. You don't handle it as well as you think you do. Even if she doesn't land a punch, I see how it messes you up."

I rolled my eyes at Ollie's worrying, but neither Von

nor Ezra were in the mood for blowing Ollie off. "I didn't call so you could scare Ezra. He's already done enough to be cool to me. I called so he would know I wasn't lying."

"Oh, right. Well, October doesn't lie, especially not about that stuff. I can't tell you how many times I came home to find her and Allie shivering in the corner under blankets because Bev didn't pay the heating bills. She had enough money, but she spent it on her 'treasures', buying crap she didn't need and forgetting about the people who depended on her to pay the heating bill. Allie and I worked after school to keep the heat on and buy groceries for the three of us. We decided we didn't need electricity or water. We couldn't get to the bathroom anyway, since Bev filled every inch up with garbage."

"Please tell me you're joking," Ezra begged, his voice hollow.

Ollie's voice lowered. "You ever see a three-year-old cry because there wasn't any food that day? It changes you."

My hands were burning with the desire to scratch them. I didn't like having my secrets spilled out all over for Von and Ezra to dissect at will, though I knew it was necessary to save Mariang from Bev. I took my arm from around Von and raked my nails down the backs of my hands, alternating from left to right which one needed punishing.

"October, stop scratching," Ollie said, as if he could see me. He knew me like the man who raised you should.

"I love you, Ollie." I tried to keep the emotion out of my eyes.

"I love you, too. It'll be okay. If you trust Ezra, then he'll do the right thing. You've got a good gut about most people. I should've said something when we first met him, but I was being selfish and thinking only about how good this would be for you if he took Bev off your hands."

Ezra cleared his throat three times before he could speak. "Thank you for sorting that out. You're always welcome in my home, son. Please stop by when you're in town next."

"Thank you, sir. If you could send Danny to check on my sister after it all blows up with Bev, I'd appreciate it. If you tell Bev I ratted her out, she probably won't go off on October, but you never know. Sometimes it's just the nearest one who gets hit when Bev's in a mood. I'm moving back home in two weeks, but I'll worry until then."

"Of course. Anything either of you need. Allie, as well."

Ezra ended the call and stared at the phone, willing it to have given him better news.

I wished I had it for him.

I wished I had it for me.

17

IN THIS

Ezra excused himself, running straight into Danny, Mason and Finn, who'd not gone downstairs as I'd thought, but eavesdropped on the entire conversation. "Gentleman, down to the kitchen with you. I'm sure Lynna's got something you can eat to distract yourselves from the things you were not meant to hear."

The bathroom door closed, leaving me in Von's arms in the warm water. I pulled away from him, standing in my soaking clothes between his legs. "I think I'm good now. Just totally tired. Is it cool if I crash in one of the rooms?"

"I think it's the only thing Ezra would be cool with. I can't imagine him sending you home right now." Von stood, and I realized how very naked he was in just his boxer briefs compared to my fully clothed body. "I'm going to rinse off. I've gone from freezing to sweating to freezing to sweating too many times to be able to seduce anyone tonight."

I sniggered, melting in his arms when he wrapped me in a hug as we stood in the tub while it drained. "Thanks for making a joke. Sorry you had to hear all of it. You win the friend of the year award for staying with me through it all while my body was freaking out."

"Does that come with prizes? I'm only in this for the prizes."

"As a matter of fact, it comes with a unicorn. All the magic you could ever want, packed inside one of the zoo's least stocked animals."

He rubbed my back as he held me to him, and I felt a sense of peace envelope me like warm chocolate, making me sweet on Von in the privacy of the bathroom. "You forget that I chose this. But if you could add in the occasional, 'Von, you're so sexy,' I wouldn't be opposed."

"You think *you're* sexy? Check out my new bathing suit." I motioned to my sweater and jeans that were clinging to me and making me about nine kinds of uncomfortable.

His voice went low and husky. "Oh, baby. Flash me a little wrist," he teased.

I indulged him, rolling up my sleeve in slow motion while he bit his lip in feigned lust. "Is that how you like it? Oh, you're filthy!" I covered up my wrist to reclaim my dignity, my nose in the air and a smile on my lips.

"That's what you love about me, darling." He pressed

his lips to my smile, making sure it was a light peck, and nothing that would ruin our treasured friendship, or invoke the euphoria that really kissing an Omen would bring about. His smirk at my blush gave us back a little of our levity to bring us out of the funk that conversations about Bev always mired me in. He tugged lightly on my weighted sleeve. "How about I turn around and promise not to peek at anything that would stop my heart. You can leave your clothes in here and dry off before you get changed."

"Thanks. I didn't want to ruin Ezra's bathroom floor."

Von made a show of turning around and peeking a few times before he promised to keep his nose to the wall. "I could eat a horse right about now. Any chance you can choke something down?"

I considered this. "Maybe, but only if it's actual horse meat. I'm on a strict diet."

"Well, obviously. That's why I suggested it."

I peeled my soaking sweater off and tugged my shirt over my head, accidentally whapping Von across the back with it. The simple act of raising my arms to undress was taxing. I hated that reaping made me such a wuss. "I know I should eat, and I think I can probably keep something down. I just can't decide what's more appealing – food or sleep."

"Food, and then sleep. Lynna's the best cook in the world."

"It's settled then. Eat until we zonk out." I made quick

work of peeling off my jeans and underwear, and stepping out of the tub to wrap myself in one of the toasty warm towels Ezra provided for us. I was shivering, and couldn't tell if it was a normal cold or a reaping-related chill.

"Mrs. Brady? Be a love and put these in the sink," Von said after starting up the shower. He handed me my pile of clothes with his underwear on top through the side of the shower curtain. His fingers brushed mine, pulling a bit of the chill from me. He yanked the curtain so his head poked out the side while his body hid behind it. "Seriously? You're cold again? Stubborn little bugger. Let me rinse off, and I'll do some more pulling."

I pursed my lips, taking in Von's unending team spirit. "I wonder at what point you'll start resenting me for always being in your space."

Von leaned his head further out and pecked my cheek, the utter nudity of the situation making the simple sweetness feel far steamier than a kiss to my cheek otherwise would've been. "You forget I grew up with five brothers. Being around a beautiful woman all the time? Not as much a chore as you make it sound."

"But what about the Hot Nurse in Pink? You got her number and then had to hold my hand. I'm seriously going to cramp your game."

"I'm up for the challenge. This face, this body, plus my charm and accent? It was getting too easy. I'm in this, November. You don't have to worry about me."

"Thanks," I said as he disappeared behind the curtain

again to rinse off. I got dressed in the black fleece pajama pants and pea green thermal shirt Ezra provided for me. The socks were fuzzy and had picked up a bit of heat from being in front of the vent. I brushed out my hair, handing Von a towel when he turned the water off. He came out with it wrapped around his waist, looking like, well exactly like a TV vampire might look with water dripping off his eyelashes and clothed in only a towel.

18

JOINING THE FAMILY

It felt like every time I paused chewing, another cannoli was shoved toward me. Lynna was an amazing cook, but after lasagna, carrots, garlic bread and soup, I was pretty much full. Add two cannolis to that, and I was ready to crash. I had Mason on my left and Von on my right, both of them sucking residual buildup from the excessive reaping while they ate an inhuman amount of food. It was a wonder Lynna could keep up with the demand.

"Is there more garlic bread?" Mason asked.

Finn blanched. "How can you still be hungry?"

"Of course, dear." Lynna filled his plate with more bread, giving his hand a tight squeeze before she went back to the kitchen.

"Pulling a normal amount makes me starving, but as

much as we did today? I can't keep up. I swallow, and it's like a drop in an ocean. I'm so hungry."

"Sorry, guys," I said with a frown. I hadn't thought about how my crusade to get it done ASAP would affect them. "Look on the bright side. We only have twenty-four more to do tomorrow. Then we can crash for a whole day. You can eat till you puke and sleep in as late as you want."

Von gave a noise of assent between mouthfuls, his hand on the inside of my knee as he ate. With Mason's hand on my shoulder, the weighted feeling of never ever having a moment alone dawned on me afresh, sinking like a brick in my gut. I finished my cannoli with a heavy heart, knowing Ezra would drop the gavel on Bev in the next day or two. I wouldn't have the space to deal with ruining the best thing that ever happened to her, or to handle any retaliation she threw at me.

Finn, Danny, Mason and Ezra were talking shop about what to pack for the trip through Silo, Kabayo's land, but I couldn't have been further from paying attention. I was glad only Von and Mason seemed to notice when I pushed my chair back from the table and grabbed my plate to take it to the kitchen.

I rinsed off my plate in the sink and put it in the dishwasher. Then I started in on the rest of the dishes, rinsing and stacking to lighten the massive load I'd unleashed on Lynna by overworking the guys. My body was still aching, but cleaning felt like a balm to my weary soul.

I caught an earful when she came back into the kitchen

from refilling Von's plate yet again. "No! No, Lady October. You don't do dishes here. Put those down and go back with the others." Lynna's wrinkled hands went to her face, fanning with too much anxiety over something so small. Her white bun atop her head was pulled tight, making her wide eyes seem even bigger when she was upset.

"It's no big deal. It's my fault you've got so many dishes to do. Finn's here because he's curious about Omen duties. Plus I made Mason and Von work too much today. They each count for like, five grown men with how much they're putting away."

"I won't hear of it. Now you go on out there before Ezra sees you doing housework!"

I couldn't help the much-needed smile that played at the corners of my mouth at her fretting. "What's Ezra going to say about me pitching in? Does he really think I'm so useless that I can't load a dishwasher?"

Ezra strolled in, his shoulders rolled back and his empty glass in his hand. "Useless? Of course not. But your job is to be the Death Omen. Save your strength for tomorrow. You're my guest. I don't ask guests to do their own dishes." He took out a bottle of wine and refilled his goblet, making Lynna that much more high-strung now that two people were doing things she should have been tending to.

"Hello, I'm sleeping here. I'm your daughter. That hardly makes me a guest exempt from chores."

Ezra's hand was on my shoulder in the next breath. "You *are* my daughter. It's good to hear you say it."

I chuckled, waving off his earnest expression. "Alright, alright. I'll feel better about freeloading if I do something to help out." I finished filling the dishwasher, scrubbed my hands three times, and then turned to find both him and Lynna watching me with resigned expressions. "I think I'm going to turn in, if that's alright."

"Of course."

Lynna went back out to the dining room to replenish the no doubt depleted supply of lasagna, leaving Ezra and I in the kitchen. "Ezra?"

"Yes, dear?"

I had a hard time looking at him; he was just too nice a guy. "I'm real sorry for everything. For what it's worth, I like you. I don't want to take something away if it makes you happy. I feel like I did the wrong thing upstairs, telling you all that."

Ezra put his wine glass down on the counter. "On the contrary. You treated me like a family member. You looked out for my interests, even when they conflicted with your own. You told me the truth, which is more than most people do for me."

I crossed my arms over my chest, bewildered. "You can't be this nice a guy."

Ezra chortled at my skepticism. "Play poker with me sometime. You'll see my vindictive side."

"Deal me in next time you play." I couldn't help but share in a portion of his welcoming smile. He was so genuine; it made no sense. "Did Mariang have a good day off?"

"She did. Danny and I took her to a museum today. She never gets to do things like that anymore. Thanks to you, she got to see some art, went shopping with Danny and had a meal where she ate her fill, and Danny didn't eat for four. You did a good thing for her. Don't think it goes unnoticed." He extended his hand to me.

No matter how honest I'd been with him upstairs, I didn't want to tip my hand to the crazy so soon after being brought into the fold. Though there were germs aplenty, I muscled through and shook his hand. "It's no trouble."

Ezra winced at the contact. "You're still icy." He gripped my hand tighter when I tried to pull away. "While I appreciate what you did for Mariang, don't think that you can keep up this pace. I'll not sacrifice one daughter for another."

I tilted my head to the side, sizing up his sincerity. "I think we both know you would, but for my sake, I hope it doesn't come to that."

19

THE PRICE OF MURDER

I'd gone to sleep by myself in the guest bedroom I'd been given, and woke to Von sliding in beside me sometime in the middle of the night. "Oy! You're a popsicle." He took my hands and tucked them under his shirt, wrapping his arm around me to give me a steady pull while he massaged my shoulder. I hadn't realized how cold I was, but it felt like they'd turned the thermostat down by at least seven degrees.

"I'm f-fine. Just tired."

He took his phone from off the bedside stand and swiped through until he found the person he needed. "Danny? Get up here and send Mason. Does Ezra have an electric blanket? She's stone cold again." He ended the call and tore off his sweater, shoving the hoodie over my head. He tucked my messy bun inside the hood and kissed my nose. "Clever girl. Make yourself into a human ice cube in order to get me naked. Didn't you know? All you had to do was ask."

"Rats! That was funny. All I can think of is something about you thinking you have a hot body, and me giving you the cold shoulder. Give me a m-minute. I'll think up something better."

"I'll be on the very edge of my seat. Come closer, love. There you go," he said as I wrapped my arms around him. His leg hooked over mine, drawing me so close, it felt like we were one body. "I really need to get laid. All this cuddling's no good for me. You're turning me into a nice guy, and that isn't the man you fell in love with."

Despite my stiff limbs, I laughed. "After this sagrado business is over, how about you take a weekend of debauchery to make up for lost time? If I won't need to reap so much, I can get by with just the one Puller for a few days. That is, if I can ever warm up."

"I won't leave you with Mason." He rubbed my back to soothe me. The smell of him was everywhere, now that I was wearing his sweater. It wasn't a bad thing, but very intimate.

My voice shifted, not bothering to hide my worry. "Von?"

"Yeah, love?"

"What's wrong with me?"

"You have terrible choice in men. I'll do your screening next time so you don't get swept off your feet by some good looking dog."

"Von?"

"Nothing," Von assured me, pressing his cheek to mine and pulling in longer drags than he usually did. "There's nothing wrong with you at all, darling. Everything will work out alright. It always does. I'm here, aren't I? There's nothing we can't figure out together. Have a little faith, Mrs. Brady."

Despite myself, I laughed. I'm sure we looked a little raunchy with our arms and legs wrapped around each other, but when the others came into the room, we didn't pull apart. Mason, Danny and Ezra entered, turning on the light as Mason joined us on the bed to warm my back with a rub of his hand. "Something's wrong, Ezra. I c-can't keep my body heat."

Ezra placed his hand on my cheek and pulled it back as if I'd stung him. "Danny, how does this keep happening? She's freezing!"

Danny waved away Mason and pried me out of Von's arms. I sat on the bed, my legs curled to my chest. I shivered as Danny checked my pupils, my hands and even tugged up the tail of my shirt apologetically to check my spine. Something about my spine made him gasp. "Okay, Ezra? Go make October some tea. Von? Plug in that electric blanket and crank it."

"What's wrong with m-me?" I chattered, needing a Puller to give me some body heat.

Danny waited for Ezra to leave before he knelt on the bed next to me, looking me in the eye to make sure he had my full attention. "Shut the door and lock it, Von." He ran his hands through his hair as if gearing up for something big. I was nervous, and wished the dramatics would tone down a little so it didn't all seem like such a huge deal. "Listen to me, kid. Something happened that's making it harder for the souls to completely detach from you. That happened to Mariang once when she..." He shook his head. "She reaped a person after they died somehow. Something about the way he died made the soul stickier, so Von and Mason might feel like they've gotten it out, but part of the soul is still stuck inside of you. It's a slow torture. Starts out with your hands just being a little chilly every now and then, and then weeks later, you turn into this." He showed me his hands to prove their innocence before reaching around and touching a spot near the base of my spine. It was more tender than any other part of my back for some reason. "Feel that? I can see it holding on right there." His head whipped to Von and Mason. "How can you not have seen this?"

Von shot his brother an incredulous look. "Um, because we're not having sex with our charge. We see you naked about as often as we see her naked."

Danny shrank. "Oh, right. Well, we have to get it out, or this cold feeling might set in and become permanent."

I chewed on my lower lip as I clutched my knees tighter to my chest. "Like a deep clean?"

Danny let a hint of a smile touch his face to lighten my anxiety. "Exactly. Do you know what you did when you first felt the deep cold like this? It would have been a week or two ago, judging by how big the spot's grown on your back."

"No. I mean, it was freezing in Geon's dungeon, but I think that's the nature of dungeons. But I couldn't get warm even after that in the hot Sakuna weather."

"Then something that happened in the dungeon gave that skip to your system."

"Do you think it's when I killed Andy?" I asked, my voice quiet. "You said Mariang reaped someone who was already dead."

Realization dawned on Danny. "You murdered Andy. That's right. You killed him, and then you must've reaped him after he died. Same thing happened to Mariang. Andy must've been a half-breed. Part Duwende and part human."

Von's voice lowered. "Whoa! Are you saying Mariang murdered the person she reaped post-death?"

Danny looked around at the audience with worry painting his features. "Never mind about that. It was an accident, and she was trying to defend herself. From here on out, if you murder any more half-breeds or full humans, stay away from them once they hit the ground. Far, far away."

"That would've been nice to know months ago, Danny," Mason glowered.

"Stop saying 'murdered'!" I begged. "It was him or me, and I did what I had to do."

Danny raised his chin and made a show of exhaling so I'd calm down. "Point is, I can get it out, but it has to be now. It might already be too late."

"Well, do it!"

Danny moved the pillows off the bed and patted the mattress. "It's going to hurt. Lay face-down here. Von, Mason, pay attention. If I'm not around the next time she kills someone before she reaps them, make sure one of you does this." I hated the assumption that I was naturally a killer and would go on a murdering binge like a bad habit that needed curbing.

Danny walked them through several deep breathing techniques that all just sounded like yoga to me. I could tell Von was trying extra hard to pay attention and not blow this off, as was his natural inclination. I buried my face into the mattress in embarrassment when Danny moved my sweatshirt up to show Von and Mason what to look for. "Next time you can't bring her body temperature up with a simple pulling, check her spine right here at the base."

"Whoa, is that... Is her spine turning blue?" Mason asked, transfixed.

"What? Are you serious?" I tried to crane my neck to look, but if you can believe it, I couldn't see my own spine without a mirror.

Danny shoved my head back down onto the mattress. "Lie still. This is going to hurt if you resist it. Mason's going to pull along your spine, so try not to move."

I clutched the mattress. "What are we talking here? I don't want a spinal injury, Danny."

"Then don't move."

"You are such an ass," I grumbled, gathering a bit of the sheet into my mouth to bite down on. Danny positioned Mason on my other side so he could mirror Danny's actions.

"Put your hands on either side of the blue spot, Mason. That's right. Now focus on moving it up through her."

Mason pushed down on my spine, trying to knead the ice through my body. It remained in place, though. I could feel the stubborn chill giving him the finger when he tried to move it. I waited for more than the discomfort of a rough massage to resonate through me, but that seemed to be the worst of it. "It's not moving," Mason said, stating the obvious.

Danny scratched his head. "Think of it like a magnet. Will the cold into your hands first, and then move it up after it's attached to you."

Mason rubbed his hands together and then placed them on my spine like a Reiki master. A month ago I would've thrilled at having his hands on me like this. Of course, in my fantasies, it was without the audience, and we were hot for each other instead of one of us being a human icicle. Now his hands felt wrong, and like we were both trying too hard to make it feel right. Over and over he massaged the spot on my spine, but it didn't budge. "Am I doing it wrong? Nothing's happening."

"I don't know how to explain it any different. I mean, it's hard to break down something that's intuitive. October, relax. It won't help if you resist it."

"Relax while you play psychic Operation on my spine? Sure thing, boss."

Von had been standing near my head, taking in the scene with his outsider's curiosity. "Let me take a crack at it. Mason, why don't you wait outside? It's a little crowded in here. Take a break, mate."

Mason grew frustrated, pressing down on my back and gripping the muscles on either side of my spine to squeeze the cold up. It was the worst kind of massage, making me tense up and bite down on the sheet as I fought to endure whatever this was. "Come on, October! I can feel you resisting," Mason growled as he roughly kneaded my back.

"Because you're hurting me!"

He leaned his weight down on me as his knee dug into my butt, shoving me down into the mattress with a force meant for wrestling zombies, not massaging a docile woman. I tried to let him do his thing, but each time he shoved my spine, it felt like a key grinding in an ignition that had no starter to it. I tried to remain limp while Mason pushed me down over and over again into the mattress. He ignored Danny's warning to calm down, and grunted a few times in frustration as his fingers dug into my skin.

I tried not to remember what it felt like when he'd

pinned me down in the basement to kiss me. I tried not to go there in my mind, but the distrust was real.

"It's there! I can feel it, but I can't get it to move."

"Then get off her!" Von shoved Mason off of me, and Mason shoved back. The two glared at each other in warning, daring the other to strike again.

20

RESIDUAL ANDY

I let out a frustrated growl when the two started throwing insults at each other. "Would you both knock it off? Mason, take a breather. It's not your fault it's not working; we're all new at this, so chill out. It's been in me for a while now, so it probably won't be a cinch to get out." I was still face-down on the mattress with an artic chill on my spine that was slowly turning me blue. "Von, take your best shot."

Von waited for Mason to back down before he reached out and held my wrist. "Hey, it's alright. It's just me this time. Easy enough."

Danny shook his head at his brother. "It's not easy, Von. Take something seriously for once in your life."

"You're right, Peach. Danny does look like Frankenstein's monster when he's disapproving. I never noticed before." Despite the situation, I snorted into the sheet, letting out a small chuckle. "There you go. Just relax. Where does it hurt?"

"I mean, the whole middle of my back's stiff and sore now. But it's fine."

"You owe the Denial Jar another dollar. I've been keeping track; that's fifteen dollars today alone." Instead of trying to get the troubled spot out of me, Von concentrated on gently rubbing the muscles on either side of my spine, soothing the ache and warming the flesh there. "I'm moving your shirt further up so I can see what I'm doing. Is that alright?"

"Sure. That feels nice, by the way. Thanks." I felt my sweatshirt and the shirt beneath slide up to my shoulders, hitching just beneath my breasts. I shivered as the air hit my skin, reminding me all over again that I was cold. "Von?"

"Yes, love?"

"How blue are we talking back there? Like, a little blue body paint, or have I gone full-on Smurf?"

Von sniggered, his hands relaxing me beyond what I thought possible. "It's barely a tinted shade of color." Von lowered his face to my back, and my cheeks pinked when he dragged his lips over my spine. He blew hot air over me to melt whatever resistance I still clung to.

"Is this necessary?" Mason grumbled.

"Seriously, Von," Danny groused, embarrassed at having to stare at my naked back while his brother made me moan in unladylike ways into the sheets.

"We'll see, won't we?" Von leaned down to whisper in my ear. "We're going to give it another go now, yeah?"

He kissed my cheek, and I couldn't help but melt for him. "Yeah, okay," I murmured, my eyes closed.

Von's hands were gentle on my back, trustworthy and comforting through a pretty long and confusing day. When the warmth from his pulling began to heat up, at first it felt nice. Then the toastiness began to rise beyond what was soothing, heating up my spine and then my whole back with what felt like a slowly growing fire that centered around that stubborn spot. I whimpered into the sheet as Von moved his hands up my back, burning me as he went. It felt like a white-hot knife pierced through the tender bones, slicing the vertebrae like melted butter and dragging upward until Von's hands were at the base of my neck.

"You're doing it!" Danny shouted, impressed as much as he was surprised. "Now up and out the top of her head. Draw it out like you're squeezing a tube of toothpaste."

"Oh, you're a filthy one, Danny."

"Shut it and finish the job!" he yelled, leaning in to watch the rare occurrence with Mason.

Mason reached out and held my hands, giving me something to dig my nails into when the scream erupted out of me. Ezra and Finn burst through the locked door into the room, aghast at Von performing psychic surgery on me and it actually working.

"Almost there, *hani*." Von massaged my scalp, pulling

the chill through my brain and out into my hair. My back arched as I gritted my teeth through the tearing sensation. It felt like I was being unzipped, like a doll that needed new stitching. "Breathe through it!" Von urged, and the moment I obeyed, the final rip tore through me, shooting out of my head and landing in Von's palms. I collapsed with a thud on the mattress, whimpering and sweating as I lay limp and unable to summon the strength to sit up.

Mason knelt next to my wilted body on the bed, tugging my shirt down and holding my hand as if I was something valuable.

"What is that?" Finn asked, staring at Von's hands.

Von held an ethereal ball of bluish white light that danced in his palms like a tiny octopus fairy with too many tentacles. "I pulled it out of her. It's cold. Mason, is she still cold? Did I get it all?"

I remained lifeless on the bed as Mason squeezed various parts on my arms and back to test my temperature. "She's much better than she was. I don't think I see any blue, but it's hard to say. Her back's so red. Finn, check her spine. Do you see any blue?" My top was yanked up again without my permission.

Finn leaned in, touching my back when looking would've sufficed. "Let me see." His fingers climbed up and down me, exciting and relaxing like he had a right to tantalize my body, when we both knew he didn't. His hands felt amazing, but as I didn't really know him, the whole thing was a little awkward. "I don't see a blue spot, no."

"What is it, Danny?" Von asked, breathless. The blue ball of light danced with graceful turns and twists in his hands.

"It's the soul of the person she murdered. It's the last of Andy." Danny's explanation was months too late, but finally it came. "Taking a soul out of someone who's already going to die is natural. Killing them on purpose and then taking their soul isn't. When an Omen murders, the soul sticks around in the person a little while longer, and if the Omen absorbs it, it doesn't let go so easily. It's nature's little insurance policy that you don't try to solve the famine crisis by going off on a killing spree just to rack up more souls."

"I didn't mean to kill Andy," I admitted. "He was going to suck the will out of me so I'd tell them where the stone was. I was just trying to knock him unconscious, to show Geon he couldn't control me like that."

Finn's voice broke through my utter regret. "If you're bothered by anyone again, let me know, and I'll take care of it. Then you won't have to get blood on your hands."

"If it ever happens again, you have to tell us so they can get it out right away. You'll be sore for a few days where the death buildup was." Danny put his hand on Von's shoulder, and for once I didn't see a hint of loathing. If I wasn't so out of it, I'd put my money on a glimmer of pride in Danny's eye. "That was brilliant, Von. Now you've got to eat the dead soul. Then it's done."

Von watched it a few more seconds and then popped it

in his mouth, swallowing it down like a pill that soured his face at the foul taste. "Ugh. Andy was a right foul git. Like flat cola and rancid chicken."

While the others asked Von different things about the ingested soul, Finn moved my shirt down and rolled me over carefully on the bed, as if he knew exactly how a woman whose spine had just been worked over should touch the sheets. He was careful not to let my hips move too much one way or the other, taking his time so my stiff spine didn't bend too much. When I was finally in the bed the right way with my head on the pillow, he brought the comforter up over my lap and caressed my cheek with his knuckle. "Beautiful," he said of my perplexed look up at him.

I didn't often get sincere compliments like that. Von's were always kind of a joke. "Um, thanks. You, too. Super pretty. Especially the gills."

The corner of Finn's mouth tugged upward. "I heard a lot of screaming. How are you feeling?"

"Like I've had a giant man kneeling on my spine. Then like I had ice ripped out of my back through my head. So, you know, slightly worse than your average Friday night."

Amusement danced in Finn's eyes as he shifted the pillow under my head, plumping the sides. "Is that better?"

"Actually, yeah. Thanks. I'm afraid to move too much."

"I'm sure you'll be feeling better soon, *kendi*."

Von's head snapped up, and Mason, Ezra and Danny stiffened. "Don't you dare call her that! I thought we already had this talk. She's not part of your king's harem, and she'll never be that desperate. Move along, mate." Von went from glowing with pride to irate in a heartbeat. "And you're standing about ten feet too close to her bed."

Finn cast me a lazy smile before he left, leaving Ezra and Danny to exchange dark looks. "I don't like that," Ezra stated what the guys were all thinking, judging by the furrowed eyebrows that were aimed in my direction. "King Banak's commanded Captain Finn to watch her; he can't disobey orders. I can't make him stay away tomorrow, so I want one of you by her side at all times. Understood?"

Mason and Von both nodded. "Yes, sir."

Danny showed me his hands and then reached under the comforter near my feet. He pressed two fingers to the inside of my ankle to test my pulse. "Can you feel that?"

"Yeah. I just can't move much before my spine stops me. Is that normal? It's not permanent, is it? I'm kinda freaking out here." I tried not to let images of me going through life completely limp plague me.

"Not permanent, but it might be for the night. Your back's going to be in a lot of pain, so rest up. I'll call in a prescription for you for the morning. Any objections to Vicodin?"

"I... I don't know. I've never taken anything that strong before."

"Seriously? Your old job was pretty physical. I can't believe you've never been injured before."

"I've treated too many inmates in the throes of withdrawal. I can deal with the pain. Pills scare me."

Ezra sunk down into the chair in the corner of the room, rubbing his temples as the stress of the day and the worries of his life overtook him for the briefest of moments. "I can keep them for you, if that would make you feel better about it."

"Thanks, it would. Then yeah, Vicodin's fine." The extreme nature of the chill I'd had for days finally leaving me sent a flood of intoxicating heat through my body. I closed my eyes, letting the guys hash out whatever needed talking about. I didn't even protest a few minutes later when Mason slid into the bed at my side so he could warm me with his bare-chested body. Despite the horrible things we'd gone through, he was warm when I'd been so cold. I didn't have the wherewithal to resist him anymore. "G'night," I mumbled, not sure when the others had left.

Mason dragged his fingers through my auburn tangles, taking the rubber band out of my hair so he could play in the tresses. "I'm sorry, *hani*. I know it's unforgiveable, what I did to you, but I'm sorry all the same."

"If you let me go to sleep right now and don't make me talk about it, I'll forgive you anything."

He smiled as he pressed his lips to a sensitive spot behind my ear. "Will do." He tugged at my hair with gentle pressure that made me groan like a filthy... well, we won't go there.

"You keep that up, and I'll start drooling on your arm."

Mason chuckled and kept up the steady stream of pulling while relaxing my body that had been tensed for days. "I've missed you."

"I missed me, too." If we were being honest, I would admit that I was too tense even before Terraway entered my world. That I'd needed a friend to pull the stress from me even before I took up the mantle of being a Death Omen. I wanted to trust Mason. I didn't want to see him as someone so detached from reality that he could turn on me in a blink.

Von changed into pajamas and then settled in to the chair at the desk in the corner of the room, playing on his phone.

"Whatcha doing?" I asked sleepily. What I really wanted to say was "Turn that glowing thing off that's keeping me awake, and come be sexy and warm next to me." Somehow I didn't think that would go over all that platonically.

"I'm checking the weather for tomorrow, and flipping through the news highlights."

"Why would you do that to yourself right before bed? The news never has anything good to say."

Von sighed heavily. "I know. I fear I'm a masochist tonight. I don't like all this terrorist attack talk that's always in the newsfeed. I never bothered with it all that much before, but now that I'm responsible for keeping Terraway's food supplier alive, I worry." He turned off his phone and set it on the nightstand. "No terrorist attacks in

Georgia this week. It's official. I've officially become over-bearing, fretting over bombers getting at you on a normal day."

"No bombers. Just monsters and kings and whatnot. Let's shoot for a normal day tomorrow."

When Von slid into bed on my other side, he slipped his hand in mine and looped his leg over my thigh, as was our routine. Mason was more possessive as he drifted off tonight, holding me in his arms so Von and I could only half-snuggle.

Von looked on me in Mason's arms not with the joking affection he usually did, but with pity. There were many things I didn't care for, but pity was up there in my top ten ways I hoped a great guy like Von would never feel for me. He settled into the mattress and closed his eyes without a joke, without a flirty kiss to my cheek, and without anything crass coming from his lips. When I asked him if he was alright, he simply kissed my lips once, but the pity was so thick, it was barely worth the effort of the gesture. Usually his kisses were adorable, precious and flirty. This was only one note, singing clearly a song of sadness.

I really didn't like it, so I closed my eyes and drifted off, hoping the morning would bring our rhythm back to us.

PEMBERTON ELEMENTARY

My dream was in my face with a purpose. I was immediately transported to a large room with a table, two chairs and no frills where Philip sat, as if waiting for me. He flagged me down, looking relieved I was sitting with him. "I thought you'd never come see me again," he said, his eyebrows creased in worry.

"Oh, you know I always come back for the cute ones who keep me company when I'm in a dungeon."

"You're well? I can't always tell."

"Good as new. Maybe a little tired and sore, but it is what it is."

"Where are you?"

I yawned, apparently so tired that I was even exhausted in my dream. "I'm at Ezra's, sleeping with Mason and Von. We're all actually getting along. Hold your breath so nothing breaks, right?" I spoke to him like he knew everything about my life, which since he was a figment of my imagination, I guess he probably did.

"Where are you reaping tomorrow? I heard through the grapevine of your brain that you're trying to get fifty hearts in three days. How's that going?"

"Twenty-six today, so more than halfway there."

Philip's mouth dropped open. "I'm sorry. You said twenty-six?"

"I did. And I think I'd like a little fanfare for it. Not in real life, but in my dream. Seems like a nice place for fanfare."

Philip closed his mouth into a smile and clapped his hands politely. "That's incredible. Are you blissed out? Do your Pullers have you catatonic somewhere?"

"Nope. They wouldn't do that to me."

"Where are you going tomorrow?"

"I dunno. It's wherever my gut tells me to go. Usually a hospital or somewhere."

I could see Philip was thinking hard about something. "Where will there be a lot of people gathered tomorrow?"

"Not sure. Von mentioned his daughter was going to a carnival. That might be promising."

"Where's the carnival?"

"I think he said Pemberton Elementary. Not too far from Ezra's. Why?"

Philip sat back in his chair. "Reap there tomorrow. I want to see how many you can do in a day if there was no shortage of souls."

"No shortage of souls? What are you talking about? They have to be a day or less away from biting it for me to be able to reap them. I don't think you understand how reaping works."

"I understand completely. I'm in your mind. I understand things exactly how you do, remember? Pemberton Elementary. Try it tomorrow. Do it for me. Then I want you to tell me all about it tomorrow night."

I sighed, slumping down on the tabletop with a loud harrumph. "My dreams are so boring! I could be doing awesome things right now, but I'm so boring that I'm dreaming about work! Ugh! I need a vacation."

Philip smiled at me and clicked his fingers, changing our location from the mundane table and chairs to a tropical setting surrounded by mountains, low-hanging clouds and a real volcano within jogging distance. "Is this better?"

"I don't know," I grinned up at him. "Take your shirt off, and I'll let you know."

22

BREAKFAST OVER HORSE HEADS

The morning brought a horse head to the breakfast table, so you know, business as usual. I dipped my spoon into my second bowl of grits that were cooked with the right amount of too much butter and loads of pepper to make me sneeze, which was just enough.

"I'm telling you, there are enough souls stored up. My people are dying from the poison in what little water there is left in our land. They need the sagrado stone now!" Kabayo was irate, which was no real surprise. The bigger surprise would've been him not being bossy and in my face. An even bigger surprise would've been him showing up in a dress, doing a dance for us and waving his mane over his shoulder like it ain't no thang. Would've made for a much better dining experience than a severed horse's head dripping green fluid onto the sleek wood table while we tried to eat.

Mariang was sitting across the dining room table from me, her bowl clutched to her chest to keep it from the foam-crusted maw of the horse head that stared blankly at her. Kabayo had decided it was a good idea to rest it on the long oak table, I'm guessing for dramatic effect. Her voice was quiet, but everyone stopped talking when she spoke. "If both of us are going to be in Silo, then we can't risk running out of souls. What if October gets abducted again? Three days was the agreement."

"Hey, I got abducted last time. It's your turn," I joked.

Mariang liked it when I kidded around with her. She had that only child thing that rang like loneliness and read like needing to escape the house of boys that had taken over her dollhouse. "I'll make a note of it, should Kabayo's men come after us."

"I'm telling you, there's no danger! It's a straight shot to my palace, where the main river that feeds most of the wells is. No one wants to kidnap you. All we want is for our people to stop dying. Is that too much to ask?"

Finn was sitting back in his chair at the foot of the table opposite Ezra, watching the whole exchange. Finn wore a lazy posture that served as a veil to hide his calculating eyes as they took in Kabayo's desperation. Finn also studied my tight lips as I considered just how bad yesterday was, and how nowhere near ready was I for a long journey across an unknown land. My spine felt marginally better than yesterday, but I was still moving like a robot. Ezra had offered me the Vicodin, but I couldn't bring myself to take it. The tradeoff was moving like an old lady, but whatever.

Finn addressed Kabayo, who was still in a temper. "What do you intend to do about the uprising?"

"That sounds ominous," Von muttered, shoveling a bite of grits into his mouth with no flair. He usually oozed flare like a rocket. I reached over and massaged his forearm until his eyelids drooped, bringing him back to himself a little. "Thanks, Peach."

Kabayo postured, giving a derisive snort in Finn's direction. Let me tell you, horses give the most contemptuous of all the derisive snorts, so Kabayo's opinion was made clear before he even opened his long mouth. "It's nothing but a threat. I can't believe you'd bat an eye over a few angry Ekeks."

"I can't believe you wouldn't. You should take threats to your land more seriously. If it weren't for this one killing off all the Goblins, your land might still be overrun with them."

I hung my head, not counting on a heaping portion of morning shame to go with my grits. "I didn't mean to do it."

Finn smiled at me in that cool, detached way that told me he could wear the exact same pleasant expression while he choked the life out of someone. "Make no mistake, you did all of Terraway a great favor."

"Is that so?" I met his eyes with my independence evident, and made sure not to blink so he didn't think we were on any sort of team. "I'll put you both in my books as 'in my debt', then."

Finn tilted his chin to the side slightly, narrowing his eyes to decide whether or not he could pass off my words as a joke.

Nope.

Danny, Von and Mason barely paused their ravenous breakfasting, but exchanged wary glances while Mariang and I resigned ourselves to it not being the walk in the park as advertised. Ezra put his fork down and rested his elbows on the table – a thing he did only when he was upset. He was too proper to let his elbows graze the table otherwise. "How serious is this threat from the Ekeks? Is it something Sylvia can handle?"

"If she can, she isn't." Kabayo waved off our growing concern as if we were all being dramatic. "The threat's no more serious than it will be anywhere else in Terraway. The Ekeks and Manas of Lumipad don't need the stone as badly as my people do, but they're scavengers, so they think anything's up for stealing." He shrugged, and then explained for my benefit. "They want what they want when they want it. It's a nuisance, but nothing more serious than that."

I put a dash more pepper in my grits. "Then Mariang shouldn't come." She stiffened, so I pressed on before I could be overruled. "Look, I have to go because I'm the only one who can touch the stupid stone. If I didn't, I wouldn't risk being where the... Who now?"

"Ekeks and Manas," Von explained between mouthfuls. "Sylvia's people. She's a Manas. That's short for Manananggal."

I nodded. "I wouldn't risk being around them if I didn't have to. If they get us both? You know Terraway can't risk that."

Mariang slumped over her bowl while Danny glared at me. "But the citizens of Lumipad are always going to be a problem. Isn't it safer with all of us going? Could they really get past Dad, Captain Finn, Danny, Mason, King Kabayo, Prince Langgam, Ruiz and Klark?"

"Hey!" Von was affronted, sitting up straight and scrunching his nose at her. His red t-shirt had a wrinkled washed out picture of a guitar on it, and his jeans had a rip in the thigh, but he demanded to be treated as a warrior like the others. "I notice you left me out of your little list. Next time someone snatches at you, I'll just wave my hands around and flag down one of the real men."

Mariang put her dainty hand to her forehead, chagrinned. "Of course, you too, Von. You're top of the list."

"And?" Von prodded, his nose in the air.

"And... And you're so very strong. The Ekeks and Manas wouldn't try a thing with you around. They'd run away in fear."

"That's more like it." Von sat a little taller in his chair. He bumped his foot to mine and started fighting me for elbow space to start a flirty war, reclaiming a portion of his personality.

"October's right. It's too dangerous this time around, dear," Ezra said with a heavy sigh. "Danny and I will remain Topside with you. Perhaps we'll even add a few guards so Captain Finn feels more at ease with the growing threat."

Mariang was downcast, her narrow shoulders drooping as Danny rubbed an "I hate October" circle into her back. "Alright. I so hoped to be able to go see Terraway again. I haven't been to Silo in so long. King Kabayo, please send my apologies to your wife."

Kabayo nodded. "She won't be happy, but I do think that's best. If anyone from Lumipad does attack, they'll be after October, not you. The farther you are from her, the safer you'll be."

My eyebrows furrowed, and I tried to muscle through my sudden loss of appetite to choke down the last of my grits. I knew I wouldn't be able to eat anything once we got started for the day. "How serious is this threat? Like, can I do my job today without constantly looking over my shoulder?"

Ezra waved off my concern. "Of course, dear. Ekeks and Manas don't come Topside. The only residents of Terraway who can travel Topside are those the rulers take with them, like when Mason brought up Tanga when this whole mess started. They'll wait until you're in Terraway if they decide to strike."

I jabbed my spoon in Kabayo's direction. "I knew it was too good to be true when you promised me a stroll through your land, Kabayo. Not for nothing, but I like knowing when I'm walking into a trap, guys."

Kabayo gave a loud horse harrumph, but Finn answered me in his calm, unfazed way. "You have nothing to be afraid of, little Omen. I'll be traveling with you, as will Prince Langgam. The Ekeks and Manas would be fools to attack you with us there, and I can deal with fools easily enough." Finn sized up Mason's arm draped around the back of my chair and Von's breezy smile that beamed more easily when we were joking around together. "And I'm guessing your Death Reapers would have a thing or two to say about someone snatching at their collective bride."

Mason stiffened, removing his arm from me, while Von glowered at Finn. I picked up a flaky biscuit from my plate and launched it at Finn. Not quite a weapon, but the intent was clear. Finn let the biscuit hit his chest and flop to the floor, eyebrows raised in surprise at being assaulted with the fluffy pastry. "Don't make my life sound weird. We're making the best of it, and we don't need your sideways commentary, you jackfish. I'm not hooking up with either of them. For all you know, I could run into some hottie at the hospital and have a good old sexy time, with Von and Mason high-fiving me afterwards. You're the one with the harem, not me."

Finn's eyes were still wide that I was capable of

throwing food like a ruffian born for things lower than civil chatter over a pristine breakfast. Boy didn't know the half of it. He was lucky the biscuit was softer than the rock I wanted to pelt him with. "I'll cancel the wedding gift, then."

Ezra cleared his throat to diffuse the situation like the politician he was. "Darling, perhaps nonviolent methods of communication at the table would be more effective."

"Yes, sir," I mumbled. I downed a few swallows of orange juice before standing, my posture rigid. I wished I didn't need to lean so heavily on the table. My spine was being such a wuss. "I'm ready to start the day if y'all are."

"I'm finished," Von said, standing up from the table. "Let's let them talk mastermind details. I've got violent movies that desperately need watching in the living room. Can't fall behind on the important things. Come on, love." He paused by Finn, looking down at him without the note of healthy fear everyone else did. "If you talk down about Mason, November or me again, you'll have more to fear than a biscuit."

Finn stood slowly, using his three extra inches to tower over Von, who refused to be intimidated. "I thought you knew better than to threaten me, half-vamp. Clearly you think you have nothing to lose, but you know? I've never found that to be true." His nose was just a few inches from Von's, and the slight sneer told me that Finn was growing frustrated at losing his expected upper hand. "There's always some button to press to make you kneel. And boy, have I seen you do your fair share of kneeling."

Ezra was livid. "You'll not speak to my son like that, Captain."

Mason stood, enforcing Von's threat, his hand on my hip. "Go on into the living room, *hani*."

23

OUR FIRST FIGHT

wanted to fight alongside my guys, but decided to follow Mason's instructions on this one, since my insults didn't get more creative than small penis references this early in the morning. I had a feeling I'd need to save those for when the work day actually started.

I walked into the living room, trying to find a comfortable spot for my back on the leather sofa. I was wearing designer jeans and a fitted deep blue sweater Mariang had bought for me. It was the most expensive outfit I'd ever worn, and I wasn't sure what to do with that information. It made me very aware of any kind of spills that might ruin the nice gifts that just kept on coming.

I pulled out my phone and called Ollie, knowing I needed to smooth things over with him before he went off the rails. "October?"

The sound of his familiar cadence made me soften

and retract the claws Finn brought out in me. "I just wanted to call and tell you again that I'm sorry about missing our weekly check-ins, and for hanging up on you the other day. I didn't mean to worry you. Life's been a little crazy."

"Crazy how?" I could tell he was at his desk by the sound of paper shuffling. I could hear the squeak of his chair that he liked to make creak in a rhythm to keep himself from daydreaming his work time away. Only the eek-eek matched the rolling chair in his bedroom at my house, not the one at his desk in New York. I could picture my brother leaning back with a look of concern on his face as he stared at his bedroom wall, and knew that as much as I wished he was back home, no amount of phantom chair-squeaking could make that true. Ollie was still in New York, and that was the name of that sad tune. "Talk to me, October."

I wasn't sure how to answer him. I hated keeping anything from Ollie, but for his own good, I knew the land that was sucking the life out of me couldn't go near my brother. "Crazy enough to interfere with the important stuff."

"When I couldn't get ahold of you, I left a message with the warden. He finally got back to me, and told me you quit. You get a better offer?"

No. "Yeah. I miss it, though. Did he sound mad?"

"Not really. He sounded confused by the whole thing. Said you just up and quit with no warning. He's afraid one of the inmates did something to you." His voice lowered. "Is that true?"

"No, no. It was time for a change, is all."

"What are you doing now?"

I swallowed the truth and produced a good enough half-version. "I'm working for Ezra."

"Ezra? Seriously? What are you doing for him? What kind of medical help does he need?"

"I'm helping around the house. Running errands and things like that."

I waited for the brick wall I could hear Ollie turning into on the other end of the call to respond. "Are you kidding me? You have a nursing degree! You love working at the prison. Now you're, what? Doing his grocery shopping? Why?"

"The money's better," I admitted. I could hear Ollie ramping up on the other end, so I made quick work of wrapping it up. "It's fine, Ollie. It's my choice."

"It's that Von guy. You did this so you could be around him more. Come on, kid! Be smarter than this. Don't be the girl who throws her career away for a guy with no future."

"Von and I are just friends, and you don't even know him."

"Spoken like every young girl before she throws her plans away over some lowlife. I raised you better than that."

Of course Von chose that moment to meander in and

make himself comfortable on the couch next to me. "Don't say 'just'," Von complained. "Makes it sound like I'm the consolation prize. You ever seen anyone as brilliant as me? I don't think so."

I gave him a withering look that told him he wasn't helping matters. Ollie was in a right state. "Is that him? Give the phone to Von. I want to talk to this joker."

Von heard and extended his hand for the phone, but I held it tight. "Not happening, guys. Family life separate from work life."

Von donned a dramatic wounded expression. "That's all I am to you? A job? What about last night, with all the hours of raucous lovemaking we shared? I didn't know a woman's body could bend like that." He pressed his hand to his heart, ramping up the antics and the volume. "I didn't know I could feel the way I do about you! Ditch your responsibilities and run away with me, love. I really need you to cosign a loan for me first. Was thinking about getting myself a motorbike and whisking you off into the sunset. How opposed are you to Green Card marriages?"

Ollie was distraught. "Did you seriously have sex with that clown? Your first time was with him? Why, kid? Anyone but that guy!"

I stood from the couch, palming Von's face to block the overly saccharine doe-eyed expression he wore as he batted his long eyelashes at me. Von responded by licking my palm, which was completely and totally disgusting. "Ah! Gross!" I wiped off my hand on his shirt, but I could still feel the germs crawling around like tiny bugs. I stomped off to the bathroom to wash my hands, surprised that Von followed me like an annoying chittering monkey. "Ollie, Von's being a dork. We've never even kissed."

Von mimed stabbing himself in the chest. "Now you know that's not true. Why would you lie about something like that? That's just hurtful. I kissed you last night in the bed we share. In fact, I kiss you every night between the sheets."

My mouth fell open, horrified he was taking his little joke so far. "Ollie, I have to go. Everything's fine." I hung up before Ollie could yell, and turned to Von, who was smiling like the wicked boy he was. His hands were folded across his toned stomach, his wrinkled red shirt making his gold and blue eyes almost glow. He knew exactly how handsome he was, and was unapologetic as he beamed at me, ready to play. I pointed to his chest, unmoved in my accusation. "You need to cool it. Why'd you do that to Ollie? Now he's going to be thinking we're hooking up."

"You know very well I kissed your lips last night." He said it as if we'd done something to be hidden in the dark under the sheets, instead of the innocent affection it was. Then Von frowned. "Why didn't it work? Why didn't I feel that euphoria you were going on about? I thought for sure we would be able to conjure up what you experienced with Mason."

"Because we didn't actually..." Then I stopped, my frustration turning to a smack of hurt. "You're sweet to me because you want to get high when we kiss?" I took a few steps back, wishing there was some other explanation. "You were using me?"

Von sobered instantly, all play gone. "No, of course not. I only wondered why after the fact. I swear." He shook his head. "I shouldn't have said anything. I woke up on the wrong side of the bed this morning. Everything's felt off."

"You're off! You're supposed to be the one who doesn't use me. You're supposed to know how much I hate all of this."

Von reached out to me, grimacing when I jerked away. "I told you, it's not like that. It was just a thought."

"Call me when it's time to go." Maybe I was overreacting, but I needed a minute to cool down. Von's germs were still crawling on my hand like so many microscopic organisms that screamed out to let them stay. I closed myself back in the emerald bathroom I'd once seen covered in cockroaches. It was now pristine, as if the infestation never happened. I wondered how long it would take for me to be able to look back and feel like the whole thing never happened.

I scrubbed my hands again, getting in between my fingers, rinsing and starting all over again, just in case.

I looked in the mirror and flinched. After being starved in Geon's dungeon, and then going back to work to a job that literally made me sick, my face was starting to thin out. I liked my curves, my hips and my figure that looked and felt like a woman's, petite though I was. Terraway was slowly stripping that from me. I had bags under my eyes, no color to my skin and a haunted look to me I tried to force away.

I rehearsed smiling in the mirror, to show Terraway it hadn't stolen everything from me – that I'd kept the good parts and hid them where no one could take them away. My smile was practiced and false, but it was a sign that I hadn't been defeated. Somewhere, I was still in there, and I drew comfort from that thought.

Von's knock was to be expected. Before I opened the door, I took a few steadying breaths to push the fight away from me. If what he was saying was true, he hadn't pecked my lips to use me to get high; he was merely curious after the fact as to why it hadn't worked. I couldn't fault him for that. I'd wondered the same thing on occasion. It was the initial sting that got me.

When I opened the door, Von greeted me with a submissive expression of concern. "Please don't be mad at me. I take it all back."

I stepped backward and waved him into the bathroom, not wanting to have this conversation so close to the dining room, where curious ears might lean in. "I overreacted. I was scared you were like Mason, and I freaked out for a second. I'm sorry. You're right; we're better than that. I should've had more faith in us."

Von's shoulders loosened, and the easy grin I loved swept across his features. "We *are* better than that." He motioned between us. "I've never had a best friend like this. I usually don't keep women around after I move on. So if I'm rubbish at this, you'll have to educate me on how to be better. I like our arrangement, and I don't want it to change."

"I like it, too. But don't be a tool, and don't make Ollie think we're doing things. We never kept secrets from each other, and now my whole life's turning into a secret. Don't add to that just to drive him nuts."

Von pulled me into his arms, and despite all the confusion, his embrace served to center me. I fell into him, inhaling his purely guy scent of mint and cigars that had no frills or effort to it. It was refreshing, and somewhere along the lines, Von was starting to feel like the home that always traveled with me when I couldn't make it back to mine.

He held me with one arm and raised his pinky to me with the other. "How about we promise each other that we won't end up all twisted. I won't jerk your jerk of a brother around anymore, yeah? We should promise that we won't kiss for real. I don't want what happened with Mason to happen with us. We're better than that. And I really don't want you to have no one here who's not using you."

"Deal." I linked my pinky to his, not expecting him to use our little fingers to lift my chin so he could see my face more clearly. He leaned in and pecked my lips – innocent and sweet with that constant hint of flirtation he didn't know how to turn off. I would never ask him to turn it off;

it was Von, and I knew that I loved him exactly how he was.

"I don't like that you're back with Mason." He started swaying us gently from side to side, in a slow dance while he hummed *The Way You Look Tonight*. His footwork wasn't too fancy, which I appreciated. He danced with care, taking into consideration my tender back.

I leaned my temple to his chest and let myself be romanced by our strange friendship. "I'm not back with Mason. I just don't want to hold onto that anger anymore. It's not worth it to feel so hurt all the time. It's exhausting. Plus, he seems to have shaken himself out of it. Realizes how messed up it all was. I kinda feel sorry for him, losing his wife like that, then not being able to move on because I make him think of her. It's sort of awful for him."

Von's thumb rubbed a circle at the base of my spine to soothe me. "Say what you want, but I know what I saw. You're still crushing on him, and he wants back in. It's only a matter of time. Given how often you're with him?" He checked his wrist that had no watch on it, miming looking at the time. "I give it two days before you're tangled up with him again."

I pulled his wrist down to check the freckle there. "Your watch is busted, chief."

"I'm seeing Penny tonight after work. That'll give you two just enough time together to make a perfect mess of things. Enjoy the descent into tawdry self-loathing. I've always been a fan of it."

I squeezed his waist to give him a tickle. "Message received, oh wise one."

Von's chest puffed out with pride. "Oh, I like that. I might insist it's my name from now on."

"Better than wiseass?"

"Much." He swayed with me a few more beats. "You ready for work, Peach?"

"No. Let's hide in here a little while longer."

"You got it." Von started singing the Frank Sinatra song to me, his cheek pressed to mine as he turned me to his music. His hand stroked my sore back, and then moved up to thumb the nape of my neck. The mood shifted from the lightness of our steady friendly flirtation to something heavier that quickened my heartbeat, though I couldn't tell you why. His fingers traced around to stroke the side of my neck, erupting goosebumps that betrayed the flutter in my chest. "I like this spot right here," Von admitted.

"This one?" My chin tilting back to expose the silk of my neck to the vampire I adored. "That feels nice," I murmured. My eyes fluttered shut when his fingertips stroked down my throat like I was his instrument, and he wanted to see what kind of music we would make together.

In that moment I knew; I did trust Von, no matter how foolish that choice might be. My head lolled back, my auburn curls dangling as I reveled in the new life I had that actually came with the perks of making a real friend.

I gasped when I felt his breath near my neck. My pulse accelerated, and I knew with his attuned senses, that he could smell my blood heating as it rushed through my veins. "Well, look at you," he remarked, his voice low. "You really are learning to let go. Beautiful."

I swallowed hard. Then before I could further question my sanity, Von gripped me tight and blew a loud raspberry into the vulnerable spot on my throat that was invented only to be treated nicely. "Fool! Never give a vampire full access to your neck! What do they teach you in those American schools?" He released me slowly, without too much twist to my spine as I giggled through my thrill that came fervently at his touch.

Our laughter felt like breathing and tasted like the relief we both needed to wash in. I bathed in it, oh did I bathe. My levity was the release of too many bad days stacked on top of each other, threatening to turn into a bad year on me.

But not if Von could help it. Despite everything he'd been through – being chained up, bled dry, lost his mind and slowly clawed his way back to sanity – Von was ever himself, and in that moment, I fully appreciated what a gift that was.

"You got me good," I admitted, enjoying the breadth of his laughter that could only bring happiness and never the sting of bitterness. He varied from Danny a great deal in that way, and for all of Danny's dependable qualities, Von stole my heart with his loveable flaws.

He'd been laughing as hard as me, his eyes crinkling at the corners in the best way. "I can tell you'll have handsome old man wrinkles when gray hair creeps in on you. If this Reaper-Omen bond holds true, I might just be around to get to see that magnificence firsthand."

Von suddenly sobered, looking at me with a stern expression. "No." His eyes bored into me, appearing to be sifting through too many responses to my simple compliment. "I'm temporary, November. It's important you don't forget that."

"What are you talking about?"

"I've resisted the transition thus far, but one day, something or other will prove to be too much. Make no mistake, it's in my nature. I *will* turn someday." He swallowed the lump in his throat. His gold eye and his blue were filled with regret. "I won't grow to be an old man with wrinkles. Best enjoy the look of me now."

I gripped his hands tight, willing my stubborn nature to instill itself into him. "Not if I have anything to say about it. You're not temporary, Von. You're permanent. *We're* permanent. I need you to believe that. I need you to keep trying." I blinked up at him, scared of the words that tumbled out of me so easily. "I need you."

Von's eyebrows drew together, his eyes unable to conceal how moved he was by my unswerving devotion. His expression shifted in the next blink, telling me that he didn't believe the next words that came out of his mouth, but was saying them to indulge me. "Then you shall have me. However long I'm here, I'm yours."

The corner of my mouth lifted. I leaned up on my toes

to touch his lips lightly with my fingertips, our noses barely a breath apart. Then I brushed a kiss to his pained expression to hold him in place. "Then I want you forever."

That same insecure look crossed his features again, overwhelmed by my commitment to our friendship. "Then I guess I'll be by your side a bit longer. I'll stave off my pesky transition forever, then."

"That's more like it." I nodded, satisfied for the moment that Von was the same fighter I was. "We don't give up on the things that matter."

Von cleared his throat. "On the phone out there? That was our first real fight."

"I suppose it was."

"I admit, I really didn't like it. Let's never do that again, yeah?"

I smiled up at him, taking in his sincerity that showed me that I was every bit as important to him as he was to me. "Well, if you say so."

DEATH BY CARNIVAL

Finn was in quiet mode, and I wasn't sure if that was a relief or if it made me more nervous as to what might come out of his mouth once he actually spoke. I relinquished my hold on Terence and consented to let Danny drive us in Ezra's larger vehicle, leaving Mariang at home to spend the day with her father.

When Finn spoke, it was with an edge. "Clearly you two don't know how to manage your Omen, otherwise King Banak wouldn't need a daily report. Now we're going to an elementary school on her whim?"

Von rolled his eyes. "Oh, you can't help yourself. You just want to be where the action is."

I shrugged. "If I'm wrong, then we'll go to another hospital. Unclench, Finn. It's just a thought. Big gathering place with lots of people. Can't be too hard to see if there's a person or two there who needs reaping."

"A person or two. You promised them twenty-four more hearts in the next two days!" Danny was irate, which is to say, business as usual. "You're just doing this so Von can see that kid instead of working through the day."

I was sandwiched in between Von and Mason in the back. Mason kept his hand on my knee while Von had his arm linked through mine, keeping up a constant stream of pulling to push my stress level back to zero.

I slumped against Mason, leaning into his side. He'd been sullen as we got ready, needing the occasional hug or reassuring arm squeeze whenever his mind fell to the fact that his inhuman strength was gone. He and Danny had done a round of calisthenics after breakfast so Mason didn't feel totally emasculated. It was a gentle reminder that there was hope. Though he couldn't fight off an army, he could sure as Sunday do some damage with a little determination. Danny was a good friend in that respect, coming alongside him and pushing toward action, as opposed to letting his friend flail in despair.

I didn't realize my eyes had closed until Danny barked back at us, "You're pulling too hard! She'll be asleep by the time we get anywhere. October, wake up and pay attention."

Von retracted from me, but Mason only lowered the level of pull, keeping his hand on my knee and squeezing to let me know he was doing his best. "Sorry about that."

Danny's eyes flicked back to us in the rearview mirror as he drove through town, passing businesses and nearing the school at the end of the street that had one of those weekend carnivals set up in the back. The Ferris wheel stretched high into the sky. The blue and red paint was faded in parts that looked important. I never had much confidence in the carnivals that were set up and torn down so frequently. Something about them made me not trust the nuts and bolts so much. When you're dealing with a Ferris wheel, the nuts and bolts are kind of important.

"Pay attention to your gut, kid," Danny reminded me. "We can go back to the hospital, but if you just hit it yesterday, it won't be as good today. If you feel something, shout it up here."

"I feel hungry!" Von called to the front. When Danny gave a labored sigh, Von shrugged. "What? You said to shout out what we're feeling."

"No one cares what you're feeling, Von." Then Danny started mumbling disparaging things under his breath about his brother.

Though Von was my Puller, I felt the need to tug some of the negativity that was being thrown at him away. I tapped my shoe to his in solidarity, and he tapped mine back to let me know he didn't care what Danny had to hurl at him.

I didn't expect to feel a yank in my gut before we'd even parked, but in the next second, my stomach was lurching toward the carnival behind Pemberton Elementary. "Whoa. Yeah, it's here, alright. This is where we need to be." I pointed toward the bustle of the carnival. While Danny wound through the rows of cars searching for a big enough space, my gut screamed at me. "Huh. It's more than one person. I've never felt it this strong. Even at hospice where death is everywhere, it's never been like this. How is..." I gulped when I looked at the potential death all around me. "Oh, man. Something bad, guys. Von, call Penny. Make sure she stays home today."

Von wasted no time calling Angela, a look of fear crossing his face when she didn't pick up. "I'm sure it's fine. Angela won't follow through on her promise to take Penny to the carnival. I mean, she's always doing that – promising and then flaking. Never thought I'd be praying for Angela to disappoint Penny yet again." He had a clear note of anxiety in his voice and tried the number a second time.

"How many bodies do you think?" Finn asked from the front passenger seat.

My head slowly moved from left to right. "It doesn't work like that, but a lot. Danny, this doesn't feel right. Something bad's about to happen here."

Danny parked on the grass, where several rows of drivers had given up trying to find a legit parking space and had made their own spots on the green. "Then let's hurry. After they're dead, they're no use to us. If it's going down soon, let's run."

I nodded, feeling wrong reaping here. "Shouldn't we warn someone? I mean, how set in stone is everything? If something's going to go down here that'll kill a lot of people, shouldn't we tell someone? Warn them? Somehow shut down the fair so they all have to go home?"

Danny shook his head, unbuckling and getting out of the car. "It doesn't work like that. Once a soul is ready to be reaped, it's ready. Nothing to be done about it after that." We slid out and started jogging together toward the fair, but it felt like we were running into a burning building in search of the smoldering bodies. I began to see the reason firemen got their own sexy calendar, and Omens did not.

Von nearly shouted into the phone when Angela finally picked up. "Where are you?" He clutched his chest and finally started breathing with relief. "Okay. That's good. Yes, stay at your mum's for the weekend. Give Penny my love." When Von hung up, he looked like he might cry with joy at not having Penny near the danger. I gripped his hand in solidarity.

Danny and Finn fell back once we reached the crowded fair. The throngs of people were all excited to take their turns on the rickety rides. Each metal structure looked like a giant death trap now, with rusty monster-like beams and janky loose parts that groaned and creaked ominously. I wondered which would be the weakest link that destroyed too many people in one go. Or maybe there would be a hot dog vendor who served bad meat and killed everyone who ate the food you couldn't help but smell everywhere.

Fear gripped my insides as my gut pulled me toward a group of teen girls, each of them calling out to be reaped. I brushed past them, reaping four at once, taking in their souls faster than Von and Mason could tear them out of me. "Ho! Slow down, *hani*. We have to be able to keep up. You're smaller and can weave through the crowds far easier than we can." Mason rubbed his chest, feeling the life forces sizzling there as I reaped a middle-aged couple who were debating which ride they should spend their tickets on next, and who would get sicker than the other.

I made my way through the crowd, my gut pulling me in too many directions to be able to pick just one. I lost my hold on Von and Mason, going where my instincts led, reaping as I went. The ice built in my veins more rapidly than it ever had before. I trusted that the guys would catch up, and kept going as long as my limbs had any range of motion at all.

Danny caught up with me first, his hand on my shoulder retracting when he felt how freezing my body was becoming in so short a time. "You have to slow down, kid." He put both hands on my shoulders and held me still while Von and Mason made their way to us with Finn. "We'll get everyone we can, but you can't reap more than one at a time. You'll burn out in five minutes if you keep going like this."

I looked up into Danny's brown eyes, panic growing more real with every person who passed by and practically handed me their soul. "Something bad's going down here." I felt another soul leap into me from someone that brushed up against my back, causing a shudder and a shiver to rip through my body. I was becoming too rigid for normal movement.

"Stop reaping for one second!" Danny commanded, squeezing my shoulders and pulling as much stress as he could. We both knew he couldn't take the souls from me, so he worked on the stress aspect instead.

"I'm not doing it! *They're* finding *me* now. Danny, I've already reaped fifteen." More leapt into me as errant brushes transferred the icy balls of soul without my consent. Another touched me, and I nearly screamed at Von and Mason for taking so long. "Sixteen!" My nerves were on fire with ice that froze me from the inside. I couldn't move my arms, but kept them banded around my stomach, as if that would stem the tug my gut felt to reap until I dropped. They would suffer. They would all suffer unless I granted them a peaceful death. It wasn't about my pain of the moment anymore; I had to help the too many people who would die today at the carnival. My imagination did a solid conjuring of hundreds of fair-goers screaming and writhing in agony as they slowly died amidst the happy clown faces painted on the rides. I couldn't let them go out like that. Panic married with my steely resolve, and I knew what I had to do. I would reap until I dropped, to save as many as I could from having their last moments be untold agony.

My jaw locked from the ice in my veins, and wouldn't permit me to move it even to answer Danny when he asked if I could feel his grip. His arms encircled me, and though I knew Danny wasn't a warm guy, in the valley of my own personal frozen tundra, he was the sun that kept me from icing over completely. "What took you so long?" Danny demanded when Von and Mason found us.

"She ran off! It's not exactly easy to find people in this crowd." Von and Mason each took an arm and started pulling, but it wasn't enough. Danny moved out of the way, and Von took his place, wrapping his arms around me. When movement finally started reintroducing itself back to my limbs, I nearly let out a sob of relief. The ice had been painful, and as Mason closed in behind me, sandwiching me between my two Death Reapers, the warmth couldn't come fast enough. Von lifted my arms and hooked them around his neck, supporting my weight as they pulled with probably a bit too much zeal.

Finn watched our strange threesome and then looked around at the throngs of people. "Is that all of them then?"

"No!" I moaned. "There's so many more. I can't keep up!"

"How many more do you think you can do?" Finn asked, his hand touching the red silk scarf around his neck.

I breathed more easily, now that the ice wasn't penetrating my lungs. I kept picturing the hungry, bony children of Sakuna. I could make myself uncomfortable for a day or two for them. If it would fill their tiny bellies, I could take one for the team. "Lots. I can do lots more. As many as it takes." It was with an edge of unswerving determination that I answered, his innocent question feeling like a dare I needed to prove to myself I could conquer.

"Good girl." Finn cupped my chin and tilted it up so he could examine my face. "Man, I love that fire in your eyes. I've always had a gift for spotting a good fighter."

Von batted Finn's hand away from my face.

"No," Mason ruled, looking around at the crowd. "We're leaving now. If there's this many, we'll be lucky to get you out of here conscious. This was a bad idea."

Danny's voice was quieter, but there was a planning note to it that made me pay attention. "Unless you really can do more than the average Reaper. This would be a good way to test it. Reap as many as you can before the buildup takes over." He shrugged in innocence. "The guys can always pull everything out of you."

"You can't be serious," Von chided his brother.

I met Von's eyes with steel I knew he couldn't bend with all the stubborn logic he had in him. While I didn't relish the pain I was agreeing to, I put my chips where the biggest lotto was. "Danny's right. We can clean up here. We can fuel the suns of Terraway for weeks. Think of all the kids that'll be saved if we go on a tear."

"No," Mason said, putting his foot down. "We're going back to the car."

Danny's voice stopped the guys in their tracks. "Do you think Mariang could actually get better if she had a few days off? Imagine how well she'd be if she had a week." He dangled the possibility in front of me like a toy, and like a child, I followed the lure.

25

KAMIKAZE OMEN

I cared about Mariang, and she'd been dealt a raw deal. If I could help her, shouldn't I? "I guess we could push the limits a little. I mean, like you said, we don't know what's possible, and I have two Reapers. What's a little pain if it might give Mariang a longer life? I can deal with pain. I don't think any of us could deal if she died."

Danny nodded vigorously, exhibiting more personality than his usual Frankenstein monster demeanor had on display. "Right! It's just a little discomfort, yeah? You can handle it. You're tough."

Danny's pep talk churned like vomit in my stomach. The words sounded like he was proud of me, but I knew it was a manipulation. His compliments tasted bitter. But I could see he wanted this so badly, he was willing to make up nice words out of thin air in order to get me to go along with his idea. "I mean, if it would help her live longer."

Von and Mason both whipped around to face me. Von was livid. "Are you joking right now? You see what he's doing, right? He's talking you up so he gets what he wants!"

Mason stared at his friend with deep disapproval. "Danny, care a little bit about October. Care a little and you'll see how dangerous what you're asking her to do is."

We both knew Danny didn't give a flying pancake about me, but I appreciated the show he put up on occasion. His contrite expression drew his lips to purse in contemplation. "Can't you see it? Can't you see her getting better if you do this? If you can give her more time to heal up, wouldn't you want that?"

The gleam in Finn's emerald eyes told me he loved the thrill of the danger. He wanted a good show. "Oh, I think you can do more. You're not nearly as tired as you were yesterday. They got that icy patch out of your spine, and you had two Pullers all night long. This is the day to try pushing yourself."

"Yeah, just think about it. We could have a whole week of her like how she used to be before she was so over-worked. I can take her to the movies, take her anywhere. Anything, all thanks to you making yourself a little uncomfortable for one short day." Danny reached out and touched my arm – the equivalent of begging. "Please? Do this for me? Then we'll go straight home. It's barely half a day of work this way."

Finn's amused gaze fell on me. "I'm here to see the asset in action. I know this is a one-time event. Once the sagrado's where it belongs, you can reap once a day, and that's that. You won't see nearly the wear and tear Mariang has." He cast me a hint of a smile. "I wouldn't dream of letting the fight in you die out completely, *kendi*. Let's see what you've got."

"Piss off," Von snarled.

"Excuse me?" Finn's head swiveled to Von.

"You heard me." Von jerked me tighter into his hug when he saw me considering Danny's words, teetering back and forth between Mariang's health and my safety. "Bugger off. Let's get back in the car. This is dangerous. Mariang isn't the only person who matters in this, Danny. You're a lousy git for putting that on her."

I made eye contact with Danny, nodding just enough for him and Finn to see. Then my eyes flicked to Von and Mason, who I knew wouldn't let me reap anymore.

Danny lit up and nodded, letting me know he'd distract them so I could run off and do my thing.

I tested my legs to make sure they could hold me well enough, and when Mason and Von were sidetracked by Finn's point that we wouldn't come by this opportunity again, I took my advantage. I ducked out from between the two and made a labored dash into the crowd, reaping three people in the first five seconds I liberated myself from my

Reapers. Then another, then four more. I kept going, trying to amble faster than the ice could catch up with me. My limbs were stiff and screaming at me that something would break if I didn't get the souls ripped out of me before taking on more, but even as I slowed to let Von and Mason catch up, people passing by added more to my stash. Each soul felt like I was being stabbed in the side, the poison building up in me like I'd swallowed a swarm of angry hornets.

I tried not to feel the agony warring inside of me. All these people I was reaping were going to die, and the only thing I could offer them was a peaceful passing. I was determined to help as many as I could, and save Mariang in the process.

"You can't do this!" Mason growled, gripping me and nearly pulling me over. My body had no give anymore; I was a stiff board – too cold to move at all. Von and Mason sandwiched me again, pulling so hard and so fast that the heat tried to quiet the ice almost as quickly as it came. "You've met your quota, right? Am I counting it all? Between yesterday and today, that's more than fifty. We're going home."

"Can you do more?" Danny asked.

Von spewed out a string of filthy expletives that made a nearby woman shout out an indignant scolding.

"I don't know. I mean, maybe. I'm not unconscious, so technically I probably could do one or two more." I rubbed the back of my neck, which was sore and freezing. The cold was still in me, though not as paralyzing. It felt like I was being stabbed from the inside by a thousand tiny needles, making each movement painful enough to make me bite down on my lower lip to keep it from trembling.

But it was just pain, and I could handle that. The kids in Terraway had to live with the pain of hunger every day. This was just needles in my veins.

"We're leaving." Mason was disgusted at Danny and frustrated with me. He tugged the last life force from me and pulled a little extra to take the residual crap away. The needles were still there, jabbing at me and making me try my best to swallow a whine of pain. Mason all but growled at Danny. "If something's going down here, we have to leave before it kills us!"

Danny and Finn exchanged determined looks, communicating a plan they didn't need words for. That was the only warning. Suddenly Danny jumped on Mason, knocking him away from me, and Finn tackled Von to the ground. "Run toward the car and get as many as you can! We'll meet you there. Go!" Danny shouted, wrestling Mason, who was still unsure of his strength, and was therefore not adept at using what he'd been left with. It was the worst kind of betrayal Danny could've done to his best friend, hitting him where he was vulnerable.

"Stop it, Danny!" I shouted, not willing to go along with a plan that hurt Mason and Von. This was one too far for me.

"Go, or I'll break his arm!" Danny threatened, pulling

Mason's arm back ominously. "I'll set him free the second you start reaping."

I tried to punch Finn, but my fist was slow and unsteady. He deflected me embarrassingly easy and went back to wrestling Von.

The people bumped into me, and I reaped them without meaning to. A few onlookers came to watch the fight, crowding me and forfeiting their souls without even knowing it. The agony of the ice flooded me as the people gathered around the fight, edging my rigid body out and pushing me farther away from the only two people who could help me. I collected more than a dozen souls in the span of a minute before I couldn't feel my feet anymore. I tried to get back to the guys, but I couldn't see them. I could hear Von howling and Mason calling my name.

When I finally caught sight of Von's face, it was red and panicked. I gasped when Finn delivered a punch to Von's gut. I tried to run to him, but I couldn't move. I had to watch while my best friend's punches weren't on the mark, and Finn's were. "No! Stop it!" Danny released Mason, but instead of running to find me, Mason jumped on Finn, tearing him off of Von, who spat blood on the ground.

As I tried to get to them, it seemed almost every person I brushed up against needed reaping, and the pile of souls inside of me multiplied before I could get a handle on it all. The snow storm of ice and needles swirled up in me, squeezing out a loud scream before my throat iced over. I stumbled a few more steps when the crowd knocked into me, reaping four more that put me over my breaking point. The cold reached my brain, and I tripped, taking the corroding souls with me as I plummeted to the ground.

I lay there, frozen and immobile while the kind Samaritans stopped to see if I was okay. I reaped them without meaning to. Two people stepped over me, and I reaped them without trying when their feet snagged on my legs as I became human roadkill. Now my Reapers couldn't see me, and the buildup was too much. I could feel the ice in my bones now, setting in and feeling like a thousand knives jutting out of my skin, slicing over and over while I silently screamed. More people stopped, and I reaped them. Over and over until I lost count. I lost lucidity. I lost the will to fight my way to Von.

My last labored breath drew into my lungs, which were now too stiff to move. My life began flashing through my mind's eye as panic gave way to the inevitability that I needed air to live, and I couldn't get to any.

I saw Ollie when he was younger, putting on a puppet show with Allie for me using mismatched old socks that had too many holes to be useful.

I saw Bev sitting across the table at a dinner I remembered from ages ago. She'd taken me to a nice restaurant for my eighth birthday. I'd worn my best sweater and Allie had done my hair to look fancy. I'd been so excited. I didn't realize Bev would charm the waiter into overserving her, she'd get stinking drunk, and we'd have to run out of the restaurant before the check came. I didn't realize she would beat on me when I tried to take away the fishbowl margarita she'd stolen and taken with her into the car. I'd jumped out of the car at a red light, too scared of her swerving to trust her to drive me home safely. I always blamed myself, even in what I assumed would be my last moment on earth, for not managing to snake her keys away from her. She could've killed someone, and I would've carried the guilt, since she wasn't capable of that emotion. I'd walked six miles home with a bloody lip on my eighth birthday, my fancy hairstyle ruined. I stopped believing in the magic of fancy hairstyles after that, and stuck to ponytails, buns and the like. I learned at eight years old that being pretty for a day means nothing in the long run.

I chided myself on what a crappy job I was doing of picking the right memories to dwell on before I suffocated and died. Maybe I would get it right in the next life, wherever that might be. Maybe I would just stop existing, and the cracked memories of a childhood I never chose would fade away into nothingness.

I decided that would be alright, if it would finally take the pain away.

26

THE PAIN AND THE HUNGER

I awoke to yelling, which I've got to say, isn't the best way to wake up. Effective, but not the best. "I don't know how to help you! I'm pulling as fast as I can!" Mason bellowed over the screams.

Then it dawned on me; the yelling was coming from my mouth, and the screams of agony belonged to me. A thousand miniature knives felt like they were being pressed into my body all over, ripping and slicing through laughably thin epidermis that shredded like tissue and left my guts exposed.

When I opened my eyes, I wasn't bleeding at all. There were no knives, only the feel of them. We were in Ezra's SUV, and I was laid out in the backseat, stretched across Von and Mason's laps. I couldn't stop my screaming; it came out of me unbidden in response to the torment I could feel moving through my bones. It felt like tiny jagged balls of glass that damaged and mutilated as they slid through me like a pinball machine.

"We have to bliss her out!" Mason bellowed through the car in a volume that felt like it pierced my eardrums.

"No!" Danny called from the driver's seat, turning too sharp and making the guys grip the car doors. "You do that and we won't know when all the life souls are cleared. After they're gone, she might need medical attention, and we won't be able to ask what's still broken. Keep her on the edge, but don't bliss her out. Damn this traffic! It's all going toward Ezra's."

"Her house, then," Von suggested. "Turn around and head there. There's nothing slowing down the cars going the other way."

Danny barely heard Von over my screaming, but he obeyed. Movement was slowly coming back to my limbs, but it only gave them license to thrash around to rid my body of the serrated freezing fire that tortured my insides. I kicked Mason without meaning to, not even able to apologize properly. He banded his arms around my legs while Von hugged my upper half to pin my flailing arms to my sides. I howled my pain at the simple touch that pressed the knives further into my bones, but was unable to communicate actual words.

Finn was white as he watched me from the front passenger's seat. He turned in horror to see every detail of the depths of what too much reaping did to an Omen. We both got a solid education that day.

Danny drove toward my house at breakneck speed while my body acted like it was being burned by an invisible fire. I twisted as I screamed, too beside myself with pain to even let loose a single tear. Mason and Von kept up a steady stream of pulling, pausing only to shout up to the front seat how selfish and stupid Danny and Finn had been to let me run off and reap till I dropped.

It was a long drive to my house, and half an hour in, my incoherent screaming had dulled to a hoarse, "Make it stop! Make it stop!" I'd been in a fair few fights that had gotten out of hand and left enough bruising to make things sore the next morning, but this was active torture from the inside. The more the guys pulled, the more lucid I became. I was caught in this space between being given back brain function, which was good, but the only thing my brain wanted to do was shut down to short-circuit the pain. All I could feel was a bucket full of agony, and I had too much of it for one person to take.

Danny drove too fast, but I didn't care. I wanted to go home, for surely if I was in my house, it wouldn't feel like this. The simple act of walking through the door would take away the things I couldn't control and give me back skin that wasn't being grated by invisible saw-toothed knives.

"Danny? Danny! I have to eat something soon. I don't think I can make it to her house. I've never pulled this much at once before, and it's..." Von had a note of panic to him. He started tensing and squirming beneath me, throwing his head back to bang it against the seat. "I need food now, or I won't be able to resist her blood. I can smell it!"

"Is she cut or something?"

"No, but her blood's heating up, and it's all... I need food now! I need blood!"

"Stop pulling from her until I can exit at the next fast food place." Danny squinted as he watched the signs on the side of the freeway. "There! Okay, hold on just another few minutes."

I heard a handful of emergency vehicles going the other way. My stomach sank when I realized they might be headed for the carnival we'd just left. Something big had happened, though I couldn't guess what.

Von was breathing through his teeth, hissing and trying not to look at me as he took his hands off my torso and started clawing at the roof of my car. "I'm sorry! I'm sorry! I can't control it! Her blood, Danny! I remember how it tastes. I can't stop myself. Pull over! Pull over now! I'm going to bite her! Let me find an animal or something!"

A handful of seconds after Von stopped pulling the corroded souls from me, the knives I was trying to breathe through lit themselves on fire, ramping up my sweaty whimpers back to full-blown screaming. Von raised my upper half off his lap and all but shoved me at Mason. Each movement was so painful, I couldn't process language enough to tell him to stop. I started convulsing in Mason's arms, my body spasming with too much going wrong to right myself on my own. My body needed both Reapers, and when it was granted just the one, the howling torture was ramped up to full heights.

"I've got you!" Mason growled, wrestling me in the backseat that was too small for his long, thick leg muscles. He pulled the souls from me as well as he could, but it wasn't enough. He couldn't keep up at a rate that dulled the pain even a little bit. Though Von had been the one to push me off of him and onto Mason, he still hovered, his mouth open and inching toward me hungrily, as if I was a giant donut that desperately needed biting.

Finn flew toward us from the front passenger's seat, his hand on Von's chest to remind Von of the distance he needed to keep from me. "Wait it out. You do this, and it's all over. If you drain her, you lose your job, your girlfriend and yourself. Fight it!"

Von strained against Finn's arm, craning his neck to reach mine so he could bite down into my flesh. If the pain I was in hadn't been so forget-your-name blinding, I would've had several things to say about the whole situation. As it was, I just kept screaming, since it seemed language had left me.

Danny was beside himself trying to manage the chaos from the driver's seat. He pulled over onto the side of the freeway and ripped the backdoor open, yanking Von out seconds before he bit down into my skin. "You can't bite her, but you can bite me!" Danny offered, clutching his brother in a bear hug on the side of the road that looked equally emotional and aggressive.

Von's cry of self-loathing broke my heart. "I'm sorry!" he wailed just before he bit down on Danny's neck. Danny grimaced, but held onto Von, gripping him with strong arms that banded around his back.

"Easy, brother. Easy." Danny pried one arm from his brother and used it to brace himself on the car door. "It's my fault. I'm the one who pushed her to reap that much. I didn't think it through." His eyelids started to droop after a minute of Von sucking blood from two puncture wounds on his neck. "Okay, that's enough. It's too much, Von." He started to grow nervous, his voice climbing in pitch. "Stop, Von!"

27

INSATIABLE

Finn was on the two in the next second, firmly extracting Von from his meal. He lowered Danny down into the driver's seat and dragged a shaking Von to the front passenger's seat so he could take a breather from being so close to the temptation of my blood. "Here you are. Sit tight, and we'll be on our way to real food, so your brother doesn't have to be your whole meal." Finn observed Von's sweaty form and shook his head in dismay. "Doesn't look like your snack did you much good. But at least it bought you enough time to get you to a restaurant."

The cars whipped by, not having paid any mind to the brothers who'd been hugging it out on the side of the road. They didn't notice Finn slipping into the backseat with Mason and me. Everyone went about their day as if nothing abnormal was interrupting their lunchbreak. Finn took my legs and moved them to drape across his lap, wincing at the ice in my skin he'd not been expecting. He held onto my shoes when my amped up howls informed the men that touching my skin at all caused me untold amounts of torment.

Danny was slumped in his seat, but had just enough in him to coast the car forward on the shoulder and putter to the nearest exit. When he pulled into the parking lot of a crappy fast food joint, he sighed with a breath of victory at the hill he climbed. He turned off the ignition, taking his wallet out of his back pocket and handing it to Finn. While Finn was totally out of his element, he was the healthiest one among us at the moment. "Grab as much food as you can carry and bring it back here. I need a minute." Danny had napkins from the glove compartment shoved to his neck. His breath was labored and he was paler than looked passable.

When Finn hesitated at my ramped up screams, Mason nodded him toward the door. "Go quickly. I can keep Von away from her. Just hurry. I'm not a vampire, but part of me is a wolf. If I turn, there's no telling who I won't attack for quick meal." He let out a whine of distress into my hair. "I'm fighting it, but it's coming. Go!"

Once Finn was gone, Mason smoothed the stray hairs from my forehead, holding me tight on his lap, as if nothing shady had ever happened between us. "Is the pain going down at all?" he asked as I seethed through my teeth when my voice tired from all the screaming. Shaking my head hurt, but I couldn't form words, so it was my only option. "I'm pulling, *hani*. I'm going as fast as I can." Both his and Von's stomachs rumbled in a rolling thunder that kept going. Mason let out a loud cry, and I could hear his distress, his pain that I'd caused by considering Danny's cracked-out plan instead of going straight to the car.

It took exactly a hundred years for Finn to come back with several armloads of food. Von snatched at the nearest burger, chewing barely as much as was needed to choke the thing down. Mason let out an animalistic growl at the meat, warning us he was on the brink of transitioning, and that it wouldn't be pretty. "There's plenty for all of you, so keep going." Finn passed an orange drink up to Danny, who clutched it with clammy and weak fingers.

The boys made gratuitous noises of gluttonous bliss, tearing through the meals that were meant to feed several families. It wasn't until tears started streaming down my face and I couldn't hold back my screams any longer that Mason divorced his gaze from his burgers and remembered what he was supposed to be doing. "Oh, I'm sorry. I know I'm not pulling as hard as I should."

Finn snatched away Mason's burger, a rare bit of personality showing through the cracks of his military boss perfection. "You can take a break from eating to pull some of this from her! Von, are you sane enough to switch yet? She's barely holding it together back here."

Von plowed through another burger as he got out and traded places with Finn. The feeling of one Reaper tugging the atrophying life forces out of me was like a mild pain reliever when I needed anesthesia. When Von added his efforts, I was able to breathe through the pain that seemed never ending.

Von snarled toward the front of the car. "For the record, this is all on you and Danny. We're cleaning up the mess as well as we can. But every scream's on the two of you. I hope it haunts you. I hope it's all you hear when you try to close your eyes tonight."

"You'll watch your tone, half-vamp." Finn wasn't a fan of correction.

Von wasn't a fan of Finn. "You'll watch your neck around me, and your back around Mason. You're not in Dagat anymore."

I leaned forward and screamed into Mason's neck, praying that the fighting and the agony would come to an end.

MAKE IT BETTER

By the time Danny took the exit to my house from the freeway, the pain was only excruciating, which was a far sight better than it had been in the beginning. I could speak a little and keep it to a quiet bleat through the worst parts, which were all when I was bumped or moved. My torment was kept private after I regained enough of myself to be able to form a whole sentence worth of thought. My misery was contained to silent crying into Mason's thick, hairy neck. "It's alright, I can fix it," he assured me, though we both knew he was lying.

I bit down on his neck to muffle my scream when Danny hit a pothole that jarred my bones. I let my tears fall down his back and into his black t-shirt.

"Who's car is that?" Finn asked as Danny turned off the engine.

I glanced at the car and groaned. "Oh, no. It's a rental. Ollie's here! He can't see you guys. He can't see me like this."

Mason handed me off to Von. Gentle as he was with my body, each movement felt like my bones were being ripped from their sockets. I bit my lip, distracted from the torture only when Mason transformed into his wolf body right next to us, shaking off his clothes to the floor.

Danny hung his head in defeat. "Did you know Ollie was coming home?"

"No, and I just talked to him this morning." I whined through a torrent of pain that was so cold, it burned my insides, if that makes any sense.

"I'll take care of it. If he sees you like this," Danny looked over his shoulder at my splotchy face that was wet with tears, and grimaced. "He'll go out of his mind. Any chance you can look... not like that?"

I wanted to leap into the front seat and beat on Danny, but I couldn't move without screaming. Mason growled at Danny for me, which I appreciated.

Ollie busted out of the front door, his worry face on high alert. "October? Is that..." His eyes fell on me in the backseat, limp in Von's arms. "Get your filthy perv hands off my sister! What did you do to her?" Ollie ran around to my door and ripped it open, yanking me out of Von's arms.

The knives sliced into me at the separation from both my Reapers, terrifying my slowly numbing nerves into full-on action again. My scream could no doubt be heard for miles, if not whole continents. I'm pretty sure the midafternoon clouds shading the sun from shining down on my pain heard my plight and sent me a sympathetic "oh, girl" chuck on the shoulder.

Ollie was startled and lowered me to the concrete. "October, what's wrong? Is something broken?" His tone changed from fear to fury. "You! I knew you were no good! What did you do to my sister?" He whirled on Von, who knelt on the pavement at my side, his hands working to dull the endless abyss of agony. Mason hopped down from the car on all fours and laid against my other side, doubling the opiate that kept me from losing my mind.

"Let's get you inside, Peach."

Ollie was confused, but knew where he wanted to direct his anger that could turn volatile on a dime. "Touch my sister and die."

"As jolly as that sounds, I'm the only thing keeping your sister together right now. Danny can explain everything, but not here." Von's arms were careful as they tucked under my back and beneath my legs. He lifted me fluidly, but unfortunately nothing was seamless. I bit my lower lip through a scream, my skin sweaty. "I know, love. I know it hurts." When Ollie stood in his way, Von lowered his voice in a threat. "Let me lay her down first. Duke it out with Danny. See if you can knock some sense into him. Not all brothers care about others the way you do. This one's on him."

Mason ran ahead through the door Danny opened

with a somber expression. My wolf scampered to my bedroom and pulled back the covers so I had a soft place ready for me to lay.

Ollie didn't know where to direct his anger anymore. Poor guy was completely in the dark, and I'd been the one to keep him there. Now he would know everything, and I wasn't sure if I should be scared or relieved. Ollie's fists were clenched as he spoke through his teeth to Von. "Get out of my sister's bedroom. I'm here. I'll take her to the hospital now."

Von kicked off his shoes, flipping his middle fingers to Ollie and Danny, who stood in the entrance of my room, unsure where they should be. "Danny, get him out. Mason and I can clean up the mess you made." He pointed his middle finger at Danny. "Sure, I'm the screw-up, but you did this. Never forget today. You jeopardized the whole kingdom and nearly got the strongest Omen killed. You'll be lucky if we can get her to zero at all today. Keep the food coming and have fun breaking The Truth is Out There to the only brother who's more clueless than you. Then you'll call Ezra and tell him all you've done."

Von tried not to move my legs at all as he untied my shoes. He snapped his fingers at Mason. "Up you get, Mason." He waited until Mason was snuggled into my side before taking off my shoes, ensuring I was sedated enough to get through the simple task that jarred every bone in my leg.

"You'll not undress my sister," Ollie fumed.

Von pulled a cigar out of his backpack and cast me an apologetic look as he slowly turned it to give it an even burn on the tip with his gold lighter. He puffed out a mouthful of smoke, and I knew all the pulling was making him hungry again. "Look, not for nothing, but don't tell me what to do. I know every bit of subterfuge November's been up to for the last couple months, and you don't." He puffed again, ignoring my glare that came with gritted teeth and muscles so tense, I wasn't sure they'd ever relax. "I'm not pleasant when I'm irritated. Far more charming when I'm being told how amazing I am. Now Danny, be a love and fetch me something to use as an ashtray so I don't give my darling a conniption." When they didn't move, Von bared his fangs at his brother. "Don't make me ask twice."

Ollie took a wary step back, figuring he might not know everything about the situation unfolding before him.

Danny narrowed his eyes at Von, but knew he had to take whatever cockiness was thrown his way. Once he closed the door, Von lowered himself to the bed, toeing off his socks and climbing in next to me. The second his hand reached over me to rub my arm, the pain decreased from pure torture to just really bad. I could handle really bad pain just fine. I melted into him, letting the tears run down my cheeks now that it was just the two of us. Well, plus Mason. For some reason I didn't hesitate so much around wolf Mason. It felt like having a dog who loved you for all the things you were to him, even if they weren't true or all that impressive.

Von rolled me onto my side, shushing me through the searing that made me bite off a whimper I hated myself for. He draped my arm around his neck and wrapped me in a one-armed hug I loved him for, while Mason leaned against my back. "More contact means we can pull it all out of you better." He kissed my wet eyelashes when my eyes squinched shut through a shudder. "I can make it better."

"Mm-hm." My voice was pinched and unable to conceal the pain I refused to scream about anymore. "V-Von?"

"Yeah, love?" He took a puff of his cigar and blew it away from us, but the sweet smell still landed on me. I could only hope he didn't ruin my perfectly white carpet with the ashes.

"I n-need you to bliss me out. Please, Von. I c-can't feel this. Hurts... too... much."

He paused a few seconds. "Call me your big, strong, sexy man."

I ignored Mason's low throat growl. I would've called Von Mayor McCheese if that would've sped things along. "You're my b-big, strong, sexy man."

He drew his mouth to the side. "Huh. I thought that would've done it for me, but still no." He kissed my cheek. "See, if you bliss out, then you can't tell us when the souls are completely gone, or if you've still got something swimming around in you. The only way we'd be able to tell is to look for your skin turning translucent in parts, like Mari-ang's." He kissed my other cheek and then brushed his nose back and forth across mine. "As much as I'd love to get you good and naked so I can stare at your peachy skin, I prefer my women conscious. Old fashioned, I guess." He puffed his cigar through my sobs of defeat. "Hold tight, November. It's you and me till the end, remember? I'm right here, and I'm not going anywhere."

29

FLIRTING WITH DISASTER

Danny came back in with a cereal bowl for Von to use as his ash tray. "Pizza will be here in twenty. Can you wait until then?"

Mason stood up on all fours on the bed, shaking his head and jumping off the mattress. He scampered out the door, no doubt to raid the refrigerator or chase a few squirrels. The second he broke contact with me, the pain ramped up again, but I found I could breathe through it as my body writhed against Von's.

"How about you, Von? Can you hold on until then, or do you need more blood?"

Von groaned. "Oh, don't say blood. I'm alright. I can make it fine until the pizza comes. How's Ollie handling the whole thing?"

"Bad? How's one supposed to take something like this?" Danny shrugged. "Finn's giving him the breakdown of the different countries in Terraway. It's a geography lesson at best right now. He's not gotten into October's role in all of it yet. Expect a lot of yelling when that happens."

Von moved the cereal bowl to the other side of my head on the pillow so he could keep his arm around me. "I'll be simply waiting on the edge of my seat." He took a puff and turned to blow the smoke in Danny's direction. "I'm surprised you're sticking around to do damage control on the mess you made for us. I expected you to be off honeymooning with Mariang by now. This is what you wanted, isn't it? November barely able to lift her head, screaming in pain so that Mariang can go to the prom with you?"

"Sod off. You know I didn't want this. I didn't know it was even possible to reap that many in a day. It was an experiment gone wrong."

"Yes. An experiment you never would've risked with Mariang. You threw October away, Danny." Von's upper lip curled at his brother as he clutched me through a quiet sob that rose up in me at Von's choice of words. "You disgust me. Clean up the mess you made with Ollie and get out. You and Finn both. Don't let me see his smug mug again until we have to go back to Terraway."

Danny shoved his hands into his jeans pockets and stared down at his shoes. "October? I'm real sorry. I didn't—"

"No!" Von snapped, flashing his fangs at Danny. "You don't get to apologize for something like this. Not to her, not to me and not to Mason. Go take your self-loathing to Mariang and bed her the way you've been missing it. This is exactly what you wanted."

Danny's face hardened, but he wasn't the type to defend himself. He wasn't usually wrong. He watched the tears fall down my face with something that looked like regret while I cried silently in Von's arms. "Whatever you think of me, I am sorry. I'll stay with Ollie until he understands everything. I'll make sure he doesn't bother you with questions until you're ready for it. I'll keep the food coming for the guys. Then I'll go home." He rubbed the back of his neck. "I've got to ask how you knew there'd be so many bodies to reap at the carnival. You suggested the place before we were close enough for you to feel any sort of pull."

"Lucky guess," I worked out through gritted teeth. It was a valid question, and one that scared me. How did Philip know? Philip was a figment of my imagination. How did he know something I didn't?

"Well, I've been watching the news, and there was a terrorist bombing at the carnival. They're still counting the casualties."

I gasped and Von clutched me tighter. He all but barked at Danny, "Do you think adding more stress is helping anyone right now? Save the details for another day, Danny. Out you go."

I buried my face in Von's neck as soon as Danny shut the door behind him. A few of the faces of the people I'd reaped flashed before me in various stages of bloodied and blown apart. I let out my grief over all the terrible things in the world into Von's skin, shuddering and wetting his collar with my tears that had no end in sight. "It hurts! It hurts," I whispered, confessing my weakness to the one person I trusted enough to be careful with my vulnerability.

"I suppose this is a bad time to tell you that you shouldn't have hesitated when I told you we were done for the day."

"Bad time," I agreed, calming a little when he rubbed my back. His leg draped over my thigh, pulling my knee between his as we enveloped ourselves in each other, soaking in the comfort that felt intimate behind closed doors. "Finn hit you!" I wailed. "I c-couldn't get to you. I just stood there and watched it all happen while my body froze over."

"Not the first time I've taken a punch from him, the fishy bastard."

"I was so scared for you! You can't get hurt, do you hear me? That k-killed me!"

Von paused, his cigar in his teeth as he studied my distraught face. "You really were scared, weren't you? Scared for me while you were on death's door."

"You're my treasure," I said meekly. The second the words were out of my mouth, I wished for better ones. Less embarrassing ones. "Oh, forget I said that. So dorky."

Von was at a loss, which thankfully meant he didn't say

anything to call me out on my overemotional response. He ramped up the pulling, and my shoulders started to droop. "I think I might like dorky." We looked into each other's eyes, saying too many things we shouldn't have even let our eyeballs converse about.

"I'm sorry you got punched," I offered, swallowing the strange feeling that tried to introduce itself to me. I batted it away, certain my emotions were off because of the almost dying and the whole nature of the job thing. "Where'd he get you? Does it still hurt?"

Von rested his cigar in the bowl behind me and reached his hand between our bodies. "It's not so bad." His fingers snuck under the hem of my shirt to thumb my navel, making my stomach go concave. My body thrilled at the sexy touch I could feel above the icy stabbing that was finally starting to dull. "He got me right here."

"Here?" I reached my hand between our pressed together bodies and dragged my knuckles up and down over his abdomen, tracing the dip when he sucked in his stomach with a lusty hiss. "Does it feel better now?" I worked out in a whisper, unsure of what I was doing, or the madness that drove me there. I could feel the second the goosebumps erupted on his skin, his grip on my back tightening as his whole body responded to my simple touch.

"Oh, keep doing that," he breathed, his hips moving against mine in a seduction that was entirely new to me, but one he was well-versed in.

"Does it still hurt?" I traced a circle around his navel, thumbing the light smattering of hair that trailed downward and disappeared below the waistline of his jeans.

"Easy, baby." Von shifted against me, throwing his head back as we held each other. "Oh, you're driving me mad! It's been too long since I've had sex. Or blood."

I pulled my hand away from him and leaned back to give him a few inches of breathing room. "Sorry about that. You alright?" I wiped the tears from my face, finally calm enough to compose myself.

His heavy breathing started evening out as he kept up a high dosage of pulling to mute a little of my pain. "Blood and sex, that's what I need right now, and I won't be getting either from you, you little strumpet."

I clumsily palmed his face and chuckled as I came down from the tease neither of us had a right to indulge in. "You should write Christmas cards. That was downright poetic."

He took another puff of his cigar and then rested the brown stick in the bowl. Von took my hand and slid it across his face, drawing out a hiss from me when his tongue laved over the inside of my wrist. The pain went down another notch to make room for the unbidden pleasure. Now it was my turn to erupt in goosebumps.

"Your blood... Mm. I can still remember the taste. I don't care about the different kinds of wine, but blood? There's a difference between someone from Terraway and a pureblood human. Terraway's overly salty, humans are far too sweet. But you? A mix?" He inhaled my skin, his lashes fluttering as his eyes rolled back. "I wish you were anyone else. I wish you were ugly and mean and selfish. Then I could work out some kind of logic where you didn't smell so delicious to me. If you were haggard and covered in warts, I could resist you on lack of package appeal."

"I can work on getting some warts. I've already got the haggard thing down," I said of my bedraggled state.

"Not haggard. Captivating." Von dragged his lips over to my ear, making my back arch and my body slide against his in unladylike ways that were all primal instinct. I couldn't feel the needles. I couldn't feel the cold. I was on fire, and all I could feel was Von.

Von's lips tugging on my earlobe.

Von's lips sucking on my jaw.

Von's hips grinding into mine while my knees parted and trembled.

Von's lips dragging down the slope until they puckered the skin at the juncture of my shoulder and my neck. I was utterly twisting in the sheets beneath him as he tortured my neck like only the best vampires knew how to do. "I can almost taste you," he murmured, tugging my skin with his lips just to hear me moan. "Delicious."

I let out a gratuitous soft whimper of longing I couldn't keep inside anymore.

30

SEE WHAT YOU WON'T DO

I was writhing beneath Von's lithe body when he froze. "I... we..." He extracted his lips from my neck, suddenly scared and apologetic from his position atop me. "I don't know what I'm doing. It's been an off day all around. I'm... I should not have done that."

"If you don't want me to feel all the... you know, then you probably should stop sucking on my neck. Vampire stuff aside, you know it makes me... And we're not." I'm pretty sure that was the point my cheeks turned the brightest shade of crimson. "I shouldn't have touched your stomach like that. This one's on me. Sorry, Von."

Von leaned down and kissed my cheek. "Let me go outside and take a breather. When I come back in, we'll start over with something very platonic, like farting or belching contests."

I cast him a dubious look. "I feel like you don't know many women you're not sleeping with."

He batted his hand at me. "Oh, you."

The pain ramped up when we broke contact for the briefest of seconds, going from almost a two to a solid seven. "Ah!" I'd been so distracted by the Von of it all that I'd forgotten the true purpose behind our entwined bodies. That's the thing about a really sexy vampire.

Von came back to himself, scooping me up in his arms and calling for Danny. When Danny ran in, Von's tone was sharp. "Get me something to eat before I bite into her."

Danny bolted out of the room and came back a few seconds later with a box of cereal Von looked insulted by. "What? It'll tide you over until the pizza gets here. Then Mason will come back to help you."

Von dug his fist into the box of off-brand cereal and shoved as much as he could into his mouth, getting crumbs in the bed. Luckily this distracted me a fair amount from my aching bones. I didn't allow food in my room, least of all food that made crumbs. I made a mental list of all the things I'd have to do when I felt better to get my room back to what it should be.

I expected Danny to leave, but he leaned against the wall near my window and crossed his arms over his chest. "Ezra's on his way over to help with Ollie." He hung his head. "Lang's here. Showed up with Ruiz and Klark. Lang wanted to check how close she was to reaching her goal to see if we could start the trek early."

Von glared at Danny. "You go tell them you're the reason she won't be going anywhere today, and why she'll be taking the day off to rest and be a person tomorrow. We'll leave as scheduled, *if* she's better by then. She'll not be bullied by you or the council."

Danny ran his hands over his face, tired from the half day we'd survived, and weary from his life that was spent always on guard. "October, can I get you anything?"

"Percocet?" I asked, only half joking. "Hammer to the head?"

"I wish I could get you something like that. But Von and Mason have to get you back down. If medicine dulls anything, then they won't know if the corroded souls are totally gone. It could really hurt you if they're left inside you too long. I know it's painful now, but they can keep you from getting the scars I know you won't like. Mariang hates hers."

"We won't need you anymore once Ezra gets here, so you can go back to your precious girlfriend then." I could tell Von's anger wouldn't die down anytime soon. Von tipped the box up to his mouth with his free hand and started pounding cereal like he was afraid of being without something to chew.

Danny's tone iced over, only able to play the submissive dog for so long. "Listen, slacker. You've been at this only a few months. Mariang's been by my side for years. We've seen each other through every moment. Try being October's Puller for as long as I've been at this and see what you wouldn't do to make sure she lives." He held up his hands when Von reared on him. "I know I stepped over the line. I get it. But once you two stop denying what's obvious to everyone else, I don't want to know the depths you'd stoop to in order to keep her alive."

If Von was capable of leaving me, I know he would've leaped at Danny and knocked him one right good. I rubbed Von's arm. "It's over. It's fine. The pain will go away. Danny didn't know any better. He was just testing a theory. And look! Tomorrow you can have the day to yourself to go see Penny. Won't that be nice?"

Von threw out his free hand in exasperation. "Are you pleased with yourself? You've got her sticking up for you."

Danny shook his head, his blue eyes actually earnest instead of stuck in their usual harsh glare. "It's already happening. You're already more attached to your charge than you realize. You look down on me now, but give it a year and see what you won't do."

Von reached his breaking point, gripping me hard and sending the reminder of pain through me. "Get. Out."

Danny obeyed, which was a relief all the way around. Von settled back into the bed with me, resting his head on the pillow next to mine with his arm wrapped under my neck to make sure I stayed close. He was serious, and I didn't like it on him. Von was much better with that playful grin that told me he was up to no good. He stuck out his little finger between us, linking it through mine gingerly, so as not to hurt me with too much movement. "I swear to you, we won't end up like you and Mason. We won't make a mess of a good thing." Then he tapped his chest with his thumb. "You," he said, indicating the residence I'd taken up in his heart.

Then I tugged our joined hands to my chest, pressing my thumb to my sternum. "You," I admitted.

Mason was a fantasy – a Viking king who made my heart flutter with girlish intrigue. My friendship with Von was real, and that was enough to center me when my world felt impossibly tilted.

31

LETTING VON HELP ME

The afternoon gave way to evening before Von and Mason got me down to where I could sit up on my own. I breathed with new independence when I was strong enough to shuffle around with only mild pain. Whatever. I was the sexiest senior citizen for at least five miles. It would be worse later, when I would actually need help with things, like changing into my pajamas for the night. I wanted to, but was too chicken to try it on my own or ask for help from the all-male crew who'd taken up residence in my house.

Mason had turned back into a man when the pizza came, and stayed that way most of the day and on into the evening. I was sandwiched in between Von and Mason on the couch, who were still eating like they'd never seen food before.

"I honestly don't understand how you're still eating.

That's eleven whole large pizzas and who knows how many breadsticks and buckets of chicken wings," Ollie remarked from the recliner, his mouth open in half-awe and half-disgust.

"I'm starting to slow down. Wouldn't say no to some ice cream, though." Von rubbed his stomach. "You almost finished with your one piece of pizza, featherweight? You know, you're losing the eating contest by a mile."

I hated looking like the girl who couldn't stand on her own enough to feed herself. It looked like I'd developed an eating disorder overnight, but I hadn't. I wanted to eat like a normal person, but every bite felt like a gamble as to whether it would come back up or not. "This is my second slice," I lied to get him off my back and to keep Ollie from slipping into parent mode on me.

Mason scoffed, but Von laughed. "Oh, that's cute. Your eyes get real wide when you lie. Did you know that?"

"Oh, shut it. I'll be sure to aim my chunks your way when I eat too fast and it all comes back up."

Ollie was in heavy observation mode after having asked as many questions as was humanly possible to Ezra. "So these two are moving in with us? I don't know how I feel about that."

Now I was the one with the questions. "I thought you and Gabby were moving into her townhouse."

Ollie picked a pepperoni off his slice and laid it in the box. "Nah. Not yet. Maybe not ever. You know that on again, off again thing we've got going? It's off again.

Something about me not being able to commit or whatever."

My shoulders slumped. "Oh, Ollie. I'm sorry. It's really over?"

"I honestly haven't thought about it at all today, so I'm alright with it. This whole Narnia thing's blowing my mind a little. My sister's connected for life with a vampire and a werewolf? I can't believe how much I've been missing, living in New York."

Mason grumbled, "I'm not a werewolf. Those aren't real. I'm Matruculan, like her father was. Werewolves bend to the moon, right? I bend to no one."

"Dum-dum-dum!" Von said ominously, bringing about a comical amount of doom. "He's a shapeshifter, is all. His animal just happens to be a wolf."

Ollie's mouth fell open as more of the puzzle began to reveal itself. "Do you know our father? You know the D-bag who ran out on us? Because I gotta tell you, I'd love to meet the good-for-nothing myself."

Ezra was funny to me, eating a piece of pizza in his business outfit, looking all pressed and perfect, sitting in a chair he'd pulled out from the kitchen to lounge around in the living room with us. "It's not as simple as all that. Matruculans are drawn to human women who are pregnant. We have an unnatural desire to eat freshly born babies. Your father no doubt left to ensure he didn't kill you. I cannot speak to whether or not he was a 'D-bag', as you put it, or why he didn't come back."

Ollie put his whole slice down in the box, his nose crinkling in distaste. "Okay, where do we start? The eating babies part, or the fact that you said 'we'?"

That was pretty much how the evening went. Ezra, Mason, Finn and Von filled Ollie in on everything he'd missed, even down to the mission and how it had gone awry so early on. They were getting closer to the bit about the battle with the women launching their bomb babies at the bad guys when I decided I didn't need to hear the rest. It was barely six o'clock, but I was beat. "I'm tired, guys. I'm going to turn in."

Mason was eating his weight in chicken wings, and though I knew it was my fault he was so hungry, the sight of them eating so much made my stomach churn. He paused his feeding frenzy to meet my eyes. "I can pull while you sleep. Von, you go ahead and eat as much as you need. I was slowing down anyway."

Von stood, brushing the crumbs off his pants onto the carpet. I cringed at the mess. "Oh, no. I don't think so."

"Why not?"

"For a million obvious reasons why not. She's barely upright. Ezra's rule still holds that you're not to be alone with her, yeah?" Von confirmed with Ezra's answering nod. "See? Kosher as things are, you're not out of the doghouse." Then he sniggered. "A wolf in a doghouse. Get it? I'm funny."

Ezra kept a polite expression on his face. "That, you are. And Von's right, Mason."

Mason sat back on the couch, finally freeing himself up enough to speak his mind. "Okay, let's put things into perspective, here. What I did was wrong, of course, but Von almost killed her! How can what I did be worse than that?"

Ezra folded his hands over his knee that was crossed over his other leg. "Von, are you going to bite October Grace tonight?"

"No, sir. I'm full. I'll be fine until I leave to see Penny in an hour."

"See? There you go, Mason. I do appreciate you trying to be helpful, but the rules still stand. You need distance. That you're not a wolf right now is a tribute that she's starting to trust you; it's not a sign that it's time to test boundaries. After Von leaves, you'll stay a wolf until he returns." Ezra stood to help Von lift me off the couch. Each of them held an arm and gently tugged in slow motion. Even though their movements were fluid, my bones and joints were stiff, not lending themselves to being moved with ease.

Ollie was at a loss watching me move like an old woman, too fatigued for proper dinner company. "You're still in pain? I thought the pulling stuff was supposed to help with that."

"It has. The souls are out of me, but I'm still a little sore. That much poison at once hurt me on a bone level. Not cool." I leaned heavily on Von and Ezra. "It's fine,

Ollie. I promise. I'm just being a baby about it tonight. I'm a little tired, is all."

Ezra and Von helped me to the bedroom, lowering me to sit on the bed. Ezra's formerly composed face was contorted with concern. "I can tell you've been putting on a brave face for your brother."

"It's only pain." I managed a wan smile for the man who looked genuinely concerned for me. "I'm alright. Hoping unconsciousness will cure what ails me."

Ezra smoothed a few stray hairs away from my face. "That was so dangerous, darling. I hope you realize how lucky you are to have two Pullers to fix the damage."

"It was worth it, and you know it. Now Mariang can take a few days off, instead of just one or two. While we're marching the sagrado stone to Silo, she can rest. Maybe heal up a little. Give her a fighting chance."

Ezra stared into my eyes with an unfathomable expression. "You have to stop sacrificing yourself. This isn't what I want for you. I won't trade one daughter for another." He'd said as much to me before, but it wasn't sinking in.

"'Fraid that's not up to you, chief. My job, my call. Danny was fine with it. It worked, right? I mean, I won't be trying it again, but it all worked out."

Von's tone turned sharp. "Do you want me to lose my temper? You're daft if you think everything worked out."

Ezra's even tone leveled off Von's spiking edge of frustration. "Yes, well, never again. And I'll be having words with Danny."

Von was rummaging through my dresser drawers, making a mess of the piles I had my clothes neatly folded in. "See that you do. The whole thing was his cracked idea. He's bent, Ezra."

Ezra was talking to me, but I had a hard time paying attention to anything. I don't know if it was the malnourishment, the exhaustion that came from doing the job, or the ringer my body had been through, but whatever it was, I was beat. "Did you hear me?" Ezra asked, waving two fingers in my field of vision.

"Huh? Yeah, whatever you said." I yawned through Von's snigger. "I'm tired, though. Can it all wait until tomorrow?"

Ezra sighed. "Certainly. I'll be on the couch with Finn if you need me."

I frowned. "No, no. You take the bed. Mason, Von and I can share the couch."

Ezra tilted his head at me, amused. "Do you honestly think I'll allow that?"

"It's not right for you to be on the couch. You're a grownup."

Ezra chuckled as he kissed my forehead. "Thank you for the offer, but the couch is fine. Goodnight, October Grace."

After Ezra left, I cast over to Von with a sleepy, "I'm going to get changed, so you know, give me a minute."

Von put my pile of clothes atop my dresser and folded his arms over his chest. "Let's see you get up and come over here to pick up your clothes. Then I'll believe you can do this by yourself."

I rolled my eyes at him and placed my hands on the bed, readying myself for the jolt my limbs would endure if I simply stood. It took a few tries, but I finally got off the side of the bed, moving with care and determination toward the dresser. I stopped halfway there, debating whether my pride was worth the pain or not. I took another step, biting my lower lip to keep from letting Von know how badly I was hurting. My tendons were too tight for use unless I had a Puller on me. I was hunched over, unable to stand up straight. So, you know, I was your average sexy beast.

"Okay, you obviously can't do this yourself. This is just painful to watch. Here. I'll help you." The moment his hands touched my elbow to steady me, half the ache evaporated, melting me and my posture as I slumped in his arms. "Whoa. Alright tiger, let's sit you back down, yeah?" He brought me back to the side of the bed and knelt at my feet, slowly working my socks off.

"You don't have to do that. I can figure it out." I grimaced when his hands touched my bare feet. "Oh, gross, Von. You don't want to touch my feet. They're dirty."

Von smiled up at me, half sweet and half too much flirtation to ever be taken seriously. "I don't mind. And your feet aren't dirty. They're fine. Relax, Peach. I'll take care of it." He tilted my foot up and placed a few kisses across the tips of my toes, making me cringe and melt simultaneously.

I don't know how he could say the simplest things and get me to believe him, but as he rubbed my feet, I started uncoiling from the pain I'd been so married to. My spine relaxed, and I let him take care of me, knowing I would never let anyone else do this. "You're being nice to me."

"Would you prefer I yelled?" He stood and took the clothes from the dresser, placing them on the side of the bed. Without a word, Von slipped my blue sweater over my head, smiling down with affection at me as I covered myself to keep him from seeing my lacy teal bra. "Sexy," he murmured before shoving a pink cotton t-shirt over my head.

"Oh, hush," I scolded him with a blush.

One thing I learned about Von that really didn't surprise me: he was great at undressing women. He had my jeans off with minimal movement of my sore limbs, pausing the slow and sweet seduction with a snort and a laugh he tried to cover unsuccessfully. "Now, that's just adorable."

I laid back on the mattress and covered my face with my hands when I remembered the underwear I was wearing. They were white cotton with little cartoon rainbows on them. I'd thought they were cute, and since Beto and I never ventured to that region, I bought what I liked, not caring how a guy might be turned off my something so childish. "Well, don't look!"

"It's too late, I've seen you in your knickers, and I'll never dream of another woman again. For me it's only girls with rainbows on their..."

"Shut up, you dork!"

"There's a joke in here about 'tasting the rainbow,' but I'm too much a gentleman to say it." Von's wide smile told me how very pleased he was with himself. His elation crashed when his gaze fell on the spot I prayed he wouldn't see. "What's this?" He thumbed the puckered line on the inside of my thigh, giving my body the guilty kind of chills.

My thighs slammed shut. "It's nothing. Just an old scar."

"How does one acquire a scar there? Seems a pretty off the map place for danger to roam."

I lowered my voice and checked to make sure the door was locked. "I got a little bit stabbed at work a long time ago. It's totally fine. I healed, and that's that."

Von stood and leaned over my supine form, his knuckles supporting his weight on the mattress as he caged me in. "An inmate stabbed your thigh?"

I rolled my eyes, making sure my voice was quieted to a whisper so we weren't overheard. "You remember Judge and Darius? They have a brother in lockup, Terence, who I knew when I was younger. He goes by T now, though. I was treating an inmate when the patient grew hostile. I got sliced a little, and Terence rescued me. It would've been a lot worse if Terence hadn't been there."

"I can't believe Ollie didn't make you quit after that."

I scoffed. "Ollie doesn't know, and he never will. He's got enough to worry about without him having to come running every time I get a paper cut."

Von's whisper turned indignant. "This is not a paper cut! You've been stabbed twice? Once on your arm and once on your leg?"

"It's fine, Von. It was a long time ago."

"That's a dollar for the Denial Jar." He paused, examining my face before he migrated to the scar on my arm. His thumb swept over the pink line before he pressed his lips to the wound. "Does it feel better now?"

"You've got the healing touch." I couldn't keep the smile off my face at his sweetness.

Von's gaze hardened with something darker that made my breath catch in my throat. His body shifted, and my eyes widened when he sunk down between my legs, parting my thighs ever so gently. I let out a rough gasp when his lips brushed across the scar I tried never to think about. He lingered there, and suddenly the torn skin I'd always thought was ugly started to feel beautiful under the tenderness of Von's healing touch. He sought out my most war-torn parts and sent loveliness into them, redeeming the portions of me that seemed beyond repair. I clumsily propped myself up on my elbows, catching his lidded eyes with a look I hoped communicated my deepest gratitude for caring about things like healing in a world where I was constantly being broken. "Thank you," I whispered. "That's my ugliest part, and you made it feel beautiful."

"Darling, every part of you is stunning." Von kissed my scar again and leaned back on his heels, shaking his head to clear it of the PG-13 position our friendship would never survive.

He slid my pajama pants on as if they were the silky panties I wished I was wearing. He made quick work of stripping down to his boxer briefs before he climbed into the bed with me. He kissed my cheek, and then lowered his lips to my neck, giving me the shivers that only encouraged him to misbehave more.

CONFESSIONS FROM A MALE PROSTITUTE

ow that he was touching me, my body was far more pliable. We tangled around each other in ways that were entirely indecent, and needed to be shrouded under cover of bedsheets.

He started playing with my hair, relaxing me to the point where I had to remind myself not to drool. "Von?" I asked, my voice barely above a whisper. "What's the deal with you and Finn? You two know each other from a long time before this."

"Everyone knows Finn. He's King Banak of Dagat's top dog."

I knew he was trying to brush off my question, but after all the secrets I'd had to give up, I didn't feel like shrugging off this one. "Von?"

A dark cloud settled over Von as he slowly twirled a

curl that hung at the base of my neck. "I passed through Dagat a few times. Got into a little trouble. Nothing more than that."

I kissed his nose. "Okay. You don't have to tell me. You're allowed a few secrets."

Von looked at me as if considering just how deep and true our friendship went. "Fine, but just so you know, Danny doesn't even know what really happened. No one but me, Ezra and Boston do."

"Your youngest brother? Bishop's twin?"

"Yeah. Boston's great. He's filled with lots of terrible fun you only get into when you don't care what happens to you in the end. The two of us went to Dagat on holiday a few years ago. We had a blast, going off with the Mermaids and getting ourselves into all sorts of mischief. One night we worked our way into a high stakes card game with the Kataw."

"That's what Finn is, right? The Mermen without tails?"

"Yes. I was handling myself like the smoky gentleman you adore, but Boston was reckless, as he always is. Bet way too high and lost more than either of us had. Infinitely more." Von's eyes hardened and then closed as pain shaded his expression. "He was scared. The Kataw are ruthless, and the great Captain Finn was there. He's the worst. Has a reputation for being cruel that's well-earned."

"Did he beat you guys up?"

Von swallowed. "No. He offered us a way out. He told Boston he'd let him work off his debt, selling his body to the king's son by joining the harem."

A rock sunk in my stomach. If I thought reaping made me sick, it was nothing compared to that. "Oh, no. Tell me he didn't."

"Boston was so scared. Actually cried, which if you knew him, you'd know how big a deal that is."

"I don't blame him."

"I couldn't let him do it. He's my baby brother, and I'd brought us there in the first place. So I talked to Finn and took Boston's place."

The pulling couldn't counteract the ice that froze in my veins at that blast I hadn't been expecting. My heartbeat pounded in my cheeks as my tongue stuck to the roof of my mouth. "Please tell me that means something different than it does in my world."

Von shook his head, looking at the wall as he lay propped up on his elbow next to me. The lamplight illuminating a few choice features, making him look truly haunted. "I sent Boston home and signed over the worst three months of my life."

I wrapped my arm around his waist to let him know that he wasn't back in Dagat. He was safe with me in our bed. "You got sold to the king's son?"

"Yep. Like a pack of cigarettes. Duwendes down on their luck make for good prostitutes. We can make people feel better, so they think they've had the best night of their lives afterward. Always a satisfied customer." He tried to make it come off as a joke, but it fell flat. "Julius was a little harder to subdue. Violent, sick pervert. It took a long while to get him to think he had a good time without... It wasn't pleasant."

"You couldn't have bitten him? Sucked him dry and killed the bastard?"

"I hadn't been turned yet. This was years ago. I wasn't even sure Finn remembered me until he made a crack about it." The second Von's eyes watered, he cleared his throat. "Sorry. It was a long time ago. I'm fine now. Just a rough patch."

"Now who owes the Denial Jar a dollar." I rolled on my side to face him, holding his hand between us as we'd done when we'd pinky promised we wouldn't kiss and ruin the great thing we had. "I can keep your secrets, Von. Let me be your Duwende. You can talk to me." I leaned forward and kissed both of his shut eyelids. "You *should* talk to me."

Von was quiet for half a minute, so I wasn't expecting him to tell me what he'd been through, to unload some of his burdens onto me and trust that I'd be strong enough to hold him through it.

But that's exactly what happened for the next forty-five minutes. By the time he had to leave to go see Penny, he'd cried in my arms, let me kiss his face and told me more horrible, disgusting details than a qualified shrink could ever sort through. He kept feeding me a new degradation he'd endured while reading my expression with caution to see if I would pull away from him, turn on him and use his confession against him. I could tell he'd been in need of someone who could carry his secrets, to treasure him when he admitted he'd been used and abused so brutally.

I kissed each of his tears, whispering, "You're a treasure. You're *my* treasure."

"I'm filthy. No one who's done the things I've had to do can be called a treasure."

I held him tight as he fell more irreparably apart in my arms. "You saved your brother from that nasty man. That doesn't make you filthy. It makes you a good dad to Boston."

Make no mistake, it was all filthy, but even the clean freak I was couldn't turn away from Von's mess. I couldn't wash my hands of his past, nor did I want to. I held him just as he was, in the same way he'd done for me when I'd been half a human and a whole disaster.

Von shook his head, brushing his damp and reddened nose against mine. "I don't deserve you. The way you look at me sometimes, it's scared me for months that I'd lose that hung-the-moon adoration from you if you knew all I'd been through."

"Oh, honey. You're only more heroic now." I shook my head in dismay. "How could you let Danny call you a male escort? That's how you passed it all off?"

"Boston was scared, so we came up with a story that I'd

been the one in gambling debt, and I chose to sell myself to wealthy women in Terraway to pay off my debts. That's why I was kicked out of the Academy. Word got around that I had a gambling problem, and that I was whoring myself out to women to pay my way."

I was furious when I added up all the male escort cracks Danny had made at Von's expense. "Why don't you at least set Danny straight?"

"Danny sees me as he would like to. If he can't love me as a male escort, then I don't need him to love me as a sex slave." He clung to me as I laid his head on my breast, running my fingers through his hair and over his shoulder to soothe him. "You deserve to know me, though. You loved me even when I was a prostitute." He clutched my pink shirt as a fresh handful of tears rocked him. "And now it's ruined! I'm dirty, and you like things clean."

Guilt sunk deep in me for inflicting my neurosis on Von as I held him tight. "You listen to me, Von. You are not dirty. You're my treasure. Always my treasure. This changes nothing about how I see you, only that you have too much on your shoulders. You're too good a person. I don't know many who would do that for their family."

Von broke all over again, crying into my breasts until the waves of haunting emotion calmed. Finally he lay docile, utterly spent after reliving the trauma he kept tight to the vest. "Thank you," he whispered.

Von was a storm of trouble, but in my arms he was a

sweet, lost puppy. I loved the puppy in him. I loved the proud man in him, as well as the lost boy. He kissed both my cheeks before he left to go see Penny, and I realized with all the subtlety of a gong that I hopelessly and deeply loved Von.

33

RICOTTA CHEESE AND KALE SALAD

I had a day of rest. Beautiful, blissful rest where I got to play video games with Ollie, clean my house the way it was meant to be scrubbed and eat food like a normal person who wasn't vying for the trophy in the Miss Young Adult Skeleton pageant.

Watching Mason try to figure out the video game controller was the best entertainment. He kept moving the controller up and around whenever he wanted his avatar to jump. He finally gave up and lounged on the couch, eating his way through seven tacos while I kicked Ollie's butt. My brother was sorely out of practice on the things that mattered.

Ollie didn't bring up much about Terraway, asking the occasional non-confrontational question, but never making me feel bad for not telling him sooner. He hovered, though, which wasn't completely unexpected. I didn't so much look like death warmed over, as I had the day before, but I wasn't exactly winning beauty contests or running any marathons.

I got to go shopping with Gabby, though it wasn't the kind of shopping she liked to do. Grocery stores weren't nearly as fun to her as the department store treasure hunting she loved. Mall shopping gave me small bouts of anxiety, complete with flashbacks of watching Bev spend the money we needed for food and bills on sweaters and makeup. Grocery shopping was safer.

Ollie had asked me if he could tell Gabby about Terraway, but I was firm. I'd rather look like a weirdo with two shadows than bring anyone else into the world that had only threatened to tear me apart. Plus, their relationship status seemed to have gone from moving in together, to breaking it off, to grocery shopping together in the middle of the day while they held hands. I couldn't keep up with Ollie's commitment issues. Though, kudos to Gabby for trying.

While Ollie was handling Terraway like a champ, I knew Gabby wouldn't be able to be as cool about it all. She could barely keep a lid on her excitement at meeting my two bodyguards (though she'd met Von at my house once before). I'd gone from borderline nun to a girl with two new guys since she'd last seen me, apparently. I was having a hard time spinning how very normal a trio we were. I may or may not have pretended to not be able to hear her prodding whispers when she asked which of them I was hooking up with. Thank goodness for the overhead PA system announcing every little sale.

I let out a quiet groan when we pulled over to the deli section with our two carts, and my favorite girl wasn't at the counter.

"Yes! Your stories about this guy always make my day." Ollie pumped his fist in the air like he'd won the lottery when the mid-twenties dude came into view behind the deli counter. Deli Frank had bloodshot eyes and a mole cluster in the shape of Cassiopeia on his forehead. He breathed with his mouth open after he called our number. "Oh, I've been waiting for this," Ollie rubbed his hands together eagerly.

"What?" Mason inquired, clutching my hand tighter as if anticipating danger. I relished the warmth of the gentle pull he shot through me. It relaxed my sore muscles and took away the lingering ache in my bones.

"Nine pounds of salami, sliced thick," I requested to start out my order. Von and Mason went through a ton of lunch meat. When Frank looked blankly at me, I repeated the order with a polite, "Please."

Frank looked at the case in confusion, though he'd been working there for over a year. "Salami? Like, sliced, or like sticks?"

I pursed my lips, unsure how I could've said it any clearer. "Sliced, please. Nine pounds of salami, sliced thick."

"Right on, right on. Hold up. Let me see if we have any."

Ollie giggled while I pointed to the log on sale that clearly read "salami" on it. "I think it's that one."

"No. That's turkey. I'll look in back."

I leaned my forehead to Mason's shoulder, while Ollie and Gabby let out a loud laugh. "He usually makes it through at least one item before he has to 'look in back.'"

When Frank returned, his bloodshot eyes fell on me with no recognition. "Can I help you?"

Gabby's giggling couldn't be helped. "She'd like nine pounds of salami, sliced thick, please."

Frank looked around and grabbed the mesquite chicken and took it to the slicer. "Right on. Right on."

Von frowned. "But that's..."

"It's not worth it. He never gets the order right. You all like mesquite chicken, right?"

Von shook his head at the whole situation. "No, no. I didn't really care what kind of lunch meat you got, but now I'll go to the mat that we need salami." He squeezed my side before detaching from me and letting himself in behind the counter.

"Von, you can't be back there!" I admonished him, looking around for the supermarket police. I expected a SWAT team clad in the store's orange polo uniform to descend on us at any given moment.

He shrugged innocently. "Looks like I can." Von jerked

the fat roll of salami from the case and handed it to Frank. "Here, mate. My girl wants this one."

Gabby pursed her lips through a giddy squeal that Von had called me his girl. I shot her a "be cool" look, but it was a completely wasted effort.

Frank sliced up about four pieces of salami, bagged it and handed it over the counter to me. "Anything else?"

"Um, can I have nine pounds, please?"

"Nine pounds of what?"

"Salami. I need nine pounds."

"Of what?"

I wanted to shout "Salami!" at him, but as I'd actually done that before with no lasting results, I closed my mouth. Ollie, on the other hand, was laughing so hard, he was red. I'd complained a great many times about Frank to my brother on the phone.

Von turned Frank around and pushed him back towards the slicer. "Let's try this again, shall we?"

Von stood next to Frank until the mountain of salami was sliced, bagged and handed to me with no further incident. Nearby shoppers grabbed tickets, now that someone competent was behind the counter. The line went from one to fifteen in the span of however long it took for Von to flash his charismatic smile out across the counter. I can't imagine the loss of business Frank had caused the store. With Von's charming grin to greet them, it seemed everyone wanted a nice salami.

Von stood next to Frank behind the counter with a pleasant look on his face. "What else would you like, love?"

"Really?"

"Truly. Frank and I are your servants."

Frank's dilated pupils didn't seem to absorb much, but he remained at Von's side, breathing in and out through his slack mouth. "Can I help you?"

Ollie wanted the game to go on forever. "Sharp Cheddar cheese, please. How much, October?"

"Nine pounds?" I requested, and then Mason jerked his thumb upward. "Ten pounds, please."

"Ten pounds of what?" Frank asked with a glazed-over expression. I wasn't even positive Frank's idiocy was because he was always baked. I think part of his dysfunction had to be genetic or something, coupled with massive amounts of pot.

Von tugged out the brick I wanted and handed it to Frank. "Start slicing, and I'll tell you when."

"You're a miracle worker," I smirked over the counter at Von.

He pressed his hands to the waist-level surface and leaned his tall frame over to close a little of the gap between us. "Tell me I'm your hero."

My smile stuck on my face as my cheeks flushed. I shook my head bashfully. I could feel people watching him openly flirt with me while I held onto another dude's hand.

Mason answered for me. "You'll be *my* hero if you can

get some of this turkey over here. That looks good. And you know nine pounds won't be enough. Just have him slice up the rest of the log."

"On it, my good man." Von lowered his voice to me while we waited for Frank to finish up with the cheese. "I'm waiting, November. Tell me I'm your hero."

I shook my head again when someone nearby whistled suggestively at the cuteness. Public displays made me introvert all over the place. "You're incorrigible."

A mama with three irritable kids hanging on her basket pressed her hands to the case with mild desperation. "You'll be *my* hero if I can just get a pound of the cheese he's already slicing. Just one pound."

"Frank would be delighted to help you with that." He turned back to me. "Tell me I'm your hero, or I'll sit back here and eat the entire order by myself while you watch."

"Gross! You will not."

"Say it," Von begged, his eyes turning sweet, endearing me forward.

I kept my chin down with chagrin. "Fine. Von, you're my hero."

A broad beam swept over his features, his chest puffing out with male pride. "Ah, you didn't have to say that." He winked at me, ignoring the commotion that was gathering around us. "What else would you like?"

"Really? I usually only get one thing before I get frustrated and move on."

His eyes met mine, saying too many things I hoped no

one else heard. "It's okay to ask me for what you want. There's nothing I'd hold back from you."

I swallowed, pushing aside Gabby's squeal of anticipation. I think she was hoping I might ask Von to throw me down on the counter and make love to me right then and there. "Thank you." I pointed over to the premade food portion, excited that I was finally able to try out some of the salads I'd not had the patience to order before. "Can I try the kale salad? Like, just a small container of it?"

Von waved Frank over after the cheese and the turkey were sliced and bagged. "Three big containers of the kale salad, mate."

Frank looked to the case in confusion. "The what?"

I hung my head. "It's honestly not worth it, Von."

"The kale salad," Ollie repeated through his chuckle.

Frank grabbed a large plastic clear container and pointed to the meatloaf logs. "This one?"

"No!" Mason replied, indignant. "I'm not even from here, and I know what she's asking for. The kale salad!" When he realized the alien implications in what he'd just uttered, his neck shrank into his shoulders.

"This one?" Frank asked, perplexed as he pointed to the water-logged block of ricotta cheese.

Von intervened before Mason had a conniption and I lost my patience. Ollie had fallen to his knees, clutching his stomach while he roared. "It's ricotta cheese!" he howled. "He thinks kale is ricotta cheese!"

Von steered Frank to the correct bowl, watching with

his mouth open in confusion as Frank attempted to get the kale into the cylindrical plastic container without the use of a serving spoon. He stabbed at the salad with the lip of the cup, scooping some inside, but scattering much of it out of the bowl and into the bottom of the case.

I dropped Mason's grip and squeezed my fists in frustration. "It's not worth it, Von."

Von arrested the cup from Frank and turned him back toward the slicer. "Why don't you go cut up the rest of that log of salami for anyone else who wants it. I'll handle this part." He shot me an expression that read, "Yikes. *This* guy."

My blood pressure dropped when Von used a spoon, scooping enough kale salad from the bowl into a container for me. "What else, darling?"

Gabby's hand flew over her heart as she swooned on my behalf.

I narrowed my eyes at Von. "Whatever you guys want is fine. And don't call me 'darling' in public."

"Very well. Only in private then, my love."

"You know you're just trying to get a rise out of me."

He grinned at me like the boy who would never apologize for tracking mud into the house. Von took Gabby's order, Mason's and, when Ollie collected himself enough for speech, my brother's. Everyone at the deli took their bagged portions of salami and ran with gratitude, delighted that finally they could get something without having to deal with Frank.

The commotion died down as we shopped around the store, making our way through the aisles until the cart was so full and difficult to maneuver, Mason took over pushing it.

"You want more honey?" I asked Von after putting ten bear-shaped plastic bottles in the cart.

"Do I want more what, sugar?" he teased. Then he reached to the higher shelf to grab down the econo size tub of honey I couldn't reach.

Gabby counted the jars and laughed. "What could you possibly be using all that for?"

"I'm trying my hand at making mead," Von answered without missing a beat. He smiled down at me, and I saw the practiced patience in his eyes that warned me this wasn't his ideal day when Frank wasn't there to mess with.

I pulled Von aside when the others moved ahead and whispered in his ear, "Hey, you want the day off? Like, to go spend with Penny or something?"

"Aw, that's sweet of you. Penny's at Girl Scouts, though. I'm alright playing fifth wheel. Pretend I'm not even here."

"Why don't you go call Katrina? You don't want to be here for the boring stuff. Before you know it, you'll be domesticated, and then what would the world do? Take advantage of the space while you can."

He was wary of the gift. "But what about you? You could barely move without screaming yesterday."

"That's the thing about Pullers who're good at their jobs. I feel fine. Plus, Mason's here if I'm not."

"Really?" His eyes darted to Gabby, who was preoccupied fixing Ollie's collar so he looked more "dashing". "You wouldn't mind?"

"Of course not. You're going to start resenting me if you don't get a breather every now and then." Though I was a stranger to relationships, I understood the mechanics well enough. I made sure Gabby couldn't hear us. "You said you needed to get laid and drink blood. I can't help you with the second part, but Katrina's probably more than happy to help you relax. She gets off work at four. Go surprise her, dude."

"Best work wife ever." He drew me into a tight hug, pecking my lips just to make me blush.

"We're in public, Von," I murmured, my cheeks heating as I lingered in his arms.

"I love when you say saucy things like that. Don't you know? Embarrassing you is the high point of my day. Oh, let me slap your pert little backside in front of Gabby. Just a little pat. It's been absolutely begging for it."

I thrilled at the blatant flirt, but quickly swallowed any kind of lean toward a green light. I ducked out of his arms with a glower I pretended was sincere, though neither of us bought it. "You're dismissed. Run along, Mr. Brady."

"Oh, don't turn me on with that sexy talk." He feigned a shiver and then broke out in a handsome grin, presenting his fist to me for a quick bump of friendship. "Thanks, November. See you later tonight? Call if you need me."

I slipped into my southern accent just for kicks. "But if

you're gone, who'll I get to tie my shoes and hold my purse? What shall I do without my gentleman caller?"

"I think I should like you to only refer to me as that. Your gentleman caller. It's more dignified than 'dude'."

"You'll have to behave like a gentleman, then. It's the one catch."

"I'll stick with Mr. Brady, then." He lingered, almost as if he was reluctant to leave. He pulled me in for another hug, using the closeness to tickle my ear with his whispered, "Thanks for last night, and for not dodging me today. You're top shelf, you know."

"I'm well aware of my general awesomeness. Enjoy your day. Go have double-jointed fun." I kissed his cheek, braving public affection to make sure Von knew that he was treasured.

"You, too." He winked at me and then gave a meaningful look toward Mason, who was trying to figure out how the grocery store worked, his eyes wide at commerce in action. "He's been a good dog, but don't you think about giving him all your treats."

I shooed Von away and moved toward Gabby, who'd caught just enough of our public affection to give me a giddy grin. I shook my head and looped my arm through Mason's, who was trying his best to blend in and not rock the boat with me. He was soft-spoken, and offered me hesitant smiles as we moved through the store. My body was still moving slower than my usual let's-get-this-done speed, but Mason was never impatient, instead matching my sluggish pace. We took our time warming back up to each other, taking baby steps instead of the flying leaps we had done earlier. "Have I said I'm sorry today?" he whispered as Ollie put two bunches of bananas in the cart. I reached for seven more bunches, knowing the guys would plow through all the food in the store if I had another day like yesterday.

"Yes, and we're fine."

"How fine?" Mason asked, pushing the boundaries to see if they were still in place.

I wasn't sure how committed I was to my defenses, so I shrugged. "Fine enough to enjoy a day with you, not so fine that we'll be kissing anytime soon."

"I'll take what I can get. You and Von aren't..."

I winced. "No. Of course not. Von's my friend. My best friend these days. He's off hooking up with one of my girl-friends."

"Best thing you've said to me in weeks." Mason slipped his hand in mine, alerting the entire world to the very rela-tionshippy thing I wasn't known for.

Every time Mason did something nice, Gabby could barely hold back her squeal. "Man, I leave for a month or two, and you're serious with a new guy who's all mature." I knew she'd meant to say "old," but kept a lid on it to be polite. "Boyfriend?" she inquired to Mason.

Mason answered with a quick, "Yes" before I could respond with the truth. "We're trying it out to see how it fits," Mason told Gabby, squeezing my hand. "I'm loving it so far."

I didn't like the caged-in feeling it all gave me. "We're not serious." I huffed at Mason's squint that told me he was about to argue. He'd moved from doghouse to my bed, though I couldn't imagine why he still wanted to be there. All I did was remind him that he wasn't ready to move on from his wife, even though it seemed he still wanted to try.

Gabby motioned to our joined hands. "Um, yeah you are. I know the difference between you serious and you with Beto. You're holding hands in public! Good for you!"

"Thanks, and hush up about it," I murmured, completely embarrassed. I removed my hand from Mason's and shoved it in my pocket. My back immediately felt the ache of stiffness without his stream of pulling.

"I wasn't talking to you," Gabby said, her nose in the air. "I was talking to Mason. Good for you, man. You're the luckiest SOB in the world right now. Our girl's the best there is, even if she doesn't return phone calls." It was the third time she'd jabbed me for that, though I couldn't blame her. I hadn't even listened to my voicemails yet; I was too afraid I'd hear the warden's voice asking me to come back – or worse, him not asking.

Mason gave Gabby a modest smile and tucked my arm into the crook of his elbow. "I am pretty lucky."

Mason was lucky, Gabby was giddy, Ollie was wary and I was unsure.

34

OLLIE'S LITTLE SISTER

That night, Von snuck into my bedroom where Mason was spooning me, completely asleep. I watched as he undressed silently and in slow motion just to amuse me, doing his best impersonation of a male stripper. He pulled on pajama pants for Mason's sake and slid into the bed, trying not to wake Mason. "Thanks. I needed that. Katrina was a great stress relief," he whispered.

"Good." My eyes rolled back when Von ran his knuckles over my cheek, giving me the double dose of pulling I'd been missing. "Oh, I needed that."

"She's angry I didn't stay the night again." We both shrugged at this, knowing Von's capacity for commitment wasn't much greater than my own. "How'd things go with Fido?" he asked of my time with Mason. The whisper between us felt like kids planning the future, holy and laced with trust that bespoke of something grander than just our fort.

"It was nice. Not as nice as you and Katrina. Going slow, still pretty platonic. Feeling our way around the landmines."

"That's my girl. Good for you. The slower the better. Or, you know, the never the better." He yawned and stretched, bringing his hand back down to hold mine, ensuring I didn't scratch my scabs open while we slept. "Goodnight, darling." He leaned forward and smooched my lips, our eyes closing in sync with each other.

That night I slept soundly, wrapped in Mason's arms and holding Von's hand. With any other guys it would have felt claustrophobic, but with them it felt right. Peaceful. I didn't feel the need to conjure up Philip to come meet me in my dreams, though I had questions for my fake boyfriend aplenty.

I awoke to Mason kissing a line down the back of my neck, which incidentally, is the very best way to start your day. A knock sounded on my bedroom door, and I wondered how long the person had been trying to wake us. "October!" Ollie's whisper sounded through the door.

"Come on in," I murmured, not totally awake.

Ollie hissed, waving his hands like there was a stench in the air, his voice carrying enough to wake Von. "Get off my sister, guys. I know you have to be touching her to do your pulling thing, but this is overkill."

I refused to feel bad about the weird sleeping arrangement, since I hadn't been the one to choose any of this. "It's fine, Ollie." I sat up and stretched, smiling down at Von, who refused to wake up if at all possible. The stretch felt amazing, without a hint of the pain or stiffness I was growing accustomed to. Von wrapped his arm around my legs and snuggled his face into my hip, looking totally precious. I reached down and ran my fingers through his hair to wake him more gently.

Mason sat up next to me, yawning loudly and rubbing his stomach. "Is there breakfast, or should I go hunt up some squirrels? I'm starved."

"Do I look like your maid? Fridge is in the kitchen." Ollie was in a mood, so I knew to step lightly.

"Is everything alright, Ollie?" I asked quietly.

"Get dressed and come on out. Bev's been calling all morning. What'd you do to her?"

"Huh? Nothing. Why would you even ask that? I've been in Terraway or working Topside the whole time. The last time you saw her was the last time I saw her."

"Well, something's wrong. Normally I wouldn't care, but I picked up your phone when she called, and she was crying. Actually crying. Said if we don't come over, she's coming here." He motioned to Mason and Von. "I don't think you want her in on this freak show. I could barely understand her on the phone. We should go before we have to get to Ezra's to leave for Terraway."

I did a doubletake, blinking up at my brother. "We? Who's we? You're not coming."

Ollie reared back. "Oh, yes I am! I'm not sending you off with any number of dangerous monsters without some sort of supervision. I'm gone for barely two months, and look what's happened!" He motioned to Von and Mason as the source of his problems that particular morning.

I climbed over Von and retrieved a fresh outfit from my dresser, not willing to engage with Ollie before I'd had a shower to get myself fully awake. "Is Gabby still here?"

"No. She left just before I came in here. You know I don't usually care about Bev's latest drama, but this sounded different. She sounded scared, kid."

"Huh. Alright. We can make a stop there before Ezra's, but you're still not going. You don't know the first thing about how dangerous it is down there."

"All the more reason for me to go to keep you safe!"

"*I'm* the one who'll have to keep *you* safe. Don't you see that?" I shook my head and shut myself in the bathroom, ignoring him when he shouted through the door that we weren't finished discussing this.

Showers were one of the few times I was truly alone, so I took my time soaping myself up. I luxuriated in the scent of the shampoo I knew I wouldn't get to use again for a while. When I came out, all dressed with my damp hair in a bun atop my head, Mason's hand found mine. He drew me to his side at the kitchen table, proudly displaying the breakfast he'd made everyone.

"Oh, thanks. It looks awesome." I plated more food than I could reasonably eat, but knew I somehow had to. I was behind on the whole getting enough calories thing, and wasn't sure what kind of food we'd get our hands on when we went down to Terraway, since everyone down there lived off the *buhay* shoots.

My phone rang, but before I could tell Ollie to leave it, he answered for me. "Yeah?" His brows furrowed as he cast me a wary look. "Hey, Crayfish. Whatcha need October for?" He paused, and then handed the phone to me. "Can you two play nice?"

"Hey Darius," I said, cradling the phone with my shoulder.

"So you *can* answer the phone. I had no idea. Didn't you get my messages?" Darius' strained lightness told me he hadn't smiled in a while.

"No. I was out of town. Sorry about that. Did I miss anything important? Your brother buy a mountain and paint his face on it or something?"

"Not yet. We've got a bit of a situation here."

"What kind of a situation? I gotta tell you, if it's anything short of a unicorn parade showing up at your house, I don't really have the time for it right now."

"Bloodier than a unicorn parade. One of our guys was shot. He's... Can you come by?"

I chewed on the inside of my cheek, instantly torn and on edge. "Was it you or Judge?"

"No. We're fine. It's... You know, it's probably best you don't know his name."

I clung to my boundaries with resolve I willed myself

to feel undivided about. "I'm sorry, hun. Unless it's you, Judge, Terence, or maybe Big Mike, I'm not available."

"We can pay you."

My temper swung, as if money was the reason I wasn't running to help. "I don't need your money. I'm not coming because I don't want to be part of Judge's world. You can tell him to shoot himself in the foot if he wants me to help him out, which is basically what he does every time we talk. Hospitals are wide open. If you're still a good guy, you'll take Random Drug Dealer #27 in and get him help. I'm not interested in doing favors for a drug lord."

Von's eyebrows tented, and Ollie frowned, but thankfully didn't intervene. It bolstered my confidence that he trusted me to handle friction with the McCray brothers.

Darius handed the phone to Judge, and at the first sound of his voice, my spine straightened. "So now you're not only turning your nose up at me, you're too good for the sick people you swore to heal? Isn't that part of your nurse's oath?"

I tried to sound bored, and not like he'd poked at my sore spot. "I totally would be there in a heartbeat, but I've got plans today. I was thinking of getting my nails done. Man, if only there were emergency rooms for just such an occasion. Sorry I'm leaving you with no options, like you know, the EMT you already have on payroll." I paused at his intake of breath. "That's right; I know things."

"I don't want our EMT. You're closer. I need your help."

"Wow. You uttered the word 'need'. That had to be painful. Might want to sit down."

"October," he warned me, his velvety timbre turning sharp.

I let out a gust of feigned boredom, though my insides were twisting at turning my back on someone who was injured. "You should probably let your man bleed out while we go back and forth."

Judge sighed, and I could tell he hadn't gone to sleep. "Fine. I'll call the doc. You've turned cold, baby girl. I don't like it."

"You raised me. You break it, you bought it." My voice lowered, and I loathed that I had a weakness for this sort of thing. "Put pressure on the wound and get him to the emergency room right now, Judge. I mean it. And don't call with stuff like this again. I'll help family, not criminals. Call me next time someone shoots you in the head for being a jerk. Then I'll come running with Band-Aids and whatnot." I hung up before Judge could eke out another word that would break my heart. "I'm just going to kill him."

"Easy, now. Tell me where he lives. I'll take care of him for you," Mason offered as Ollie handed the phone back to me.

"He lives on his own planet of subjective morality. It's fine. Just annoying. And insulting, come to think of it."

I started eating, sitting in between Mason and Von with Mason's hand on my back and Von's leg looped over mine so our thighs touched. Ollie looked over our arrangement with a frown he didn't bother hiding. "This is dysfunctional. How long does this last?"

I swallowed my bite of food along with the lump in my throat. "We're doing the whole thing with the sagrado stone so Mariang and I don't have to reap so much. Right now we have to do seven souls a day between us. After the stone business is handled? We can do one a day total, and that's that. I don't guess I'll need both Pullers then, but I don't really know. That's all down the road."

Mason and Von both chewed more slowly. "We'll always be your Reapers, Peach. Our threesome just means that Mason or I can take a week off here and there, and it's fine. That's after the stone's in place, of course."

Mason squeezed my shoulder, trying to communicate something to me I needed actual words for. But all he said was, "We should put more food in our packs this time."

I ignored the waves of impending complications, hoping they would resolve themselves before I had to deal with them. I would've thought they would be relieved not to be chained to my side until their dying breaths, but they both looked like I'd told them they were ugly.

We finished breakfast enough for twenty people and packed up the car. I tried to take Ollie's backpack out of the trunk, but he was resolute. "I'm coming with you. Don't you dare try to fight me on this." He held onto my shoulders, making sure I was looking right at him. "Before any of this, it was you, me and Allie. Now it's you and me, alright? No matter what, I'm in this as long as you are. Where you go, I go."

"What are you, her father?" Von asked, shooting off at the mouth and shooting himself in the foot.

Ollie straightened, pulling the keys out of his pocket. He had the only other key to Terence, which spoke worlds of the absolute trust we had in each other. "Yeah, that's right. I'm her father. *I'm* her brother. I'm her mother. I'm her doctor. I'm her teacher. I'm her mechanic. I was the Easter Bunny, the Tooth Fairy, Santa Claus and anything else she needed to get to where she is today. I won't leave her for you two to look after."

I tilted my head down. "Ollie, I'm all grown up now. It's okay to let go. I'll come back home to you."

He stared at me and then jerked me into a tight hug that told me exactly how scared he was for me. "You have no idea the things that went through my head when you missed your check-in. I'm not going to worry like that again. No. It's you and me, and we're not going out any other way. I worked too hard to keep you alive to get careless now. I already lost Allie. I'm not losing you!"

I wrapped my arms around Ollie, grateful that the guys got in the car to give us a moment. "Hey, it's alright. Okay. If you want to come along, you can take it up with Ezra. You're not losing me. I'm just going on a little camping trip. Nothing as fun as ours used to be, but it'll have to do."

Ollie let out a one-noted laugh filled with too many

nerves. "You think they'll tell ghost stories and make up fake constellations that look like butts?"

"If you're there, yeah. You make everything better." Then it dawned on me that I'd consented without meaning to. "You're really coming?" I tried to swallow my dread and focus on the positives. "That might be fun. I've missed you so much. The phone's not the same."

Ollie squeezed me tight, and I began to realize that he needed me as much as I needed him. "Oh, kid. You have no idea."

35

SHOCK AND ALL THE SPECIAL THINGS

Of all the things I wished for, visiting Bev's trailer before going to Terraway wasn't on my list. Ezra called on the way and said he was going to meet us there so he could surprise Bev and see her place for the first time. Needless to say, I had a strong desire to shred through the backs of my hands. Mason held my left hand in the backseat while Von held my right wrist. Ollie wasn't a fan of all the hovering they did, but after several reminders, he understood it was all just part of the job. "You can really get her to stop scratching her hands?" he asked as he turned the car onto Bev's street.

My anxiety rose more than the normal throat-choke because Ollie was there. I knew they would fight; they always did. I could rely on Bev saying something mean to me that I had to pretend I didn't hear. I only wish there weren't witnesses to the hurricane we were about to walk into. Mason had already seen my childhood home, but Von had only heard stories. "Maybe just Ollie and I should go in. I mean, it'll be so boring inside."

Mason squeezed my hand. "I can feel your anxiety shooting through the roof. It's okay. I've seen it all before, remember?"

"I don't want to do this!" I squeezed out, my voice threatening to lock down.

Ollie parked the car and turned in his seat, giving me his most serious business face. "Hey, we've got nothing to be ashamed of. This place isn't us. This trailer has nothing to do with who we are. It's a pile of garbage, and nothing more." He paused, making sure I was paying attention. "Are you a pile of garbage?"

I swallowed, imprinting his words in my mind. "No, Ollie."

He snapped his fingers twice to make sure I wasn't drifting off in my mind. I was never thrilled when he did that, though it was effective. "That's right. You're *my* kid, not hers. You've got a degree, a house, friends, no debt—"

I held up my hands. "I get it. I don't need the pep talk. I just don't want them to... Guys, could you wait here? We'll be in and out."

Ollie shook his head in time with Mason. "No. They're in your life. This is the pit of it. If they're supposed to know everything about you to keep you safe or whatever, they need to know about Bev. They need to see how dangerous she is if she's given an inch."

My eyebrows furrowed when Ezra's sleek black car saddled up next to ours. "Fine. Whatever. Let's get this over with." I pointed my finger in Ollie's face. "For the record, there's no forgiveness for what we're doing."

"We're saving Ezra! I thought you liked him."

"I do, but we're ruining Bev. Like it or not, she's your mama. You're supposed to protect your family."

"Never once has she protected you. Don't stick up for her. I'm telling you, I can't take it today."

"She's sick, Ollie. We're not. We know better; she doesn't. Big difference. We're taking someone good away from a sick woman."

Ollie's voice lowered. "She deserves what she gets for being the way she is."

I paused before taking Mason's offered hand after he slid out of the car. My voice was quiet, which to Ollie was worse than me yelling. "You raised me better than that. Better than payback. No matter what, she's still our mama."

Ollie opened his mouth to argue, but closed it again, slumping in his seat. "You can be right about that, but this is still necessary."

Mason took my hand and helped me out of the car, saying nothing of my trembling fingers. "We're right here," he assured me.

For some reason, that only made me feel worse. "Hold on a second." I turned back and slid into the car again after Ollie got out, shutting myself with Von in the backseat.

"It'll be fine, Peach. Really. Your mum loved me the time we met, and she'll get used to Mason's surly mug in time."

"It's not that. You know how you didn't want people to find out all that awful stuff Prince Julius made you do to pay off Boston's gambling debts in Dagat?"

Von's expression darkened as he ducked to make sure our conversation had no chance of being overheard. "I thought we agreed we didn't need to talk about that anymore unless *I* brought it up."

"I know, and I'm not talking about it really." I motioned to the trailer. "This is my secret shame. This is everything that's wrong with me, and I don't want you to see it."

Von softened, his shoulders lowering and his head tilting to the side. "*Hani*, I promise I won't think less of you. Mason told me everything; it's Bev's dysfunction, not yours."

"But it *is* my dysfunction! How would you feel if someone forced you to talk about all you had to go through? You *chose* to tell me that stuff. Aren't you glad you had that choice?" Von looked up at the ceiling to avoid my pleading eyes. "Please, Von. Just wait in the car for this. I'm begging you. I'd send Mason back, too, but he's already seen it, and I know y'all won't be thrilled with me going anywhere by myself this late in the game. Please just let me have this one thing."

"What are you afraid of?"

"Other than tetanus? I'm afraid you'll take one look at

my childhood and think that's who I am! I'm afraid you'll think I'm garbage and you'll throw me away, and that would kill me. Everyone else can, but not you. I need for just you to not look at me like I'm garbage."

"I would never." He cupped my face so my vision was filled with his sincere pledge. "You told me I'm your treasure? You're mine, darling. My shiny, strong and beautiful treasure. Nothing in that trailer could change that."

I closed my eyes, lest I look at him for one more second and burst into tears. "Please, Von. Please give me this one thing."

Von let out a long and loud gust of air through pursed lips, bathing my face in cigars and mint. "If it's that big a deal to you, I get it. I can wait out here." I thought he would drop his hands, but he cupped my chin with a gentle, stern grip so he could look into my eyes that jerked open. "But listen good, sweet Peach. We're in this for the long haul. At some point you're going to have to let me in more than this. I think I've earned the right to at least be let in through the front door."

It was hard to talk when I couldn't move my chin, but I managed. "Bev's front door doesn't open all the way." I shrugged, offering him a weak smile. "That was a little metaphor joke."

"Clever little college girl." He brought my face forward and smooched my lips. "Go on. I'll wait here like the good dog I am."

"Thanks, Von. You're my best friend, you know."

"Tell it to the backseat I'm stuck in. Hurry up. Ezra's looking impatient. Gets downright unpleasant when he's anxious. Starts saying "No, thank you,' instead of 'No, thank you, kind woman.' Surly git."

I got out and shut Von in the car, breathing fifteen percent easier now there was one less person surprising Bev. I went to the trunk and pulled out gloves for everyone and a brave smile that looked more like a grimace of pain than actual happiness.

I waved at Sandy when he came into view, but my dog ran away from me, which was unusual. The pit bull next door loved me, and had never acted afraid of anything. I could tell he didn't like the look of Ezra or Mason. I blew him a kiss and let him have his space, though I wished for his sloppy kisses right now more than anything.

"You ready for it?" Ollie asked me, not caring how Ezra and Mason felt about the whole thing.

"Do it to it," I replied, hunching my shoulders and moving to the trailer that groaned with too much emotional and physical baggage. "I'm sorry," I whispered to Ezra. "I really did like you."

Ezra was in nice gray dress pants that looked too expensive to be worn by a real person, brown leather shoes, a brown belt and a crisp blue dress shirt with thin white pinstripes. "I won't desert you," he promised, though I doubted how accurate this vow would be after he saw the woman he loved as she truly was.

I paused at the door, swearing under my breath about

thirty times before banging my fist to the flimsy glass pane. I knocked four times before I heard a cry coming from inside the trailer. It wasn't a cry of distress, but more a moan of pure loss. "Bev? You okay?" I opened the door, expecting to only be able to force it the usual one and a half feet open so I could slip inside. I was shocked and confused when the door opened all the way.

My eyes intended to do a quick sweep of what used to be a living room, but my gaze froze when the mountains of garbage, trinkets, broken toys, clothes and rotting food only amounted to mere hills of crap. The narrow passageway lined with stacks of newspaper, towels and brown things that didn't use to be brown was now wider, and would allow even Mason to walk through to Bev's bedroom near the back of the trailer.

I covered my mouth and let out a muffled shriek. "Bev? Bev!" I faintly heard her crying inside, but couldn't see her. If what looked to be a third of her treasures were gone, I couldn't imagine her mental state. "Ollie, she's been robbed! Bev, hold tight! I'm here! I'm coming! I'm so sorry, Bev! I shouldn't have stopped coming by for our weekly visits. This is all my fault! Are you hurt?"

"No, October! You'll wait outside." Ollie insisted, letting Mason pull me out of the house so Ollie could step inside. His hand went over his mouth to muffle his outcry, as well. Though Ollie hadn't been home in years, the drastic change was not lost on him. "If she really has been robbed, they could still be in here. Get October away from the trailer, Mason!"

I whirled on Mason, jerking my arm from his grip. "Don't you dare 'tiny little woman' me. I used to fight inmates before you came along. That's my mama in there!"

"Give us a minute," Ezra said, his hand on my shoulder. Ezra followed in behind Ollie, grimacing at the stench you couldn't quite put your finger on, but it was a swirling aroma of animal feces, tuna and mold. You know, the stench of child-hood. "Ho! What's happened here? Burglars did this?" Ezra ran back out, his eyes watering. He drew in semi-clean air as if the trailer park was the sweetest thing he'd ever smelled.

I gotta tell you, it's not.

"No. Robbers cleaned it. Let me through." I shook off Mason and bolted into the house after Ollie. "Bev! I'm here. Come on out. I know you must be mad, but I promise you, Ollie and I didn't do this." I kept my arms up just in case she flew out at me and aimed for my face. "I would never steal your treasures, Bev."

Ollie waved me over, a dark look of powering through clouding his features. "What did they do to you? Did you see their faces? We'll file a report first thing."

I moved slowly to Ollie's side, gasping at Bev's besotted state. I'd never seen her with no makeup, but there she was – tearstains down her face, old sweats I'd never seen her in before and wreaking of rum. She was drunk, her pupils unfocused and her hand slow as she reached for Ollie from the floor. She'd built herself a fort out of folded towels – some new and some too old and disgusting to be anything but fodder for rats' nests. Her blonde hair hadn't been combed in days, and she smelled like... Well, I could smell her beneath the stench of the rotting trailer and the booze, which was saying something.

"Did I do this?" Bev asked, clutching the bottle of rum like it was a precious puppy. "Was it all real?"

Ollie fought hard to keep his fight face intact. We'd never seen Bev with a hair out of place. In the land of refuse, she was the perfect Barbie doll who stood tall and much, much too proud. "Let's get you some fresh air," Ollie offered. I was surprised he was being so civil. He was gentle as he lifted her off the floor, pausing when she cried out.

"My foot! I stepped in some glass yesterday, and I can't get it all out of my foot!" Her cries brought Ezra back inside to brave the elements, though he was too stunned to make it past the entrance.

It was then I noticed Bev wasn't wearing shoes – a serious no-no inside the trailer. "Oh! You're bleeding! What happened?"

Her cheery pink sock was stained through with a thick puff of blood. She cried harder as she leaned on Ollie. "I woke up a few days ago and saw the trailer like this, so I started cleaning. Throwing things out." She sobbed loudly. "The things I did to you both! Why would you ever come back here? I'm sorry! I'm so sorry! I'm a horrible person!"

Ollie reared back as if he'd slapped her. Bev's apology hit me like a crack across the face with her leather belt she'd gotten on sale for $9.99. The apology was shocking and somehow hurtful, though I couldn't pinpoint why.

Ollie held up his hands slowly after Bev was able to balance on one leg. "Alright. Um, I don't know what to do with that, so let's start with the basics. How'd you hurt yourself?"

Bev's pink face pulled with what actually looked like self-loathing. I'd never seen her do that emotion, so I couldn't be sure. "I stepped on a broken bottle and cut my foot. I haven't been able to get up, and I can't find the charger for my phone! I called you!" she accused, and then turned mournful again. "I called you, October Grace, but you didn't come! You shouldn't have come. I can't believe you came! I'm horrible! I'm a monster!"

"I'm sorry, Bev. I was out of town. Let's get you out of here." I positioned myself at her side, looping her arm around my shoulders while Ollie took her other arm.

She cleaned. She threw things out. She actually did it. I didn't make for a good crutch, since I was shaking so badly. Years were spent begging her to let us clean just inches of the trailer so we could use the bathroom in our own home, but it was met with furious beatings and hurtful words that sizzled as they cut.

Bev threw things out. Bev apologized.

It made no sense.

We rounded the corner of takeout boxes filled with

cockroaches, maggots and viscous slime, giving Ezra a full view of his bride to be in all her glory. "No!" Bev screeched in agony, her worst fear realized. Her wail almost brought tears to my eyes, but I'd promised myself long ago that I would never again cry in front of Bev. "No! You can't be here! Go away! Get out! This isn't me! It's not me!" Her pain tore at what was left of my heart.

Ezra was lost until she verbally pushed him away. Then he found his purpose, directing his fiery gaze at her disheveled state. "I told you I loved you. A little mess doesn't change that." He barreled toward us, and before I could warn him to be careful of the floor that wasn't all that solid in parts, he scooped Bev up in his arms, carrying her like a bride over the threshold, and out of my walking nightmare.

36

BRUCE CAMPBELL ISN'T REAL

I didn't know what to do, think or feel. All I knew was that Ezra sped Bev to the emergency room, with Ollie driving us right behind him. The check-in was quick, the doctor less frazzled than we all were, and they started treating her foot and the shock she seemed to be steeped in.

Bev wailed semi-coherently the same story over and over – that she woke up one morning a few days ago and discovered all the wrong she'd done with her life. It would've been any cast-aside child's dream come true, only I couldn't feel anything. I was numb, my arms banded around my stomach as Von and I waited in the hallway. Ezra and Ollie stayed with her through the doctor's examination while Mason made himself useful as a Duwende, pulling the stress from Ollie, Bev and Ezra when necessary so they could focus on the matter at hand.

"Okay, you have to stop rocking like that. It's demented, darling." Von rubbed my back, but the pulling he did was only a fraction of what I needed.

I hadn't realized I was rocking back and forth, but the second he mentioned it, I saw the depths of my twisted gut. "She said she was sorry to me," I muttered quietly, as if uttering the words too loud would make the faulty floor beneath them drop out and expose the lie in the apology. "Bev doesn't apologize."

"She looked pretty turned about. Not how I remember her at dinner when they got engaged."

"I've never seen her like this. And why did she look scared? It was like she didn't know how any of the stuff got there. I'm worried, Von. Seriously. Every piece of crap in that trailer was her life. She beat me something awful on my fifth birthday because she brought home a dollhouse, and I started playing with it. I thought she'd brought it home for me." I blinked twice, not seeing anything except that awful day. I could still feel my little heart pounding as I ran through the trailer, trying to escape her while Ollie and Allie were at work. I shouted apologies and begged for her to stop, but I'd broken Bev's rule – don't touch her special things.

"You're exaggerating."

I stared at Von, confused. "When have I ever exaggerated?"

"Fair point. But there's got to be more to the story than that."

"Sure. She bought herself a dollhouse on *my* birthday, and got me nothing. We're not allowed to touch Bev's special things, and I touched the dollhouse, thinking she'd gotten it for me. I didn't realize she was taunting me at the time, but I learned. My fifth birthday was the first time I tasted my own blood in my mouth. That's the whole story. Never an apology or even a flicker of regret."

Von's hand stilled on my back. "I wish you were exaggerating."

I swallowed, and because only Von was there to hear it, I confessed the crux of my dysfunction. "I was never Bev's special thing."

Von didn't say anything at first. He simply laced his fingers through mine and brought me closer to his side, kissing my temple. Then quietly, he whispered, "You're my special thing. My very own glittering treasure." He squeezed my fingers and chuckled. "Yeah, that was dorky."

"I like dorky."

The hollow, scared look in Bev's eyes haunted me. It was like she was an entirely different person who woke up and discovered she'd been walking around in a foreign body. My skin was itchy all over, so I scratched my stomach and my arms with long rakes over my skin. I moved slowly enough that I hoped Von didn't see. I couldn't force the universe to make sense. Even after all the half-horse, half-fish, half-vampire, half-wolf people I'd met, Bev's whole new personality scared me the most.

My gut tugged in the direction of a man being wheeled

past us by a nurse. "Let's get some work done. I need a distraction."

"Really? You sure? Mason isn't here."

"Mariang only has Danny, and they hold up just fine. You up for it?" It didn't really matter if he was; I couldn't sit and wait anymore.

"I guess so. You're sure, love? I mean, maybe we should wait on your mum to see what's what."

"Look, the only logical explanation is alien inhabitation, and I just can't handle one more bit of magic right now. Let's do some reaping. See how far that gets us."

"Alright, but just one or two, yeah? I don't want you wiped out before our trek."

Something about this grated on my nerves, but I couldn't get a proper read on my emotions to know if I was overreacting or not. It was sweet that he cared, but it felt like paternal scolding, and I hadn't needed a father since birth. I walked toward the man in the wheelchair, noticing his yellowed skin that sagged unnaturally in parts. My fingers brushed against his, and I felt his tired soul leap into me, sending out an electric chill I wasn't sure I'd ever get used to.

Von jogged to catch up, surprised I was already on the hunt. His arm snaked around my waist, pulling the soul from me. He pressed his chest to my spine, warming me from the inside and the outside. His lips parted and attached to the nape of my neck. I shivered as he exhaled hot air right where I needed to feel it. His biceps flexed, holding me tight as his black "You Thought You Knew" t-shirt stretched across his taut muscles. "Slow down, Mrs. Brady. I didn't realize you were already going."

"I need to not feel this. Bev's face? I don't know what to do with that. Maybe the cold will numb it." Though Von felt like the best warm blanket in the world, I squirmed out of his grip. I was too comfortable, which made it too easy to break down. I couldn't have that. "Not now. It's too much," I explained of the distance I was determined to put between us. I didn't look back at his confusion, but let my gut pull me forward. We were in the ER, so there was no shortage of reapable bodies.

I walked toward a man with a loud hacking cough that had a rattling wet rasp when he breathed in. He was in his mid-fifties, and would never know what the swinging sixties might feel like. I didn't even bother with a preamble. I just walked straight up to him in the waiting room and clasped him on the shoulder, not even offering a kind smile to get him through his last day on earth.

Von reaped the soul by looping his arm around my shoulder as if we were old pals, which I guess we kind of were. That day I felt like a sinking ship, though, and didn't want anyone to go down with me. "Okay, that's two. That's enough for today. You're still on the mend, darling."

"I told you, I'm fine." I cast him a look that told him I was in no mood. "And if you could not call me 'darling' in public, I'd appreciate it." *I'd already said as much in the grocery store, but whatever.*

"You have to put a dollar in the jar," he reminded me of our game in which I lived in denial, and he refused to let me. I friggin' hated that game.

"Bill me." I stalked off toward the entrance, where an elderly woman was being wheeled in by what I assumed was her daughter. They had on hand-knitted cardigans in two different colors and their hair was up in matching buns. I don't know why the sight made me unbearably sad, but I was in no mood to be patient while the melancholy of a life filled with motherly love I would never know passed by me. I skipped over the gloom and went straight to pissed. It was the wrong moment for Von to hold my hand. I shook off his grip and glared at him. Before I could stop myself, I spewed venom meant for my childhood in his direction. "Would you give me some space? Jeez! You're not my boyfriend!"

Von reared back, the initial slap of hurt confusing him. Then a wash of anger slid over his features, turning him from my favorite flirty pal to a man I didn't recognize. "Oh, really? How sad. I was just begging for the job. And make no mistake, you are the job."

I knew I'd crossed the line, but Von was dancing clear over it. "Shut up, Von. You're just being a jag because I was short with you. I get it. I shouldn't have snapped like that."

"I love that you think I have nothing better to do than follow you about, like I'm your groupie." He donned a girly voice and clapped his hands together with sarcastic glee. "October Grace, what shall we do today? Oh, you want to work till you drop again? How fun! It doesn't affect me at all. In fact, I'm so slit-my-wrists in love with you that I don't mind that I'm starving. Looking at your pretty face is enough to sustain me." He narrowed his eyes and threw his hands in the air. "Think about Mason and me for a change! Don't just go off reaping, thinking it's only you who's affected."

I took a breath, knowing I'd been the one who set us on this downward path. I held up my hands in surrender. "Look, I'm sorry, okay? I was being a jerk. It's barely noon, and it's already been a long day."

"I'm so glad you set me straight that I'm not your boyfriend. I think I'll have a good old cry tonight on my pillow about the virgin queen who turned me down." He cried dramatically into his palms. "October Grace doesn't want to be my girlfriend! What'll my mates on the playground say?" He pulled out his half-smoked cigar and unwrapped it, lighting the thing smack in the middle of the ER.

"You're being a brat. Do you even need me here for this part, or can you scrounge up your own audience? I said I was sorry."

"The only thing I need you for is a good pair to look at before I go to sleep." His eyes flicked down to my breasts, and for all his bravado, I could see the regret behind it all as he dove into the muck headfirst.

I held his gaze when it sheepishly climbed back up to my face. I tried to build up a steel wall against the hurt he was trying to deflect onto me. "That's how it is? This is who you really are? You're the perv who's in it for my boobs? I must say, well done fooling me. Really had me going there."

"Give me an hour in the sack, and I'll show you everything you need to know about me, baby." He took a puff and blew the smoke in my face, ignoring the nurse who scolded him and told him to take his cigar outside. "You let Mason use you easy enough. It's time I won the coin toss. For no other reason than curiosity, of course. I've never actually been with a real, live virgin before. Most virgins are like, seventeen. You get to be their queen at the ripe old age of twenty-two."

The sting cut me worse than a scalpel, slicing through the tender parts I'd trusted Von with. I knew he regretted it; I could see remorse stinging his features. I didn't know why he was lashing out so cruelly. I tilted my head up at him, my arms banding around my stomach. My words were quiet, not wanting a public scene through one of the top ten worst conversations of the year. "You never really loved me, did you?" I needed it confirmed. I needed him to tell me that I was young and foolish. That I'd trusted in rainbows when I shouldn't have. I needed him to tell me that the Brady Bunch wasn't real, and neither were we.

I needed to know he wasn't Bruce Campbell, and that Santa Claus didn't exist.

Von responded coolly by exhaling a puff of smoke in my face. "I'm not your boyfriend."

"And I guess I'm not your special thing. I was short with you one time, and this is what I get for it." A rock sunk in my gut as Von made his way on the list of people I vowed to never cry in front of again. "You're not Bruce Campbell." I wasn't mad at him; I was disappointed in myself for falling for it all. "You're not Mr. Brady."

"I'm not your boyfriend," Von repeated, as if the very idea was laughable.

"Tell me I'm a kid." I wanted to hear him say that's all I'd ever been. I stared at my shoes and waited for the gavel to fall.

"You're just a kid. Katrina, on the other hand, she's all woman. Nothing childish about her." He blew smoke in my face, but I refused to cough or wave it away. I inhaled the stink, letting it chase away the childish delusions I'd entertained that Von had ever loved me, and that I'd finally been somebody's treasure.

I don't know how I'd been so had by Von. Maybe it was his British accent that made everything sound more beautiful than it actually was. Maybe it was the flirty way he gave me little nicknames. I felt sick to my stomach, and like I was the butt of a joke when I'd been thinking I was precious to someone wonderful. Turns out, I wasn't precious at all, and Von wasn't wonderful. I wasn't Von's special thing. He could throw me away at the first sign of me being a little bit broken on a bad day. "Okay, Von. I'm going to go get some air. I'll try to stay out of your space."

I forgot about the old lady on the brink of death and

marched out of the ER, leaving Bev with Ezra, and just plain leaving Von. I was shaking with regret and self-loathing, and wished my Omen abilities gave me some sort of lightning bolt powers that could zap at will. On second thought, perhaps that wasn't the best superpower for me at the moment.

There had to be a bus stop along the main road, so I made my way up toward the grass and over-trimmed shrubs that framed the forty-five mile an hour street. I could've called Ollie, but something about calling one guy to save me from another guy felt off to me. There was too much building up inside of me. Too much wear and tear to shake it all off unscathed. I wanted to go home where I felt safe, but that would be the first place they'd look for me. I wanted actual space. A whole continent of it.

Maybe even a whole world of it.

I slid my phone out of my pocket and dialed up Danny, putting on a cheery voice that didn't match my heart-broken features. "Hey, Danny. Could you put Finn on the phone? He left something at my house."

I was leaving the mess right where it was. I wouldn't try to fix what was clearly meant to be broken. I was getting out, and Finn was the one who didn't give a rip about me. He'd let me risk my life to get the job done, and I was in a mood to be reckless.

37

OCTOBER GRACE, OUT

"Tell me again why we can't wait for Ezra, or at the very least, your Reapers?"

I huffed, already frustrated it had taken Finn so long to figure out how to use the bus system to get to me. An hour had passed after I'd hightailed it to the parking lot and stolen my rock and my pack from Ezra's trunk. The sagrado backpack was fitted tight to me to ensure no one ganked it. "Do you want the job done or not? I thought you cared about getting the stone to Terraway."

"I do, but I don't want to be known for kidnapping the only useful Omen. You can see how Ezra might not look the other way on that."

"Since when are you afraid of Ezra?"

Finn raised an eyebrow at my urgency. He fingered his green silk scarf that wrapped around the neck of his collared gray dress shirt. "Fear of war is a healthy one, *kendi*."

"Then let's do this and come back before we get caught."

"It's a three-day trek to the central city of Silo, and you're not used to our climate."

"All I need is that *baga* root that helps me breathe. Can you get that right quick when we get down there?"

"I can. But why? Why not wait for everyone? Kabayo at least will want to be there to guide us."

"No time. Let's just do this."

Finn tsked, shaking his head to scold me. "My, my. Such deception. I knew I liked you."

"I'm jumping for joy on the inside. Take me down there quick. I don't want the others to find us."

"Alright. If you insist. I admit, I never thought you'd ask me to run away with you."

I crossed my arms over my stomach, scratching at my skin and wishing for the whole thing to be over so I could escape the world that had taken over my life. "Just do it, dude."

The corner of Finn's mouth curved upward, and I began to doubt the awesomeness of my grand escape plan. "Yes, milady." He reached out and placed his hands on my shoulders, closing his eyes as he murmured a string of nonsense syllables.

It was too late for regret. There wasn't time to turn

back. I closed my eyes and let myself vanish from the earth, hoping Terraway would be kind enough to let me hide in its depths for a while.

Love the book? Leave a review!

38

TEMPT

Enjoy a free preview from *Tempt*
book four in the *Terraway* series

I was grateful when Finn let companionable silence fall between us to replace our bickering. When I looked back in the direction we'd come, I couldn't even see the circle we'd entered in on anymore. Everything was brown, brown and more brown, so landmarks that stood out were hard to come by. The famine had struck Silo in the usual way, scorching the *buhay* shoots so there was precious little for the inhabitants to eat. It also hit them in the form of a drought, drying up most of their rivers and leaving the landscape dull, dusty and bare.

The suns were setting, and we'd put a fair amount of distance between us and the entrance to Silo. With my backpack stuffed with half a dozen *baga* roots Finn had unearthed not two minutes after he'd ported us to Terraway, I was ready to get a piece of the sagrado stone to its rightful place. If we dropped a portion of the rock into the well in the main city, the suns wouldn't burn so hot, and nature would have a chance to right itself again.

I'd left my two Reapers, my brother, Ezra and a bucket full of baggage Topside when I'd made the decision to go rogue and start the mission to deliver the sagrado stone without the crew. I needed space, and they needed to breathe. A whole new world of breathing room seemed like the right move. Since Captain Finn didn't care much for rules or waiting around while the nations continued to wither away, I brought him along to be my guide.

We passed a few houses here and there that looked like thatched-roof barns, but mostly we kept to the woods, so we would go unnoticed as long as we could. The trees were dry with only crusty, shriveled leaves that held on for dear life. I looked around at the nothing all around us. There weren't even any houses anymore after we'd travelled by those first few. Just brown, dusty mountains spread out, and cavernous craters where I'm guessing water used to be. It was like walking by mini Grand Canyons everywhere.

Maybe I could deliver the stone before the guys even noticed I was gone. Hopefully they'd think I wanted to be alone at home, and would go back to the mansion for a few days. Von wouldn't look for me; he'd slung some mud in a nasty fight I knew he wouldn't take back. And Mason? Well, we were actually doing alright, but hopefully he'd have his hands full cleaning out Bev's trailer with Ollie.

Bev. I couldn't go there in my mind. Her lost expression when we'd found her in a state of shock in her trailer haunted me, and made me feel like a shell of who I was supposed to be. I'd always firmly believed in taking care of your family, but I was left spinning on this one. I needed more information, but knew I couldn't handle another word, be it apology or raging blame.

"It's quiet," Finn observed, scratching his gills. He'd discarded his scarf and dress clothes into his backpack, changing into the black soldier-wear that was common in Terraway. He'd chuckled at me when I'd turned around so I didn't have to see him half naked. He craned his neck to look down at me while we walked. "You're quiet."

"You're tall," I offered back my own observation. "Talk away, if that helps you."

"You want to tell me why you ran from your Pullers and Ezra?"

"Nope." A bat flew overhead, its wonky flight path catching my eye.

Finn studied me curiously. The growing darkness was starting to fall around us as the horizon began to swallow up the setting suns. "You're usually annoyingly chatty."

I shrugged in response, unsure how to tell him to butt out, other than the obvious obnoxious way. "I guess it's your turn for that now. Don't know what to tell you. It's your lucky day. No annoying chatter from October. Santa Claus does exist."

Finn squinted in warning at the bat that came back to circle us. The creature responded to his silent threat, flying in the opposite direction. "Sylvia. She sends out bats to be her eyes and ears."

"Did she make us?"

Finn quirked his eyebrow at me. "She's probably looking for her own people, to make sure they're not lurking where they shouldn't. This is Kabayo's land, and there've been too many skirmishes for them to be welcome here right now."

"Should we be out in the open like this? Is she going to report back to Ezra that she saw us?"

"Her spy doesn't know to look for us, I'm guessing, so there's nothing to report. You're awfully skittish about Ezra finding out. Tell me, what did you do that you're running from him?"

"Nothing at all." My eyes tracked the bat who flew off into the distance. "How worried do we need to be about monsters trying to ambush us?" I voiced the concern I'd felt for a while.

Finn quickened our pace. It took two of my steps to equal one of his long strides. "Not very. The Ekeks and

Manas will be expecting you to travel in an entourage. Smart thinking to keep it just us."

"I daresay that sounded almost like a compliment."

"Well, it almost was." Though Finn had been a little harsh, in control and kind of sleazy when we were Topside, he seemed to be taking his post seriously. It was just the two of us on this mission, and we were both determined not to screw it up.

Finn cleared his throat next to me. "I don't spend much time Topside. What do you think of our world so far?"

My thumbs looped in the straps on my backpack, pulling them like suspenders. "I don't think I can judge it just yet. The only times I've been in Terraway have been with the suns all wonky and the government trying to abduct me. So, I guess that's a thumb's down so far."

He chuckled at my assessment. "Silo has been suffering a drought for too many years. Occasionally the morning brings enough dew to keep things going, but they've had to borrow more water from us than they can ever afford to pay back."

"Yikes. How do they buy it? Like, do you all have the same currency? I can't tell how separate the different countries are."

"Gold is the universal language we all speak. Goods, women. The usual."

"Not for nothing, but don't let anyone trade me for a cup of water." I shivered, despite the heat that made my clothes cling to my skin. "Let's just do this and get back home."

"You wouldn't be attractive to Tikbalangs." Then to clarify, he added, "Horse on top, person on the bottom half. And I can promise you that my king has all the women he could ever possibly need." His eyes flickered to me. "Though if you ever meet King Banak, you may want to keep your head down. He has a thing for mouthy women with legs."

My eyebrows furrowed as I tried to keep Finn's pace. "Your king likes women who have legs and mouths? I can't imagine I'd be all that rare if he's casting that wide a net."

"You forget the women in Dagat are Mermaids. No legs. And they know better than to talk back. Something tells me you wouldn't fall in line so easily. Everyone has a healthy fear of our king because he has me to carry out his dirty work. They all know I'm bewitched to carry out his will," he said bitterly. King Banak wanted Finn to watch me to make sure I was performing up to par, which was why he'd been Topside in the first place.

Finn informed me that he had also been instructed to keep an eye on me to make sure I wasn't some giant walking danger. I'd kind of accidentally murdered off an entire species – taking Goblins clear off the map in a single terrifying blow. I couldn't really blame this Banak guy for wanting me observed. "No, we don't get many mouthy ones anymore in Dagat. They know better than to cross me."

"Because you're a big, scary man?" I teased with half a grin.

"Oh, *kendi*. I love when you toy with me in that sexy, coy way you do. It'll make your fear that much sweeter when you see me in my element and off Ezra's leash. I bet you're a beauty when you're terrified."

"You know, I think you try to sound sleazy out of habit. I don't think you really care all that much about hooking anyone, least of all me. But it's nice of you to pretend, I guess."

Finn quirked an eyebrow at me, confused that I wasn't shirking away from his fat mouth. "Nice? I think that's the first time I've been called that. Perhaps I should be offended."

"Oh, sweetie. My nickname was Jailbait. I treated men in a prison for a paycheck. If I cared about intimidation tactics or sex jokes, I wouldn't have a leg to stand on. Fire away. I really don't care. If you need to be big and scary, I'll play along once the stone's delivered. Until then, I've got too much on my mind to pretend I'm afraid of you."

Finn looked down at me as if I was the strangest animal. "I don't know what to say to that."

"Well, that's good. I'm not really paying attention anyway."

Finn let out a loud, guttural laugh that looked so foreign on him, it confused us both. We walked along the forest's edge toward the village in the distance with decidedly less tension between us. I kept looking over my shoulder to make sure my Reapers hadn't found us. They were probably still on regular earth and hadn't even noticed I'd split.

Finn followed my gaze back toward the direction where we'd entered. "They're not here yet. We've got a decent head start," Finn informed me. "You're running from them, aren't you? That can't be good. Ezra's got a mean streak he doesn't often use, but it's there."

"He's preoccupied. And I don't much care if Ezra's mad at me, no more than he cares when I'm pissed at him. But yeah, I'm running. Needed a break. Having two Reapers is intense. Going from living alone to sharing my house with two grown men who don't know how to wash a dish? It's not the easiest thing for me to adjust to."

"It's more than that. You're not stupid enough to defy Ezra over dirty dishes."

I tilted my head up at him. "Do you care why? I thought you wanted the stone delivered. This is the quickest way. I'm not doing any reaping down here, so I don't need them to do any pulling. They could use some time off from the job." *And I am the job*, I reminded myself of Von's harsh parting words.

"Fine by me. Just know that I'm not Duwende. I can't pull from you, so if you see a dead body that might have a lick of human in it, stay away."

"Roger that. I only need you as a guide. If I had a map, I could've done this on my own just fine."

"You say that now. Wait until we get nearer to the town."

My shoulders sank. "Awesome. What are we about to get into?"

"It's nothing I can't handle."

Read *Tempt* and continue with the next book in the *Terraway* series.

ABOUT THE AUTHOR

USA Today bestselling author Mary E. Twomey lives in Michigan with her three adorable children. She enjoys reading, writing, vegetarian cooking, and telling her children fantastic stories about wombats.

While she loves writing fantasy, dystopian, and paranormal tales for her readers, Mary also writes romance under the name Tuesday Embers, and cozy mysteries under the name Molly Maple.

Visit her online at www.maryetwomey.com, and sign up for her newsletter, so you never miss a new release.